FORWARD MARCH

FORWARD MARCH

SKYE QUINLAN

PAGE STREET
PUBLISHING CO.

First published in 2022 by
Page Street Publishing Co.
27 Congress Street, Suite 105
Salem, MA 01970
www.pagestreetpublishing.com

Distributed by Macmillan, sales in Canada by The Canadian Manda Group.

26 25 24 23 22   1 2 3 4 5

ISBN-13: 978-1-64567-440-5
ISBN-10: 1-64567-440-1

Library of Congress Control Number: 2021936598

Cover and book design by Laura Benton for Page Street Publishing Co.
Cover illustration © Alex Cabal

Printed and bound in the United States

DEDICATION

To queer band geeks everywhere—this one's for you. Mark time wisely, right slide down a path of positivity, and forward march with your chin up, shoulders back, and eyes filled with pride.

AUTHOR'S NOTE

YOU ARE NOT ALONE.

Trigger Warnings: anxiety, depression, mentions of self-harm and alcoholism, being outed.

The Trevor Project 24-Hour Crisis Hotline: Call 1-866-488-7386 or text START to 678-678.

SEXUAL ORIENTATION AND GENDER IDENTITY RESOURCES AND DEFINITIONS

It's Pronounced Metrosexual (itspronouncedmetrosexual.com)

Gender Spectrum (genderspectrum.org)

TRANSGENDER RESOURCES

National Center for Transgender Equality (transequality.org)

Trans Lifeline (translifeline.org)

QUEER BLACK YOUTH RESOURCES

Center for Black Equity (centerforblackequity.org)

The National Black Trans Advocacy Coalition (blacktrans.org)

The Audre Lorde Project (alp.org)

ASEXUAL, DEMISEXUAL, AND AROMANTIC RESOURCES

The Asexuality Visibility & Education Network (asexuality.org)

Demisexuality Resource Center (demisexuality.org)

AUREA (aromanticsim.org)

SELF-HARM, SUBSTANCE ABUSE, AND HOMELESSNESS RESOURCES

Self-Harm Alternatives (siriusproject.org/alternatives.htm)

Teen Drug and Alcohol Abuse (drugrehab.com/teens)

The Ali Forney Center (aliforneycenter.org)

ADDITIONAL RESOURCES

glaad.org

thetrevorproject.com

CHAPTER ONE

UNLESS YOU WANT YOUR INSTRUMENTAL SECTION TO SHUN YOU FOR the entire season, you *never* start a story with, "This one time at band camp." It's an official rule of marching band, one that's been carved into the missing door of the tuba locker, somewhere between "tie your shoes" and "keep your eyes on the field commander."

But the door isn't actually missing from the locker. Mrs. Devereaux ripped it from the hinges after Natalie Portman—no, not that Natalie Portman—had been caught having sex with her boyfriend inside. I still don't know how they'd fit, even after Nadia and I squeeze inside to test our latest theory.

"Obviously, they took out the tubas." Nadia's great at stating the obvious. It's one of the things I love most about her. What I don't love is her elbow currently wedged between my ribs. She's standing on top of a muddy tuba case, her forehead against my temple to avoid hitting the shelf above our heads, the bottom of which is covered in wads of old, still-tacky bubblegum. "But Matt is tall, and Natalie has a bad knee. Maybe they did it on the floor?"

"I don't know." I shove my hands against Nadia's boney shoulders, her bronze skin slick with a sheen of sweat from rehearsal.

"But I'm pretty sure there's gum in my hair, and I think I smell mold in here." I tilt my head forward, and my hair snags on something that feels gross and sticky and that I might have to cut out of my curls later. With my back pressed into the far corner of the locker, Nadia pushes against my front, her knee digging painfully into my hip. "No one's cleaned this locker out for months," I say glumly. My hair snags again, and I groan; this is why gum is illegal in the band room. "Not since Natalie tainted it. Let me out before I die of something worse than suffocation."

Nadia snorts and sprays my cheek with spit. Her dark eyes gleam a golden brown like the polished brass of her trumpet, except maybe with a touch more deviance. She's kissed a few boys in here, too, but she swears that the mechanics are different. I've never cared enough to ask how, and I still don't know why Nadia brought me in here. Bellamy or Evelyn would've done this with far more enthusiasm. "Natalie wasn't the first to get laid in here, you know."

"No," I say dryly, wiping off my cheek. "But she's pregnant and people think it's cursed."

"It's not cursed, Harper, for God's sake. Natalie poked a hole in the condom."

Tomayto, tomahto, who cares? I don't want to be in this locker.

I twist my hips and force Nadia off the tuba case. She slides down with a grumble of protest, then stands in the doorway and narrows her eyes, pondering a new theory. "Let me out, Nadia. It's hot, you're sweaty, and I feel gross. I want to take a shower while there's still hot water in the bathroom, preferably before the color guard takes it over. The mystery of the sex-locker can wait."

Nadia hops out of the locker and stumbles over a flip-folder with sheet music from next week's halftime show. She kicks it aside, knowing I'll slip on the folder's plastic pages and break my neck if she leaves it there. "Shower after dinner," Nadia says. As soon as I'm free from the locker, she loops her arm through my elbow. "You promised to help me clean the dorm, and I won't let you weasel your way out of it again."

Our dorm is on the south side of campus, tucked behind the empty field where the band practices every afternoon. It isn't messy, per se; Nadia's half of our shared bedroom is spotless, not a book out of place or even a shoe left out on the floor. She likes it that way, the sparkling cleanliness that makes my skin crawl. I thrive in the organized chaos that's my half, my clothes and books and a pencil or three scattered across the stained beige carpet. Everything I have has a place, on the floor, beneath my bed, or on the rotting window-sill, but at least I know where everything is. As organized as Nadia might be, she can never find anything she's looking for.

And if there's a week-old slice of pizza that's still sitting out on my desk, well . . . it's entirely Nadia's fault. She shouldn't have Door-Dashed pizza last weekend.

"The room is starting to smell, and I don't know how you can even tolerate it with your asthma. Honestly, Harp, you have no self-preservation. If not for me, you'd be—"

Dead. I don't need the reminder.

If not for Nadia Juliette, I would have died last spring when our boarding school's cafeteria served seafood for the first time. On top of forgetting both my allergy to fish and my EpiPen, I'd forgotten to make sure that a piece of shrimp hadn't swum onto my plate by accident. Nadia had stabbed me in the leg with one of the extra pens she keeps stashed in her backpack for emergencies, hard enough to leave a bruise that lasted for weeks. She never lets me forget it, though it's usually more of a reminder for me to take care of myself than it is for her to boast about having saved me.

It depends on her mood that day.

She has one of my emergency inhalers, too, stuffed into the special "Harper Bag" she'd made for her backpack after I'd collapsed during band camp sophomore year.

I wouldn't say I'm forgetful, but Nadia begs to differ. Things just slip my mind.

"Can we not talk about how much I suck at being a human?" I ask, shoving open the back doors of the band room.

A warm blast of stifling, end-of-summer air heats my sun-burnt skin. I breathe in deep and can smell the rain on the wind, can feel the sticky mugginess that plays hell with my lungs and makes my shirt cling to all the wrong parts of me. "Is it supposed to storm tonight?"

The clouds above are an ominous gray and rumble low in answer. Nadia's smile is sympathetic. "We can blast Demi Lovato if you want?"

"I knew there was a reason we still live together."

Nadia and I have been rooming together since we were seven, when my mom became the dean of Golden Oaks Academy and Nadia's father uprooted their family from Indonesia for better job opportunities. We transferred late in the semester, and since there hadn't been anywhere else to put us, they shoved us both into the smallest room in the dormitories. It was either that or a broom closet.

We've come a long way since then—now we have the *second* smallest room on campus. Mom keeps offering to place us in one of the empty suites in the faculty building, but I don't want any special treatment. Being her daughter already makes me the school pariah. Besides, no one wants to live with their teachers, and Nadia and I have a good system: I keep my chaos contained to my side of the room, and Nadia won't smother me in my sleep. It works best with a limited amount of space for me to dirty up.

Beyond the faculty parking lot that stretches like an inky sea of black, blistering pavement, our sprawling green practice field is a flurry of stick-spinning motion. The drumline always stays late after rehearsal to practice their crappy cadences. They draw in crowds from all over campus, mostly upperclassmen who clap and cheer and stomp their feet in sync with the snares and bass drums. They'll beat on their drums for hours, crashing their cymbals until my skull is splitting and I hide beneath a pillow to escape it.

Drums are my absolute least favorite instrument. They're loud, and our drumline sucks.

Nadia and I trudge through the muddy grass, the blades trampled flat from the day's long hours of high-stepping. The yard lines, painted fresh every morning, are nearly gone from the abuse of slides and crab-walks. They'll disappear entirely if it rains tonight. But the lines that mark out the end zones are still clear, and the drumline has gathered in the nearest one in a circle. Stick a pentagram in the middle and they're a cult.

"Drummers," Nadia scoffs, the word like acid on her tongue. She tugs on my arm and we give them a wide berth on our way back to the dorm. Zander Bryant purposely beats his mallet through the warped head of his bass drum and cackles. "I can't believe I dated one freshman year. It's like all they care about are sticks and mallets and banging on a drum until it breaks."

I stifle a snort behind my fingers. She says it loud enough that they probably hear her. "That's not nice, Nadia. That's like saying that all trumpets are obnoxious and only care about blasting their horns in people's ears."

"We *are* obnoxious, and it's not my fault that trumpets are naturally loud."

She's not even the slightest bit wrong; I've never met a trumpeter who wasn't full of themselves. "Truer words have never been spoken."

Nadia bumps my shoulder and grins at me, her lip gloss from this morning still shining. Or maybe she put more on. She keeps a mirror in her trumpet case. "What do you think they say about people who play the saxophone?" she asks.

My freckled shoulders are the color of a lobster left in the sun for too long, properly baked and overdone. Shrugging them at Nadia makes me wish she had some aloe in the drawstring bag she carries around with her everywhere. "We're wise."

Nadia's hoot of laughter cleaves through the field, and I pretend not to notice the heads that swivel in our direction. "Have you met Michael Briggs? That is absolutely not true."

"Hey, McKinley! Wait up!"

I whirl around on my heels, a quick "to the rear," like the call of my name is a command given by Mrs. Devereaux. My shoes twist into the mud with a gross squelching sound, and Nadia squeals as I wrench her around with me. "Christ, Harper, a little warning would be nice!"

A snare drum and harness thud into the grass from inside the drumline's circle, splattering mud on a set of sparkling blue tenors. A pair of multicolored sticks clack against the snare's silver rim, and discontent ripples through the drumline in the form of cursing and groans.

Margot Blanchard squeezes between two bass drums, phone in hand as she jogs toward Nadia and me. I don't have the slightest idea why Margot would ever want to talk to me, though the drumline doesn't need her, not with ten other drummers still harnessing their snares. But as their fiery section leader, she's the only one among them who can keep a steady beat while screaming at the football team on game nights.

I've never spoken to her before. Margot transferred here from Canada in the eighth grade because her dad is the ambassador for the Canadian embassy in D.C. I've seen them together at fundraisers, but in the great wide world of politics, my dad doesn't like Margot's dad because, apparently, he's "too damn liberal."

Nadia raises an eyebrow and nudges me with her elbow. "How do you know Margot?"

"I don't." I smile nervously and raise my hand in greeting. "Hi, Margot."

"Hey." Margot stops in front of me. She rolls her shoulders and stretches her arms until her spine cracks like a glow stick. Snares are heavy and even though they're padded, their harnesses look uncomfortable. As little as she is, I don't know how Margot even carries one. "Look," she begins, panting to catch her breath. Margot has a slight French accent, a pretty lilt I could listen to for days if she were anyone else. "I know that we, uh, don't really know each other, but . . . do you think we could talk? Just for a minute. It's important. If you're busy, I won't keep you, but we really need to talk."

I tilt my head and take this opportunity to stare at her. Margot will have to take it out once classes start, but she's biting on the back of the silver stud pierced through her thin bottom lip. "Talk about what?"

Margot glances at Nadia and shifts her feet in the mud. "Do you mind if we talk alone?"

Nadia bristles, crossing her arms and puffing out her chest like a bird whose feathers have been ruffled. "Anything you want to tell Harper, you can tell me, too. We live together, and I'll find out anyway."

"She's right," I warn, not unkindly. There's nothing I keep from Nadia. "What's up?"

Her sigh is more annoyed than resigned, as if we've given her the runaround. Margot drums her fingers against the back of her phone, and I notice her nails are painted black. "Look," she says again. She turns to face me and ignores Nadia entirely. "I really appreciate that you think my hair is cool and that I rock some lesbian aesthetic, or whatever, but we are *never* going to work. I'm sorry."

It's the weirdest thing I've ever heard because it's something I would never say, especially to Margot Blanchard.

My eyes instinctually dart to the top of her head.

Margot's curly black hair is shaved on the sides and longer on top than in the back. It compliments her golden-brown skin, the smattering of freckles across the bridge of her nose, and the beauty mark that's just above her lip. But the longer I look at Margot, the more I realize she's a walking dress-code violation. Her tattered black shorts are nowhere near the required length of just above the knee. She's wearing a loose-fitting tank top with some weird indie band logo across the front, one that's dingy and sweaty and shows off the straps of her bra, and an old red flannel is tied around her waist by the sleeves.

I guess she is some kind of punkish, lesbian stereotype; everyone knows that Margot likes girls. We've all seen her kiss plenty at football games. But I've never spoken to her before now, and I've definitely never told her that I like her hair or her aesthetic. I do kind of like her combat boots, though. They're cute.

"What on earth are you talking about?"

Margot has the nerve to look guilty, her mouth pinching at the corners. "You're funny, Harper, and I like talking to you about books. But I think it's best for both of us if we stop this whole thing right now. I'm moving back to Canada once we graduate, you know? I don't want to be tied down."

Nadia's suspicion is palpable, as if she truly believes I've lied to her about knowing Margot. I can feel the heat of my best friend's glare burning its way through my temple. "Stop *what* now?" I ask, absently picking at my fingernails. I tear at a cuticle until it bleeds, a nervous tick that I've been trying to break for years. "We've never even talked before today."

Margot frowns and glances sidelong at Nadia. "We've talked every day for a month, Harper. Since the end of band camp. See, this is why I said we should talk alone, in case you were keeping this a secret. I'm not judging you; I know your dad's a Republican or whatever, but—"

"Keeping *what* a secret?" My heart is beating in the back of my throat. I can hear my pulse roaring in my ears as if my head has been shoved underwater, Margot calling out to me from just above the surface with some outlandish accusation. It feels as if I'm being outed to Nadia when there's nothing to actually "out" me for. I don't know what Margot is talking about. "I don't know who you think you've been talking to, Margot, but it's not me. I didn't even know you knew my name."

Margot's frown only deepens. It carves out the dimples in her cheeks. "You really have no idea what I'm talking about, do you?"

"Not a freakin' clue."

Margot unlocks her phone. She taps and scrolls with her thumb. "I'm on Tinder," she says. I don't point out the irony that she's just told me she doesn't want to be tied down. She turns her phone around to show me and Nadia the screen. It's cracked. "And apparently it's news to you, but you're on Tinder, too."

CHAPTER TWO

I SNATCH THE PHONE FROM MARGOT'S HAND AND BRING IT CLOSER TO my face, praying that getting a better look will somehow change the familiar picture on the screen. But it doesn't, and surely enough, the photo on Tinder is of me. Someone has pulled it from my private Instagram account.

I'm standing on a pier in Oceanside, my auburn hair whipping behind me in a salty ocean breeze. My eyes are squinting against the California sun because Mom had told me to smile even though I hadn't wanted to. Smiling isn't my thing. It makes my face look squished.

"I don't understand," I say, scrolling through the rest of the photos. There's the one of me at Disneyland from our family trip to California, one of me dressed as Amy Pond for Halloween, and a snapshot of me, Nadia, and our friend Bellamy in our band uniforms, the sequins from our golden sashes scattering the light from a camera flash.

"Who would do this?"

Margot gingerly pulls her phone away, and only then do I realize that I'm holding it with a white-knuckled grip. She's probably afraid I'll shatter it. "Any enemies?"

"Have you seen Harper?" Nadia demands. I try not to look offended because I know she means well. "She's harmless. Who would do this to her?"

Margot holds up her hands, her palms facing outward as if she's trying to fend Nadia off. "I don't know what you do in your free time. Maybe you're the school pill-pusher and shorted someone on their study aid? Adderall sells for big bucks around here."

"That's not funny, Margot." I drag a hand through my hair and swallow down the horror that's starting to coil in my stomach. I hope I don't puke on Margot's boots. "What all have I—they—said to you?"

To Margot's credit, she winces and bites her lip. She's flustered, maybe even embarrassed. Good, because at least I'm not the only one who wants to hide beneath a rock right now. "You . . . might have been explicit. Sometimes. You offered to send me nudes." She rubs the back of her neck, looking like she'd rather be anywhere else. Did Margot ever ask to see them? I really hope she didn't. I want to ask, but she continues, "We were supposed to meet up at C dorm last night, in the common room. But you ghosted me."

"Ghosted you?" My voice jumps an entire octave. Margot winces. "I've never even talked to you! God, who else has this person been messaging?"

Margot shrugs somewhat uselessly. "I can show you the messages if you want. They might help you find out who did this. It sounds like they know you pretty well."

Nadia scoffs and crosses her arms. "Everyone knows that Harper likes to read. It's not a secret. Literally *anyone* could have done this if all you talked about was books."

No, I want to say, "literally anyone" could *not*. It has to be someone I know, someone from school who'd been bold enough to follow me on Instagram before I'd switched my account to private. That's where all these photos have come from.

"I'm only trying to help," Margot says, gritting her teeth. "It's not my fault this happened."

"You're right," I agree, grabbing Nadia by the elbow. I'm going to faint or throw up if we keep standing here. "Thank you, Margot, for telling me. Just . . . delete those messages, okay? Don't show them to anyone."

Margot salutes me by tapping her middle and pointer finger to her brow. "Not a soul."

I don't bother with saying goodbye, it's too embarrassing. I drag Nadia across the practice field as fast as my legs can carry me, leaving Margot in the mud. My chest is tight, like someone's tied me into a corset and won't stop pulling on the strings. Nadia's grumbling is drowned out by the incessant thud of my own heartbeat. It's the only thing I can hear, the only thing that keeps my feet moving. I need to escape into our room, to the safety of its familiar poster-clad walls where I can pace and cry and try to figure out who might have done this.

I don't have any enemies.

Well, that's not true. There's every Democrat in the United States who hates my Republican father, and then there's Rebecca Bentley. She's the junior who's been challenging me for first chair ever since rehearsals started last month. Only seniors like me are section leaders but anyone can steal first chair if they're good enough. So far, Rebecca hasn't been.

But I barely have any friends, either. I can count them all on one hand.

There's Bellamy, the marching band's field commander, but they don't have a mean bone in their tall, wiry body. Even though they like to play pranks, Bellamy never would've done this to me. Then there's Evelyn, my friend from the color guard who regularly trips me with her flag pole. Her father is running against mine for the presidency, and she *is* mean, but only if she doesn't like you or you use Bellamy's deadname. And finally, there's Nadia, my closest friend. There's absolutely no way she would do this.

We stagger through the lobby downstairs, past the high-topped desk where Mr. Clifford checks people into their dorms every night, and up the wide wooden staircase. We track mud all over the steps and down the dark blue runner that decorates our floor's central hallway, a bit of color to break up the never-ending brown planks.

The common room is empty except for a boy chatting quietly on the phone, his eyes red-rimmed and tearful. I've never seen him before. It's Thursday evening and classes start on Monday, so it's likely his first night in the dorm. On a good day, Nadia and I would have stopped to check on him, to assure him that Golden Oaks isn't as harrowing as the Google reviews make it sound.

But today is not a good day.

Nadia switches on the air conditioner the moment we're locked in our bedroom. "Calm down, Harper," she says, gripping me by the shoulders and forcing me down onto the edge of my unmade bed. "So someone stole your pictures and chatted with Margot Blanchard? Big deal. You know what all of that tells me?"

She's trying to make me feel better, so I indulge her. "What?"

"That Margot probably likes you. She matched with you on Tinder. Take it as a compliment and move on."

"This isn't funny, Nadia!" I bend over my knees and twist my fingers back into my tangled hair. The dark red strands are greasy with sweat from rehearsal. "If my mom finds out about this, she'll kill me. She will never believe that someone's made all of this up."

13

Nadia bites her lip. "I'm less worried about Dean McKinley, and more concerned about your dad."

"Blood ran cold" is such a cliché phrase. It's the kind I've scoffed at in the dozens of fantasy novels scattered across the bedroom floor. But I feel it strike me, this icy dread that starts to spread beneath my skin, like a bruise that won't stop growing. I think I might faint, or puke, or even die. My mom is the dean of this school, but Marcus McKinley is Maryland's first Republican senator since 1977, and people love him.

And *if* he had just announced his run for president in the upcoming election next year, and *if* he'd already started booking rallies along the campaign trail, the last thing he'd need is for his only daughter to be involved in some weird, almost sex-scandal.

They'd sent my brother away to military school for less, and now we don't even know where Christian is because he cut himself off from the family.

"I can get on top of this," I say, rising to my feet despite Nadia's flailing hands. She's trying to push me back down before I spiral. But I can't sit, I *am* spiraling, and I can't stop the panic from welling up inside of me as I fish my phone out of my pocket. I scroll through my contacts with a shaky thumb and find the one that's listed as "Mom's Cell" with a devil emoji. "I can call Mom right now and explain everything, preferably before it all blows up in my face. She'll know what to do, and maybe Dad can pull some strings to have the account taken down. He has a friend in the CIA who specifically oversees social media."

"All right," Nadia says quickly. She grabs me by the wrist and pulls me back down onto the bed, snatching away my phone in the process. She stuffs it down the front of her shirt and tucks it away into her bra, knowing that I wouldn't dare reach for it. "But first, you have to calm down. Talk to your mom after dinner. I can call Bellamy if you want—"

"Calm down?" I ask. My head is spinning as if we're both on a Tilt-A-Whirl; Nadia's face is starting to blur and bleed into the pink fabric of her T-shirt. "How am I supposed to calm down when someone is pretending to be me and sexting with Margot Blanchard on Tinder?"

Nadia's eyes flicker with a bit of smudged annoyance, but I can see the concern rippling just underneath it. She's worried. "Margot didn't explicitly say sexting, Harp."

I want to whack her with a pillow for taking all of this so lightly. "Don't you 'explicit' me when the word 'explicit' literally came out of her mouth!"

I gasp in a breath and immediately realize my mistake; I've gotten too worked up. My lungs seize up and everything starts to go dark. Nadia's face and the posters on the walls smear into endless oblivion as if I'm being submerged beneath the Arctic Ocean and water is filling me where air should be.

Nadia is on me in an instant. She snatches my inhaler off the corner of my desk and shoves it into my mouth. "Breathe, Harper. For God's sake. Margot Blanchard is not worth suffocating over."

The mist from my inhaler is bitter on the back of my tongue, but I can feel it opening up my lungs again, a colossal weight lifted from my chest in the forms of Margot and Tinder. I cough into my elbow as Nadia thumps me on the back, breaking up the mucus that's sitting in the back of my throat. It'll be days before that goes away now.

"Who would do this?" I ask her miserably.

Nadia sighs, reaching out to tuck a rogue curl behind my ear. "I don't know, Harp. But we'll figure it out, okay? Just let it go unless someone else brings it up. You're going to make yourself sick. Besides, Margot swore not to tell anyone about the messages."

"And we're supposed to just take her word for it? We don't know her, Nadia."

"It can't hurt," Nadia says. I don't bother telling her how wrong she is. Margot could very well ruin everything. "Anyway, did you see how awful she felt when she thought she was turning you down? I think she likes you."

I flop onto my bed and curl into a ball on my side. The mattress is lumpy and my rose gold duvet smells like Nadia's citrus perfume. "She doesn't like me, Nadia. If anything, she likes who she thought I was. Besides, I'm not . . ."

Nadia raises an eyebrow. "Into girls?"

I shrug, because saying it doesn't feel right. But neither does saying that I am, in fact, into girls, or that maybe I'm not into boys, so I answer uncertainly, "into anyone."

Nadia hesitates as she bites her lip and asks, "Are you sure?"

I want to say no because I'm not sure, she knows I'm not sure, but who I'm into doesn't matter anyway. No one wants to date the dean's daughter whose father is running for president, boy, girl, or nonbinary. There's no way that Margot is the exception.

"I think I'm going to skip dinner tonight," I say. Nadia grits her teeth. "I feel sick."

"You need to eat something," she counters. "And I don't mean the Oreos that Dean McKinley sneaks into your laundry basket."

I bury my face into my pillow. We're not supposed to bring outside food onto school grounds because kids are irresponsible and leave it open. It's been a rule ever since maintenance spent a month trying to kill off a roach infestation. But people sneak it in anyway, my mom included, because what's the point in denying someone snack food? The ban has made people more careful, though, so our teachers turn a blind eye to any food-based contraband.

"Mrs. Devereaux should be on dinner duty tonight," I say. "Tell her I'm not feeling well and maybe she'll let you bring me something back."

"Or," Nadia drawls. "You could just come with me to the dining hall."

"I don't want to," I grumble, sinking further into the stiff comfort of my mattress. "You can live without me for a few hours, Nadia, and you'll have Bellamy and Eve to keep you company. I just want to sleep this all away."

Nadia sighs with frustrated resignation. I can tell she thinks I'm being ridiculous for letting Margot and the Tinder profile get to me. "Fine," she says, pulling out my phone and tossing it next to me on the bed. "Stay here and pout. But if I come back to Oreo crumbs all over the floor, I will push you out the window."

"Oh, but your Indomie wrappers are okay? You eat more ramen than I do Oreos." I can practically feel Nadia glaring at me, so I reach back and blindly pat her knee. "Thanks, Nadia. You're the best."

"Yeah, I know. Don't mention it."

I'm quiet as Nadia changes into her school uniform, a light blue polo with a navy cardigan and beige skirt.

"I'll be back after dinner," Nadia announces.

I lift my head to find her tightening her ponytail. Nadia is pretty, I guess. As pretty as she can be when I've never taken the time to consider it before. She's conventionally pretty, the kind of girl who doesn't even have to try. She just is. Her hair is a dark brown and hangs perfectly straight down her back, smooth and shiny, not a single strand out of place. Nadia's eyes are a rich shade of brown and her face is small and delicate, heart-shaped and all soft edges. She's tall and borders on lanky, but her legs are muscled from where she runs track in the spring. Everything about her is welcoming.

Nothing about me is conventional, welcoming, or soft, except maybe my stomach and thighs. My face is cut pointy and harsh, as if someone carved me up from the sharpest block of sandstone in God's human-making workshop. It must have been an off-day for the Creator because I always look angry no matter if I frown or grin wide enough my cheeks hurt. Nadia's eyes are warm and inviting, but mine are a glacial blue beneath a permanently furrowed brow.

I guess my freckles are cute, the ones scattered across the bridge of my nose where my glasses would sit if I wore them.

Whoever made the Tinder page was cruel. If they were going to impersonate anyone, it should have been Nadia. Not me.

Nadia grabs an umbrella from the closet, and only then do I notice the soft pattering of rain on the window next to my bed. "Do you need anything before I go?"

I wave her away and smile grimly. "I'm fine, Nadia. I just want to sleep."

Nadia shakes her head and shuts the door behind her as she leaves, letting it slam softly to remind me how much I annoy her. Naturally, she stomps down the hall until she hits the stairwell and her footsteps fade into quiet thuds.

I'm halfway through an episode of *Doctor Who*, the TARDIS's whirring drowning out the rain, when my phone dings with a new message. The 11th Doctor, my favorite of his weird incarnations, has just told River Song his name in some botched, end-of-the-world wedding ceremony meant to save the world.

There's a part of me that wishes I could be Amy Pond or River, that the Doctor could whisk me away to a different world in the TARDIS. At least then it wouldn't matter if Margot shared those messages, or if my Tinder impersonator Photoshops my head onto a naked body that's clearly not mine and sends it to everyone at school.

My phone chimes again, a small, obnoxious bell like the ones we use in concert band when the season is over. I type in my passcode, smiling wistfully at the lock screen. It's a picture of me and Nadia posing with a Dalek at Comic-Con.

A message request pops up in my notification bar. I frown.

It's from Margot Blanchard because, apparently, I don't have enough problems already.

CHAPTER THREE

NO ONE FROM GOLDEN OAKS HAS EVER DARED TO SEND ME A MESSAGE or follow request on Instagram, not when my mom is the dean. They're all too afraid that I'll tell her what they do here on the weekends.

Margot's message stares at me from a white text bubble.

Margot Blanchard: *Hey.*

Two more messages appear in rapid succession.

Margot Blanchard: *Why aren't you at dinner?*

Margot Blanchard: *Is this because of the Tinder thing??*

I don't know what to say to her or why she even cares enough to message me. It's not a world-ending thing if Margot gets caught sending risqué messages to other girls on Tinder. But my parents will ship me off to military school like my older brother if they think I've had anything to do with this.

BREAKING NEWS from Golden Oaks Academy: *Potential First Daughter Is Queer!*

I wonder who would break the story first, BuzzFeed or TMZ with a picture of my mother weeping on the website's home page. On the next page, Margot and I would have a whole spread with Photoshopped pictures of us holding hands and kissing in suspiciously dark corners. Sources close to us would say that we're happily in love, but that my dad is threatening to sue someone on my behalf because I'm a minor and the photographs are racy.

A bouncing ellipsis pops up in a new blue bubble. Margot is typing again.

Margot Blanchard: *Are you ok?*

Of course I'm not okay, but I can't tell Margot that. For all I know, she's sitting in the dining hall with her friends, laughing about the messages meant to be from me. Will Margot say they're not real, that the Harper account on Tinder is fake?

Harper McKinley: *I'm fine, thank you for asking. Enjoy your night, Margot.*

It sounds formal, but I don't know her well enough to be casual.

Margot Blanchard: *Look, I feel really bad about what happened . . .*

Margot Blanchard: *Are you sure you don't want to see the messages?*

Margot Blanchard: *If it makes you feel any better, I want to kick someone's ass.*

I frown at my phone and can't decide what might be upsetting her more: the fact that someone tricked her or that someone is doing this to me. I highly doubt it's the latter because Margot doesn't know me, either.

Harper McKinley: *That won't be necessary, but thanks for the concern.*

Margot Blanchard: *Can I make it up to you?*

Harper McKinley: *That won't be necessary, either. Have a good night, Margot.*

It's a dismissal if I've ever written one, and Margot goes offline. I toss my phone onto the bed and return to the frozen Matt Smith on my computer screen. He's always been my favorite Doctor, probably because he has the best companions. They're funny, fierce, and beautiful, everything I know I'm not. They would have known how to deal with all of this, and both Amy and River would have gladly kicked the culprit's ass for it.

My phone dings as the episode ends.

Margot Blanchard: *You live in B dorm, right??*

Margot Blanchard: *Can you meet me in your common room?*

I blow out a breath and contemplate leaving her on read.

Harper McKinley: *It's late, Margot.*

Margot Blanchard: *WTF it's barely 6:30!!*

Margot Blanchard: *Come to the common room, coward!*

Her message ends with the winking emoji sticking its tongue out.

Harper McKinley: *Why?*

Margot Blanchard: *I want to talk.*

There isn't a point in talking to her, in dragging myself to the common room to see what Margot even wants. We don't know each other, and I don't want that to change. I don't like change, not when it isn't necessary, and Margot is definitely unnecessary. If not for some fake, sweet-talking dating profile, she would never have spoken to me in the first place.

Harper McKinley: *Good night, Margot.*

I tuck my phone beneath my pillow and vow not to answer if it dings again.

Rain is still trickling in gentle streams down the screen of our bedroom window. The thunder has quieted to a dull roar in the distance, the kind that's soothing enough to rock me to sleep if I let it. Nadia will be home soon, but if I close my eyes and pretend to have fallen asleep, she might not bother me about dinner. I still feel sick to my stomach, and there's a strong possibility I'll puke up my guts if I hear the word "Tinder" ever again.

But Nadia is the president of the Harper's Full of Shit Association; she's taught herself how to interpret my breathing to know whether or not I need my inhaler, to know if I'm sleeping or awake. She returns to the dorm with a complaint on the tip of her tongue, one she bites off when she notices me curled up in bed. I can feel her staring at my back, my shoulders, counting my breaths before she sighs.

"All right, fine," Nadia announces, kicking off her shoes so they thud to the floor beneath her desk. The sound is somehow comforting. "Scoot over and make some room for me. You want to wallow? We'll wallow. But only for tonight, and on Sunday you're coming with me to church. You can whine to God about Tinder."

I huff into my pillow, roll over onto my side, and wriggle across the mattress to make space for her. Nadia slips off her cardigan and plops onto the edge of my bed. "*Doctor Who*, *Criminal Minds*, or *Family Feud*?" she asks, swiping my laptop from the foot of my bed and setting it down between us. Nadia flops back into the pillows, her head tilting against mine as she types in my password to unlock it. Her hair still smells like citrus from this morning's shower. "Oh, wait, you're wallowing. We're wallowing. We'd better not watch *Family Feud*."

I raise an eyebrow and look up at her. "Why not?"

"Because you're already sad and I don't want to hand you your ass tonight." She flashes me a grin and pulls up a browser, navigating her way onto Netflix. "Daleks or serial killers?"

"Daleks are serial killers. They—"

"*Criminal Minds* it is, you nerd. I can't lay here and listen to your fangirling."

"Spencer Reid exists," I remind her.

Nadia rolls her eyes. "So does Derek Morgan, but I don't like him for his brains."

She sets my laptop on her stomach and turns it so we can both see the screen, then shuffles closer until we're side by side. I loll my head against Nadia's shoulder and wheeze out a sigh of contentment. "Thanks, Nadia," I say quietly, then snort when she kisses my temple. Normally, she isn't this affectionate, so I must really look pathetic tonight. "You're the best."

"Yeah," she murmurs, curling in close and turning up the volume on my laptop. "I know."

CHAPTER FOUR

THE PRACTICE FIELD IS TOO MUDDY TO MARCH ON FROM LAST NIGHT'S rain, so rehearsal is held in the band room. It's our last rehearsal before classes start on Monday, and Mrs. Devereaux is pushing us hard because we don't have practice on the weekends. Most will take that time to prepare for school and finish up any last-minute shopping, but there's nothing left for me and Nadia to do except roll out of bed on Monday morning. Our backpacks are full and sitting by the bedroom door, bursting at the seams with expensive new textbooks and supplies. Nadia had taken the liberty of color coordinating our folders and notebooks during last week's shopping trip; purple for physics, red for math, and my art sketchbook is holographic. My mom drove us all the way into D.C. just so she could take us to lunch afterward.

We received our class schedules this morning. They're okay for our final year, but Nadia and I only have physics together and we're scheduled to eat at separate lunchtimes. It's a new thing they're trying out this year, splitting students into two different lunch periods to make life easier on the cooks. I don't have lunch with anyone else I know, but at least I have English and history with Evelyn and calculus and art with Bellamy.

Bellamy is standing at the front of the band room, flapping their arms and cuing Nadia for her trumpet solo. Sweat is beading along their brow because conducting this train wreck is a taxing job, and the band room is a thousand degrees. They swipe back their hair on a downbeat, throwing off the drumline into thinking they've cut off the song. Mrs. Devereaux sighs as the rest of us descend into chaos, lost without a semi-decent beat for us to follow. She shoos Bellamy away from the podium, and Nadia's trumpet gives a final blast before she realizes that Billie Eilish's "Bad Guy" has been derailed.

"Our first performance is one week from today," Mrs. Devereaux chides. She does this thing where she sticks out her jaw when she's frustrated. You can see the veins pulsing in her neck like she's seconds away from a heart attack. She picks up her baton and points it at the back of the room, where the drumline sprawls over a row of twenty-something chairs. A large mural of a family of badgers is painted on the wall behind them. "If the lot of you can't get your shit together, I'll bench you all for halftime."

It's not unusual for her to curse at us, but at least she isn't bringing out the cowbell. She beats it with a mallet to help the drumline stay on tempo, probably imagining that the bell is someone's skull. Maybe Margot's, since she can't seem to get her section together. I wonder if hitting it is cathartic for her.

Curiosity gets the better of me. I turn to look at Margot and find her slouched behind her snare. Her shoulders are caved in around her, a dark gray jacket that's too big for her tiny body sliding down her arms. She's bitten thumb holes into the sleeves, and she's squeezing her sticks so tightly that I worry they might snap into splinters.

She looks as if she's going to stab them through the head of her drum.

"I'm sorry," she says moodily. "I'll call an extra practice for this weekend."

Protests erupt from down the line: She can't do that, they have things to do, they need a break. But Margot sinks into the back of her chair and pulls up the hood of her jacket. She can do whatever she wants as section leader, especially call a sectional if they need it. And they do.

Mrs. Devereaux nods her approval even though Margot doesn't ask for it. She turns to look at the clock that hangs above the chalkboard and sighs. It's five to seven and practice is nearly over. "Before you pack up for the weekend, does anyone want to challenge for a chair?"

My spine stiffens to the point of tingling pain. My fingers instinctively find the keys of my saxophone, tapping out scales and the fight song and our halftime show, everything that anyone could challenge me on. Rebecca Bentley snorts to my immediate left, but her hand doesn't shoot into the air as it's done so many times this past month. She won't challenge me for my chair again, not tonight, but the tension doesn't leave my shoulders until I see her unclip the saxophone from her neck strap.

"Good!" Mrs. Devereaux says cheerfully, setting her baton on the podium. "Pack up, get out of here, and do not forget that I need your permission slips for the Renaissance festival signed and in my in-box by next Friday." She glares specifically at the drumline as the rest of us stuff our instruments into their cases. "Tell your parents to check their emails and message me through the school portal if they didn't receive the DocuSign invitation. You are not the go-between, and 'my mom said I could go!' isn't good enough this year."

The drumline groans, "Sarah!" in unison to the subject of Mrs. Devereaux's chiding, followed by Margot's openly annoyed,

"Tell your mom to check her fucking email."

The cymbalist sticks out her tongue before she disappears into the drum closet.

Nadia meets me outside the band room after I've put my sax in my locker. The sun is beginning to set over campus, painting the sky with hues of orangey-pink and purple. It glistens off Nadia's skin, setting her coppery complexion aflame. She looks up from her phone, grinning at me from where she's leaning against the brick wall of the art building. "There's a bonfire in the woods tonight, behind the dorm. Want to go?"

"The woods are off-limits," I remind her. Nadia rolls her eyes as if I've done her some disservice. "We could get suspended, Nadia. Or expelled, or killed, or—"

"Jesus, McKinley," says Evelyn. She pops around the corner of the art building with Bellamy, her arm looped around Bell's skinny waist. They're wearing matching denim overalls with an assortment of colorful accessories, though Bellamy is a bit more mix-matched with a sleeveless blue flannel underneath and rainbow knee-high socks. "Relax. What kind of friends would we be if we let someone murder you in the woods?"

"There's also a bonfire every year," Nadia reminds me, grinning at our friends for coming to back her up. I wonder if she'd been texting them when I got here, calling in reinforcements because she knew I was likely to say no. "The teachers all know about it, and they don't care so long as we don't set the woods on fire. It's tradition." Nadia pockets her phone and takes my hand, shaking my arm until my shoulder hurts. I can see it on her face that she's planning on wearing me down, pressing every button she knows to push if it'll get her what she wants. "Come on, Harp. Don't be such a drag. We're seniors! This is the last time we'll ever get to do this."

"Pretty please, Harper?" Bellamy shakes Evelyn loose to sidle up behind me and wrap their arms around my torso. Sometimes I forget how tall they are, how gangly their limbs are until Bellamy squeezes me with a hug. "You can be our designated curfew enforcer! Midnight strikes, and we'll be back in our dorm rooms faster than Cinderella bailed from the ball to her bachelorette pad."

"I don't think I'd call an attic a bachelorette pad, Bell."

"Semantics," Evelyn says. She nudges Bellamy with her hip as they pout. "Pretend you're Cinderella, the bonfire is a ball, and Margot Blanchard is your temporary prince. At least until we can find you someone else."

The sound that comes out of me is undignified. "You told them?"

Nadia winces and bites her bottom lip, and if looks could kill, Evelyn would be climbing into her grave. "Yeah. This morning. I'm sorry. I should have asked first."

I bury my face into the palms of my hands as Bellamy gives me a tight squeeze. I think I'm going to throw up. "Who else knows about that profile?" I cry, slumping back against Bellamy. They plant their feet and support my weight in silence, patting my back to help comfort me. "If my parents find out I'm on a dating app talking to some girl—"

"They're not going to find out," Nadia vows. She pries my hands away from my face and holds them gently in hers. "I promise, Harp. Unless Margot opens her mouth, no one else has to know about it. We'll just keep it a secret between the four of us."

"Six of us," I correct her with a wheeze. She starts to reach for her backpack. "Including the asshole who did this. Do you think it was someone from band?"

"I'm in on all the band gossip," Bellamy says, leaning over my shoulder to press a kiss to my cheek. "Perks of being the field commander. If someone in band made the profile, I'd have heard about it. Your anxiety is valid, Harp, but I don't think you have anything to worry about."

"They're right," Evelyn says, reaching for my hair and giving one of my two French braids a tug. "Out of sight, out of mind. No one's talking about it. So . . ." She gives me a grin. "Come with us to the bonfire and have fun. Fuck the profile and the asshole who made it."

I wriggle myself free from Bellamy's embrace. "What if whoever made it is there tonight?"

"Who cares?" Evelyn says. "It's not like they're gonna rat themselves out to you. Golden Oaks has a zero-tolerance policy, remember? And a fake dating profile is cyber-bullying. It's grounds for immediate expulsion."

Nadia winces. "Your mom would annihilate anyone connected to that profile. Even Margot. I would keep my mouth shut, personally."

Evelyn snorts. "Perks of being the dean's daughter." She loops her arm around Bellamy's waist again, dragging them close so she can use their shoulder as a head rest. "Come on, McKinley. Come with us tonight. It'll be fun. We won't keep you out past your bedtime, scout's honor." She waggles her brows at me. "Besides, you'll need all the fun you can get now that your dad's in the running for president."

Bellamy groans. "Can you not?" they say, stabbing Evelyn in the chest with their finger. "I want to party tonight, not discuss politics."

Evelyn kisses their cheek. "Sure, babe," she says, then looks at me and winks. "You don't have much to worry about, anyway. My dad's gonna win by a landslide, and there aren't any photographers waiting in the woods to catch you do something embarrassing. Just come out with us."

Ignoring Evelyn's jab, I want to tell them no, that I don't want to go and would rather keep wallowing in my dorm room. I can't just forget about the profile; I can't just pretend that the damn thing doesn't exist. But Nadia's eyes are unfairly wide and pleading, and Bellamy looks ready to burst. They'll drop to their knees and start begging if I don't say yes. I think of all the things we've been invited to over the years, how they always want to go but I never do, so they don't. It's unfair of me, and I know it. Even though I insist that Nadia and Bell can always go ahead without me, I always know that they won't.

"I don't know, guys . . . ."

Nadia's smile widens until all of her teeth are showing. Bellamy starts bouncing on their feet. This is the closest I've ever been to saying yes before. "Pretty please, Harp?" Nadia pleads. "I'll feed Mickey and Martha for a month."

It's not a fair trade because I know that Nadia won't feed our fish, but I sigh in resignation anyway. Nadia starts to bounce now too, knowing that she's got me where they want me. "I'll go," I say in defeat. Nadia squeals and wraps her arms around my neck. "But *only* for an hour, and if we get caught, I'll tell my mom you all drugged me."

Nadia rocks us back and forth, holding me until it hurts to breathe. I cough against her shoulder and Nadia lets me go, though her smile hasn't faltered in the slightest. "You're the *best*, Harp."

Bellamy rushes forward and presses another kiss to my cheek. "I knew you were my favorite McKinley, even if your brother was definitely my inner queer awakening."

I groan and shove them both away. "I hate you all."

It's chilly for the end of summer. The underbrush is damp from last night's rain and the ground beneath my feet is still muddy. Nadia has sauntered off with Bellamy and Evelyn to find us something to drink, leaving me alone on a wet log near the bonfire. The flames are crackling low over a pile of broken branches; someone has taken the time to lay stones around the pit to keep the fire contained. They're scorched black from several bonfires of the past, a tiny mark of Golden Oaks' rebellious bit of history.

Smoke is wafting into the air in wisps of curling gray, and I've pulled up the collar of my shirt to cover my mouth and nose. Smoke and asthma don't go together, and the last thing I need is to be whisked away from campus in an ambulance.

The seat next to me is an old, rotting tree stump covered in wet moss. No one has dared to sit there all night because they're afraid I'll tell my mom where we are. She's the only one who wants to put an end to these bonfires and has tried for years since becoming dean. She thinks they're unsafe and is afraid we'll all burn to death.

No one was sitting there five minutes ago, that is.

I catch a glimpse of Margot as she sits down, the temporary prince to my chaotically screwed-up Cinderella story.

She's dressed in black jeans and her dark gray jacket from rehearsal, the hood still pulled over her head. She's sharpening the end of a stick with a pocketknife, something she'll be expelled for if my mom finds out she has it on school grounds. But she doesn't look concerned to have casually whipped it out in front of me; perhaps she knows I'm not going to tell.

"You look miserable," Margot says. Yesterday, her tone was

sympathetic, as if she'd truly felt sorry for rejecting me over a Tinder account that wasn't mine. Tonight, her voice is flat. She doesn't care if she upsets me. "I'm surprised you came."

I clear my throat and angle myself away from her. "My friends begged."

Margot snorts as she whittles her stick into a point. "Is that what it takes?"

I frown and slide back around. "What do you mean?"

She peels back a long, curling strip of bark from her stick and tosses it into the bonfire. The flames snap it into ash. "If I begged you to talk to me, would you?"

Her words are like a punch to the gut, sharper than the blade of her knife. "I'm talking to you now, aren't I?"

Margot doesn't bother looking up at me. "That's not what I mean, and you know it."

I nervously pick at my fingernails. It's a nasty habit, but if my mouth wasn't covered by my shirt, I'd probably bite them into stubs. "I'm sorry," I tell Margot, and I hope she knows I mean it. "But I don't know what there is to talk about. If not for that fake profile, you never would've spoken to me in the first place."

"Are you serious? Shit, you are." Margot's voice has a gentle rasp to it. It's the pleasant kind of rasp, not the nails-against-a-chalkboard kind that makes you want to cover your ears. "I've talked to you plenty of times. Guess I didn't realize how forgettable I am."

I can't recall a single conversation before yesterday. "When?"

Margot shakes her head, her shoulders slumping around her as she starts to sharpen her stick again. "We've had classes together, made small talk," she says. "But your nose is usually buried in a book, and I'm lucky if I get a single word out of you."

I've come to learn that guilt is a festering, all-consuming thing.

Especially when you've made someone feel invisible, and especially because I know what that's like. "Margot, I—"

"Save it," she says. I swallow my apology. "I don't want to hear that you're sorry. But the next time you need to borrow a pencil, don't ask me for one of mine."

Her comment is open-ended, as if there's something I'm meant to say or that Margot expects to hear. But I don't know what that something is, so I watch her sharpen her stick. She flings another curled strip into the fire. "What are you doing?"

Margot glances up at me and waves her knife. "Sharpening a stick."

"But why?"

She reaches beside her and procures an open bag of marshmallows. "Everything I found is covered in dirt and mud, so I'm cutting it away to roast some marshmallows."

I frown because her reasoning seems pointless. "The inside of the stick isn't clean, either."

Margot tilts her head and stills her weird woodworking. "Have you never roasted a marshmallow before? You're *supposed* to do it on a stick."

It's only the smallest bit judgmental, but my face warms with a betraying blush. "No."

Margot blinks as if I've surprised her, then reaches into her bag and pulls out a marshmallow. She skewers it on the end of her stick and holds it out to me. "Here."

I scrunch up my nose because nothing about this is sanitary. A dirty room is one thing, but eating off a stick is like asking to swallow a termite-filled marshmallow. "No, thanks."

"Oh, come on." Margot wiggles the stick to make it more enticing. "Roasted marshmallows are a thing, Harper. People eat them around bonfires all the time."

"Eating off a stick that you found in the woods is disgusting. There're germs on it."

Margot rolls her eyes. "Sorry I forgot my Clorox wipes, princess. Just take the damn stick and roast the marshmallow. I promise it's not going to kill you."

I don't know why I take it, but the stick is warm from Margot's hands. The marshmallow burns as I hold it near the fire and watch it swell from the flames. It bubbles and browns into a crisp, gooey mess that doesn't look at all appetizing. Margot has moved closer to me and is sitting on the edge of her tree stump, her knees bouncing in what I think might be anticipation. I don't have to look at her — so I absolutely do *not*—to know that she's grinning.

"What now?" I ask. My marshmallow has caught fire and is looking a little molten.

Margot rummages through the drawstring backpack sitting in the dirt at her feet. "I have graham crackers and chocolate if you want to make a s'more, but I suggest you do it fast. I didn't bring enough for everyone."

I blow out my marshmallow like a candle. "I've never had a s'more, either."

Margot looks shockingly offended, her mouth falling open around a gasp. "You poor, poor child. I can't believe your parents have deprived you like this. Here, let me see that."

She takes the stick and sandwiches the marshmallow between two cinnamon graham crackers and a piece of Hershey's chocolate. It sticks to her fingers and drips all over her jeans, but Margot doesn't seem to care. She smashes it flat and hands it back to me, then licks melted chocolate off her palm. "Try it."

I sniff it, still skeptical. My fingers are sticky now, too, but at least it smells sickly sweet and delicious. "What if I don't like it?"

Margot snorts. "I'll finish it."

"You'd eat after me?" I ask. "That's gross. What if I had a disease or something?"

Margot shrugs, her mouth still twisted with a toothy grin. "It's a s'more," she says, as if every s'more is a good s'more no matter how you contaminate it. "I'd eat it off the ground. Now hurry, before someone sees you."

Her excitement is palpable, a thrumming vibration twanging down some invisible thread between us. I indulge her and take a bite. The marshmallow bursts between my teeth and leaks from between the graham crackers. I can taste the charred gelatin and melted chocolate mixed with gooey marshmallow. It drips down my chin and Margot laughs.

"Good?"

"You were right," I say through a mouthful. "I've been deprived."

Margot hands me the napkin she's pulled from her bag. "My dad and I used to go camping all the time," she tells me. I wipe off my chin and lick the chocolate from my fingers. "Before we moved to the States."

I frown and wonder why she's telling me this. I didn't know Margot was so open. "You haven't gone since you've been here?"

She shakes her head and skewers another marshmallow. "He doesn't have the time for it anymore. The Embassy keeps him busy. But it wouldn't be the same, anyway."

"Trees are trees," I point out.

Margot shrugs and I can visibly see her mood shift. It's in the lines of her face, the angle of her jaw as she grits her teeth and hunches over her knees. "To you, maybe. But everything is different here."

"You miss Canada, don't you?"

Margot shudders as if she's let me in on some world-ending secret. "Every day."

I don't know what it's like to miss home because Golden Oaks is all I've ever known. I can't remember anything before it. Some kids go home on the weekends, but my parents' house in Baltimore is a vacation spot.

"Do your friends know how badly you miss home?"

Margot turns her stick, charring her marshmallow all over. "Most of them don't care."

"What about your parents?" I ask.

She drags a hand through her hair, sweeping back her hood and then shivering from the chilly summer breeze. "My dad makes more money now than he ever did back home. He's happy, and I'm not going to ruin that by telling him that I'm not."

"I'm sorry," I murmur, and I am. But I can tell she doesn't want my sympathy by the way her fingers tighten around her stick. "Why'd you tell me about home? You don't know me."

Margot's smile is wry, her lips curling up in what would be a smirk if she didn't look so goddamn sad. "I figured my misery was safe with you. You'll forget all about me by morning."

Margot's words hurt, but I deserve them. I angle myself toward her and tilt my head to one side, watching her watch her marshmallow. "For what it's worth," I say. "I *am* sorry."

Her smile widens, just a little. "I know."

"Is that why you shared your s'mores with me?"

Margot tips back her head and laughs, a booming echo that rasps between the rustling leaves. I find myself liking the sound of it. "No. I shared my s'mores because your life must suck worse than mine if you've never had one before." Her marshmallow is starting to smoke. Margot pulls it from the fire. She blows out the flames and eats it whole, her mouth turning black from the charring. "Want another one?"

It's a dangerous question given that I've learned I like her laugh. I shouldn't. Margot raises an eyebrow as she rummages through her bag of marshmallows, and I bite my lip as she taps her foot impatiently. She wants to know how many more to roast.

"Just one."

CHAPTER FIVE

W E LEAVE THE BONFIRE AT MIDNIGHT ON THE DOT, AND NADIA IS SO
drunk she can't stand. I don't know where she found beer or who
might have snuck it in, but I do know that Nadia has never drunk
before.

She's obnoxious.

I can't get her home on my own, and Bellamy and Evelyn are off
kissing in the woods because they think we don't know they're still
a thing sometimes, so her arms are slung around my and Margot's
shoulders. We're dragging her back to the dorm, since she's barely
picking up her feet, and Margot keeps threatening to drop her and
leave her in the mud. I can feel the strain in my lungs as we carry
her, and my muscles ache from supporting her weight back to campus. I'm tempted to kill her in her sleep.

"Christ, Juliette, move!" Margot grunts and kicks her in the
ankle. Nadia's legs splay wide beneath her. "Pick up your feet,
Nadia, or I swear to God, I'll—"

"Harper won't let you drop me, will you, Harpy?" Nadia's words
are a slurred string of syllables, and she's never called me "Harpy"
before tonight. Margot snorts at the sound of it.

"Dropping you is starting to sound appealing."

Nadia's head lolls onto my shoulder. Her eyes are glassy, and her breath smells like something has died in her mouth. I want to stuff a sock in there and tell her to breathe through her nose. "Don't be mean to me, Harper. I'm drunk and vulnerable, and it's not my fault if GoGo is starting to rub off on you."

"Do *not* call me that," Margot snaps at her, though, in the grand scheme of things, it's the wrong thing to say when Nadia is drunk and not thinking straight.

Nadia grins and leans heavily into Margot, who groans as if she's realized her mistake. "I think GoGo is cute," she says. "GoGo, GoGo, GoGo. Harpy, don't you think GoGo is cute?"

"Shut up, Nadia. Shut the fuck up."

Margot's brow furrows with surprise. "Holy shit. You cursed."

I tug on Nadia's arm, yanking her forward until her feet finally move underneath her. "I do when Nadia is being an awful brat."

Nadia slaps her hand across my mouth. It's hard enough to sting but not leave a mark. Even her fingers smell like beer. "That's a bad word, Harpy. I might have to tell your mom."

Margot huffs another laugh. My cheeks heat with an involuntary blush. "I am going to kill you."

Margot shoulders Nadia's weight as I fumble the back door of our building open. It's rusty and covered in old vines because no one ever comes in or out of it, but I can't risk carrying Nadia through the front entrance in case Mr. Clifford is still sitting there. It's one thing to not care about the bonfire, but something else entirely to turn a blind eye to a visibly drunk student.

"I'll help kill her if you want," Margot offers. Nadia slaps her cheek and squirms between Margot's arms. She's strong for a girl her size, restraining Nadia without even breaking a sweat. It must be from carrying around her snare every day. "I've watched enough

Criminal Minds to know how to hide a body."

"Harper likes *Criminal Minds*, too," Nadia trills. "Her favorite character is Reid."

"Reid is cool." Margot hauls Nadia up the first set of stairs that open onto a small stretch of concrete. It's dusty and smells like mildew, and Margot nearly slips in a puddle of stagnant water as she starts to drag Nadia around the corner. "I like Prentiss better."

"Prentiss isn't as quirky."

Apparently, it's the wrong thing to say. Margot dumps Nadia onto the bottom step of the next flight of stairs and points a finger in my face. "You take that back right now, or you can haul this drunken, idiotic lump back upstairs by yourself."

I frown at her and struggle for speech, surprised to learn that this is a hill she's willing to die on. "I didn't say that there was anything wrong with Prentiss," I point out. "She's just not my favorite. Reid is a nerd and he's the smartest one on the team. Plus, he has a better backstory."

Margot gasps as if I've offended her. "He does not!"

Nadia doesn't seem bothered that we've left her giggling at cracks in the stairwell, so I cross my arms and give Margot my full attention. "He's a certifiable genius and recalls entire books verbatim. He's weird and complex and has a heart of absolute gold."

"Prentiss is, like, entirely queer coded," Margot argues. She places her hands on her hips. "She was originally written as a lesbian, but the network was a coward and had the writers change her character. She could have been awesome queer representation. I can't believe they wasted her potential."

"Harper only likes Reid 'cuz Reid likes *Doctor Who*, and Harpy loves *Doctor Who*."

"Shut up, Nadia."

Margot grins from halfway up the stairwell. "I knew you liked *Doctor Who*! I saw you with a Dalek on your Instagram. Who's your favorite Doctor?"

"Matt Smith," I say warily, blinking at Margot from the landing. I don't remember her ever following me.

Margot's expression is one of vague annoyance. "Ugh. I knew that, too."

I puff out my chest and glare at her; this is the hill that *I* am willing to die on. "What?"

"Matt Smith's Doctor is an asshole. Tom Baker is fucking iconic."

Nadia giggles before Margot and I can kill each other in the stairwell. "I could listen to you two argue all night," she says contentedly. Margot huffs out a breath that still sounds vaguely annoyed. "But my bed is calling my name. Harper, help me up."

I reach out my hand to help her stand, but this battle with Margot is far from over.

Nadia grips my wrist with sweaty fingers as Margot gets behind her and pushes her up onto her feet. Hanging between us, she's a human barrier that Margot and I both keep glaring around, albeit with no real heat. Margot is hoisting us all up by the railing, gripping it with surprising strength and then pulling Nadia up to the next step. Without her, I don't know how I would have ever gotten Nadia home.

Margot props Nadia against the wall while I fumble through my pocket for my room keys. They rattle noisily in the eerie silence of the hallway. Everyone on our floor must be down at the bonfire.

"Toss her onto the bed," I say, helping Margot drag Nadia through the door.

"I'd ask which one, but I'm pretty sure I know. I've watched Nadia organize her trumpet case." Margot deposits Nadia onto the right bed, the one closest to the door. It's completely spotless except for the rogue wire of her phone charger. Her floral duvet wrinkles beneath her, and Nadia's flailing to get comfortable sends decorative pillows tumbling to the floor.

Margot wanders across the room to investigate the bubbling sound coming from the aquarium. "You guys have fish?"

I'm covering Nadia with the blanket her grandma crocheted for her when I turn to find Margot with her face pressed against the fish tank. She's tapping at the glass while Mickey and Martha swim in frantic circles. "Don't scare them!" I scold. "That's rude. How would you like it if I came into your home and—"

Margot snorts. "I didn't think we were allowed to have pets on campus."

"We're not," I say, joining her in front of the tank. I grab the bottle of fish food and sprinkle some into the water. Most of it floats to the bottom of the tank and settles between the shiny black pebbles. "My mom had an aquarium in her office a few years ago, but no one fed the fish over winter break and they all died except for these two. She was going to flush them down the toilet, but Nadia and I begged her to let us keep them."

Margot nods as if she's listening, but I can see it on her face that she's not. She's thinking, her bottom lip caught between her teeth as she watches Mickey and Martha. "I know you don't want to talk about the Tinder profile," Margot murmurs. My spine stiffens. She's had all night to bring this up, but at least she chose to do it here. "But they have you all wrong, you know. Maybe they don't know you after all."

I draw in a breath through my nose. I won't tell Margot that the pictures all came from my private Instagram account. "What makes you say that?"

Margot keeps watching the fish. "Whoever they are, they're funny, and I liked that. But they didn't talk about any of the books I scoped on your floor, and they never mentioned rescuing any fish. I asked if they watched *Criminal Minds* or liked *Doctor Who*, and they said no. I don't think they know you at all."

"Doesn't seem like it." I guess those things aren't necessarily common knowledge, so maybe Margot is right. "You haven't shown anyone those messages, have you?"

Margot turns to me and frowns. "No, of course not. And I haven't even heard from you—" She uses her fingers to make air quotes around the word *you*. "—since we talked on the practice field. It seems to me that your doppelgänger has ghosted me again."

A sigh of desperate relief escapes me. I don't know why I believe Margot, but I do. She doesn't seem like the type to lie about something like this. "Can I ask you something else?"

She raises an eyebrow. "Sure."

"Why were you on a dating app if you don't want to be tied down?"

Margot coughs into her fist. "I go on there sometimes. For hookups. Nothing serious. It's . . . just a thing I do. Makes me feel something. I guess. For a minute."

"Oh." I rock back onto my heels. I've never seen her look so uncomfortable, nor felt the twist in my gut as a result of it. "Is that why you thought you were meeting me in C dorm the other night?"

Margot rubs the back of her neck. "Yeah."

"Oh." It makes me shudder to think about what Margot might have wanted from me—why she might have wanted it at all. My lack of experience in, well, *everything* isn't exactly a secret. Everyone knows everything at Golden Oaks, and I've never even held someone's hand before. "I . . . I'm sorry you didn't get to . . ."

She waves her hands in a wild gesture, telling me to stop talking. Margot looks desperate to get away, steadily inching toward the door. "I shouldn't keep doing it, anyway. They're . . . it's nothing . . . I don't know. Never worth it." Margot makes a face and drags a hand through her hair. "Not that I think *you're* not worth it, or whatever. That's not what I—I didn't mean—God, Margot. Stop talking."

I bury my face into the palms of my hands to hide my blush from Margot. This is even more embarrassing than her rejection. "Please."

"Yeah. Right. I should go." Margot makes a break for the door. I don't stop her. "I, uh. I'll see you in school on Monday. Thanks for hanging out with me tonight. Sorry Nadia bailed on you for some beer."

I turn to look at Nadia and wince. She's drooling onto her pillow. "She's not going to die in her sleep, is she?"

Margot frowns and leans against the open threshold. "Roll her onto her side in case she pukes, that way she won't choke on it. Other than that, I'd say just let her be."

My stomach churns. I'm afraid Margot's s'mores are going to reappear on the floor. "Will that happen?"

"Probably not," Margot says quickly. "So don't panic. But she will have a headache in the morning, and she'll definitely puke when she wakes up. Give her lots of water and shove some Advil down her throat if you have any, but there's really nothing else you can do."

I wish we'd never gone to the bonfire. I'm never going to sleep tonight.

"Hey." Margot has come back into the room and is standing directly in front of me. She smiles grimly, her fingers twitching like she wants to reach out and touch me. But she doesn't. "It'll be fine,

Harper. I promise."

"How do you know?" I ask. I hate that I sound so unsure.

Margot purses her lips. "Because I've been drunk before."

I gesture somewhat uselessly at Nadia's drooling form. "Like *this*?"

"Something like that, yeah." Margot crosses her arms and I realize that she doesn't want to talk about this. "I really should be going."

"Right," I say, but I don't want to see her leave. Not when Nadia is drunk and Margot seems to know what she's talking about. "I'm sorry. I didn't mean to keep you."

Margot settles for patting me softly on the shoulder. "If you need anything, just message me. I'll come right back."

I groan when I glance over at Nadia again. Margot's chuckle fills the space between Nadia's snoring and the fish filter. "Thank you for helping me tonight. I couldn't have gotten Nadia home without you."

Margot shrugs and heads for the open door. "See you around, McKinley. Message me if Nadia aspirates. Or something. If you want."

I bite my lip and nod at her. Messaging her at all is probably a bad idea, but bad ideas are all I seem to be having lately. "Good night, Margot."

She gives me a wave and is gone with a loud, "Good night."

CHAPTER SIX

M Y PHONE VIBRATES FROM THE POCKET OF NADIA'S CARDIGAN, AND I
hope it's Margot texting me good morning like she's done every
morning since Friday. The cardigan hugs my body in all the wrong
places, and the sleeves are too tight beneath my armpits. Nadia had
yanked it from her closet this morning and tossed it onto my bed
as I glared at her. "A cardigan is a cardigan," she'd said, refusing to
apologize a third time for having puked on mine the morning after
the bonfire.

The dorm had been chilly on Saturday, so I'd shrugged into my
cardigan to check on Nadia and offer her a bottle of water. She'd
been slumped against her headboard when I woke up, her face
ashen and lips cracked and bloodless. It was the worst I'd ever seen
her look—until she'd puked all down the front of me, of course.
She'd looked so terrible I'd felt it—literally.

"I'm sorry," Nadia had croaked, her eyes wide and full of tears.
I'd pay to have seen the look on my face as I processed the reeking puke dripping off of me. "I'm—I'm so sorry, Harp. I didn't
mean to."

"Take this," I told her stiffly, handing Nadia the water. My navy
blue sleeve had turned a grotesque orange. "And don't even look at

me until tomorrow."

I'm still bitter this Monday morning and she knows it, which is why I'm stuffed into her cardigan.

I fish my phone out of Nadia's skinny pocket, grumbling about the tightness of the sleeves. She flashes me an apologetic smile as I slide my thumb across the screen.

Dad's Cell: *Have a great first day of school, baby girl. I love you. Call me tonight and let me know how it goes.*

Dad's message makes me smile, and I rely on Nadia to guide me down the hall as I tap out a quick response.

Harper McKinley: *I love you too. You owe me an ice cream date, btw. My weekend sucked and I miss you.*

Bellamy and Evelyn are waiting for us in the common room. It's barely seven on a Monday, but already they're giggling at whatever is on Evelyn's phone. I shove mine back into my pocket. It's probably one of Bellamy's weird memes, the ones they make about marching band and post to the band's private Discord server.

It took weeks for someone to add me freshman year.

They sober as Nadia and I join them, Bellamy coughing a final laugh into their fist. Evelyn looks at me and grins, stashing her phone inside her bra. "Ready for breakfast?"

"I heard they're serving pancakes." Bellamy scoops up their backpack and swings it over one shoulder. They've chosen to wear a skirt today with black knee-high stockings, and I wonder if they've finally said to hell with the Academy's stone-aged dress code. They'll likely get detention for not wearing slacks, but the school doesn't acknowledge that Bellamy is non-binary, so Bellamy doesn't acknowledge their rules. "Donuts, too. I'm stoked."

I wriggle between Bellamy and Evelyn, and Bellamy slings their arm around my waist. "It'll all be gluten-free, you know. My mom's all about eating healthy these days. You should have seen her purging most of our lunch menu this summer."

Evelyn sighs as we hit the stairwell. Nadia has to stop her from climbing onto the banister and sliding down to the bottom. "Tell Dean McKinley to keep your dad's political campaign out of our school," she says. "Just because healthy meals for school-aged kids will be her little pet project if your dad wins the presidency—which he *won't*—does not mean she has to experiment on us. I will riot if she takes away our ice cream."

"She kept that," I say. "Sort of. She swapped it out for frozen yogurt."

"Blasphemy!" Evelyn cries. She's known to be a touch dramatic, and even when she's not trying to drag me to bonfires, Eve's not really my cup of tea. But she and Bellamy are a package deal. You don't get one without the other. I love Bell, so I tolerate Eve, even if she is too loud and abandons you at said bonfires to carry home your drunk mutual friend. "Your mom is a sadist, Harper. Seriously. She's the worst kind of Republican. The stick-stuck-up-her-ass kind of Republican. My mom would never take away our ice cream, and she'll have a better focus when *my* dad wins the election."

Nadia sighs as she shoves open the door of our building. "It's too early in the morning for politics, Eve. We all know you hate Harper's parents."

Frustration claws at my insides, but Nadia is right. It's too damn early, and I'm not debating with the other potential First Daughter —especially if we're not being broadcast on live television.

"I don't hate them," Evelyn says fervently. "I just don't agree with their agenda. And Harper, you'll forgive me if I vote for my dad in the primaries, right? He has a better platform than Marcus. No offense."

"I'm not even voting for him," I say, but I'm certainly not voting for Evelyn's dad, either, not when he's up against my father and has even more extreme views. Assuming his campaign ever makes it off the ground. Mayors like Mr. Holbrook are like tiny bugs in D.C.— squashed beneath the heels of rich senators like my father.

It's not that I don't support him, because I do. Sort of. He's my father. His agenda might be questionable—he strongly opposes gun control, prefers religion to science, and he's far too opinionated about abortion—but at least he doesn't want to close all our borders. Evelyn's dad wants to build a wall.

But girls like me don't belong in the White House. We aren't built for the lies, the scheming, and the constant dodging of everyone's personal agenda. I don't know if a presidential campaign will be anything like when Dad first ran for senator, if it'll be as cutthroat and brutal, but I hadn't been built for that, either. Dad must've agreed because he's stopped making me attend public appearances. His supporters probably think I died. But I guess that's better than not knowing I exist; as far as voters are concerned, Marcus McKinley doesn't have a son, and almost no one knows my brother's name.

"What do you think the White House is even like?" Bellamy asks, side-stepping a puddle to avoid getting mud on their new shoes. "Where would your rooms be if Marcus or Frank win the election? First floor, second floor, somewhere in the basement in a bunker?"

"Harper's been to the White House," Evelyn reminds them bitterly. I try not to think about the dozens of times I've been frisked by the Secret Service in the last year alone. "She goes to their Christmas party every year, and Harrison Bentley is *always* inviting her to different fundraisers."

"And I *always* turn him down," I point out. Harrison Bentley is the vice president's son and I cannot stand to even look at him.

"I'd rather be abducted by the CIA than spend a night with Harrison."

"You're so weird," Nadia comments. We're near the cafeteria now. The multi-grade campus sprawls across dozens of grassy acres with hedges and gardens planted between buildings. Sometimes we study in the central courtyard where the grounds crew, at Mom's request, installed a fountain that people like to throw pennies in. "Harrison Bentley is hot, and he has his own plane. Think of all the places he could take you!"

"I'd rather fly coach, by the bathroom."

Bellamy scrunches up their nose. "Damn, you *do* hate him."

"He called me a prude because I wouldn't sleep with him after last year's Easter egg hunt."

Nadia swipes a hand through her hair. "Yeah, okay, that's weird."

Weird indeed. Harrison Bentley is a creep known for sending dick pics that the CIA scrambles to purge from the internet. Several have landed in my Instagram DMs over the years, and every time I want to vomit. I can't even fathom asking someone to send me one, much less appreciate one I've received without consent. If Harrison thinks he's attractive, well, I'm more interested in my fish. At least they don't try and send me fin pics.

"Weird or not," Evelyn says, adjusting the strap of her messenger bag. I lean around Bellamy to look at her. "Harrison's a catch and I think you should go for it. Date at least one guy before we graduate, you know? Two if you're feeling spontaneous."

"Yes," I say, rolling my eyes to the sky. The sun is still rising, and the early morning clouds are painted with smudges of pink. "Because I just so happen to have someone else waiting around for me. If only I should be so lucky."

Evelyn snorts and gives Bellamy a flirtatious wink. "True," she agrees, then points a manicured finger at me. "So date Harrison while he's still interested. Guys like him don't like to be kept waiting. Trust me, he'll find someone else. Take your shot while you've got it. Otherwise I'm gonna finally make a move on him."

My chest feels hollow at the implication I'll never find anyone else who wants me. On a good day, I'm well-equipped to deal with Evelyn's crassness. It still stings, but I don't normally dwell on it.

"I don't want Harrison anyway," I say, and my voice must betray something because Bellamy squeezes my arm. "I'd rather see him muzzled and neutered than pictures of his genitalia in my DMs."

"Exactly!" Nadia chides. She puffs out her chest and glares at Evelyn with all the wrath she can muster up before she's had coffee. "Harper is too good for him, anyway. Harrison doesn't deserve her."

Evelyn looks at her and laughs. "If you say so. I just think it's a wasted opportunity."

"*You're* a wasted opportunity," Nadia snaps. "Can't you just leave her alone?"

Evelyn raises an eyebrow, glances between my friends, and snorts again. "Sure thing, Juliette. But when your fish run out of food again, I'm not driving Harper to the pet store. Let the damn things starve."

It's a good thing I stocked up on their food this summer. I'd sooner smile at Harrison Bentley than get into a car with Evelyn before the primaries next spring. I pray her father loses if only just to spite her.

THE CAFETERIA, DECORATED WITH GOLD STREAMERS AND A LARGE "Welcome Back, Badgers!" sign hanging above the navy double-doors, has descended into chaos. I've never seen such a mess of frantic teenagers trying to find people to sit with. The tables are small and round and hold five or six people comfortably, but freshmen don't know the rules. They're dragging extra chairs up to full tables and scrambling to grab the best seats near the open windows. Teachers will shoo them away eventually.

I don't know where to sit.

Mom had purposely not put my friends in my lunch period, no matter how hard I begged to at least give me Bellamy. But she thinks that this will be good for me, that I rely too much on Nadia and Bell, and that I need to branch out and make new friends.

In theory, she's probably right. I spent all day yesterday promising Bell and Nadia I'd be fine, that I wouldn't need Nadia to save my life like she's always been so good at doing. But in reality, no one wants to sit with me. I already miss Nadia hailing me from our usual table near the window.

I find an empty table near the back of the room. People avoid it like the plague the second I sit down. Most of its empty chairs have already been dragged away to other tables, though I'm relieved they're not here to be filled. I'd rather sit alone than with a group of freshmen expecting me to adopt them for lunch. Then I'd really be the black sheep of Golden Oaks.

At least the food is good for our first day back to class. My plate is steaming with grilled chicken and potatoes smothered in butter, sour cream, and bacon. A tossed salad sits unopened on my lunch tray. I'm starving, and I'd have already devoured half my plate if I wasn't wary of contamination. Fish is being served today, too, and my EpiPen is lying ready on the table. Hopefully, I remember which end to stab myself without Nadia here to do it for me.

"*Finally!* Someone I know!"

I shouldn't be surprised when Margot slams her tray onto the table, but the sound startles me nonetheless. It's just my luck that we'd have the same lunch period. "Christ, Margot. A little warning would be nice."

She grins and plops into the chair across from me. "We've got to stop meeting like this, Harper. I'm starting to think you might be stalking me."

I scoff and open my water bottle. "I was sitting here first."

"A very convenient coincidence." Margot rips the plastic off her salad and douses it with dressing. "This new lunch schedule is bogus. I've never not had anyone to sit with." She stabs at her lettuce and shoves a forkful into her mouth. "Not that I think you're no one."

I roll my eyes and take a sip of water. My throat is dry. "Chew with your mouth shut."

Margot glares and makes a scene of chewing her food with her mouth shut. I can still hear her chomping on her lettuce, and I want to fling a spoonful of mashed potatoes at her. But to avoid suspension so early in the school year, I ask, "How's your day been?"

She shrugs and rummages through her salad, picking out the tomatoes. "It's okay. I don't have any classes with my friends, though. Not yet, at least. What's your afternoon schedule?"

I push my food around my plate, searching for bits of seafood, and try to ignore the way my heart swells. Margot called me her friend. "Physics with Hayes, art with Callahan, and calculus with Black."

Margot's face lights up like a strung-up tree on Christmas. "We have art and math together!" she says, then tilts her head and studies me. I sink beneath the weight of her stare. Her eyes are the prettiest shade of brown, and I feel like a book she's trying her hardest to decipher, to peel apart the pages and read between the lines like no one else ever has. I don't like it. "You like art?"

"Not really," I admit. Margot deflates a little. "But it was either that or study hall. Why? Do you like art?"

She shrugs and opens her milk carton. "A little. What's that?"

Margot is looking at my EpiPen. I shouldn't be ashamed of it, but I want to swipe it off the table and stuff it back into my backpack. "I'm allergic to seafood."

Margot's face twists with a strange, deeply rooted panic. She jumps out of her seat and drags her chair around the table, moving closer to me. It catches me entirely off guard, the concern that rounds out the angles of her face as she pulls my lunch tray toward her. She digs through my food with her fork. "My sister is allergic to seafood, too," she tells me. Her panic is nearly palpable, enough to make my heart race though I know I'm not at risk of embarrassing myself from anaphylactic shock. "Her face swells up and she can't breathe if she eats it. We found out in the middle of a restaurant when she snuck a piece of shrimp off my mom's plate."

I gently grab her wrist. "Margot, hey." She stops digging through my food, so I take the opportunity to pull my tray away from her. "It's fine, seriously. I already checked for shrimp."

Margot sinks into the back of her chair and sighs. "Good. I'm sorry. That shit just freaks me out. It's scary."

"Don't apologize," I say, patting the sleeve of her cardigan. "It is scary. Was your sister okay?"

She drags a hand through her hair, flattening her curls, which look as if she's teased them to make them stand higher on her head. "We weren't too far from a hospital in D.C. when it happened. She was discharged the same night."

"I didn't know you had a sister," I say. "Is she our age?"

Margot shakes her head and idly digs through her salad, still picking out tomatoes. "She's seven. She goes to the grade school across campus, but she's not a boarder."

"That's not usually allowed."

"Isadora has this really bad separation anxiety when she's away from my parents for too long. They tried to board her when she first started school, but she cried every night and had constant panic attacks. I think she even bit her roommate." Margot gnaws on a crouton. "I tried sleeping in her dorm with her, but it wasn't enough. She wanted our parents."

There's a part of me—a small, irrational part of me that knows better—that wants to reach out and touch her, to take her hand and gently squeeze her fingers. She looks like she needs a little comfort, but I won't overstep because I don't know how Margot would take it. I know she doesn't like sympathy, though she didn't recoil when I touched her arm or took her wrist to stop her from destroying my lunch . . .

Nope, I'm not going to do it.

"I'm glad my mom made an exception for her, then," I say instead.

Margot shoves a pile of corn around her plate. "Issy is autistic," she tells me. "My parents sat down with Dean McKinley before they even enrolled her here. Your mom was understanding, I guess. Said she'd do whatever she could to help give her the Golden Oaks experience."

"Why would they try boarding her?" I ask tentatively. I don't know why Margot is sharing any of this with me. "Did they know about her separation anxiety before she started school?"

She nods. "They thought the socialization would be good for her."

"Do you get to see her?" I ask. "Since you're not a day student?"

Margot's mouth quirks into a small smile. I wonder if she and her sister are as close as Christian and I used to be. "On the weekends. My parents bring her to all the home games during the football season, and then I go home with them on those nights. Issy likes watching the band."

I smile a little bit, too. It's cute how she talks about her sister. "Is her favorite instrument the snare?"

Margot snorts. "No. She likes the clarinet."

The groan that slips out of me is undignified. Margot raises an eyebrow. "Clarinets are so *annoying*. They squeak. Tell Issy that if she wants to play a woodwind, it should be the saxophone. We're the cool woodwinds."

Margot laughs around her fork and almost chokes on a cucumber. "I'll pass it along, but she's stubborn."

"You should introduce me at the game on Friday," I say, the offer slipping right out of me. Margot coughs and takes a drink of her milk. "I could show her my sax, let her poke around on the keys. That might help change her mind."

"You'd do that?" Margot rasps. There's something in her tone that I can't quite figure out, though she just nearly choked to death.

"Sure. I'd do anything to spare her from the fate of playing the clarinet. We have so many they're like a small, cultish army of squeaking reeds."

Margot clears her throat. "She'd like that."

"Are you all right with that?" Margot and I spent the entire weekend texting, trying to figure out who might have made the Tinder profile. But texting her with a purpose and meeting her sister at a football game are two very different things. I wouldn't blame Margot if she thought it was too much. "Would your parents mind?"

"My parents won't mind at all, and neither do I. Issy doesn't say a lot, though. She doesn't like to socialize with people she doesn't know."

I frown and drum my fingers against the table. "Will meeting me upset her? Because I don't want to—"

Margot reaches over and gently touches my hand. I shut up and stare at the place where our fingers connect; her nails are painted red today. Maybe there aren't any boundaries. "Issy isn't fragile," she tells me. "I know that might be hard to understand. You just need to have a little patience with her."

"I can do that," I say. Margot pulls away and busies herself with digging through her salad again. She hasn't touched her chicken. "Thank you for telling me about her."

Margot shrugs. "She's not some secret that I keep buried in a closet. No one usually cares enough to ask about her. Your faker on Tinder sure didn't."

I flinch and play with my food, hoping that no one overheard her. "No one asks about my brother, either. So I get it."

Margot tilts her head, a piece of lettuce hanging out of her mouth. "You have a brother?"

"He's in the army," I tell her. "I haven't seen or heard from him in almost a year now."

She blows out a breath and stabs her fork into a tomato, glaring at it like it's somehow offended her. It bounces onto her tray when she flicks it off the end of her fork. "That sucks. I remember when your dad announced his run for the presidency last month. I don't think he even mentioned he had a son, just that you and your mom were his biggest supporters."

I bite my lip. Nadia and I don't even talk about him, but if Margot can share her little sister with me, I suppose I can tell her about my brother. It's only fair. "Christian fell in with the wrong people his junior year. He did some things that my parents aren't proud of, so they shipped him off to military school."

"*Things?*" Margot asks carefully.

"Alcohol, mostly. Golden Oaks was rough on him." I tear apart my chicken with my fingers. "They sent him away after Mom raided his room during class. She found a lot of empty beer bottles stashed beneath his bed."

"Jesus," Margot breathes. "When was that?"

"Five years ago." I dunk a piece of chicken into my potatoes. "They moved him out in the middle of the night and Mom expelled his roommate. She wanted to expel his friends, too, but Christian wouldn't rat them out or tell her where he got all the beer. Something about loyalty and brotherhood, I don't know."

Margot pushes her tray away. "I'm sorry, Harper."

"It's not your fault. My parents don't like to talk about him, and we don't really know where he is or if he's even stateside. Christian doesn't call us anymore."

"Not even you?" Margot frowns. "You're not the one who sent him away."

"No," I agree. "But he knows our parents are ashamed of him, and he probably thinks I am, too. But I'm not. I just wish he would have told me. I could have helped him."

Margot lays her hands flat against the table. "You were what, twelve? You couldn't have helped him, Harper. Your brother isn't your responsibility."

A soft sigh escapes me, making my lungs ache. Talking about Christian is draining. I don't know if he's still stationed in Virginia, and, of course I miss him. My heart feels like a block of lead whenever I let myself think about him. I wonder if he's okay; if he ever got the help he needed. It hurts like a punch to the chest.

"The bell's getting ready to ring." Margot stands and gathers up both of our lunch trays. She dumps them into the nearby trash can.

"You barely ate," I say.

Margot crinkles her nose. "I'm a vegetarian. I ate my salad."

I frown as I consider our lunch menu. Most of it is carnivore friendly. "Were there no other options for you?"

Margot shakes her head, but she doesn't seem bothered. "My mom sneaks vegetarian-friendly snacks into my laundry basket when I come home on Sundays. I hide them in my backpack and munch between classes if I get hungry."

"That's not—that's not healthy, Margot. You can't live off snacks and salad."

"Sometimes there are more options for me," she consoles. "Just not today. It's fine, Harper. Seriously."

I file this away as the bell rings, that Margot's lunch options are limited to whatever is in the deli. She hauls up my backpack and plops it onto the table with a grin. At least she doesn't seem hangry. "See you in art!" she says brightly. "I had physics earlier, and it was boring. You're just going over the syllabus."

I stuff my EpiPen into the pocket where I keep my inhaler. "I can handle boring."

"I'd hope so," she muses. "You live with Nadia."

"Hey," I laugh. "She's not that bad. You saw how drunk she got Friday night."

Margot snorts and swings a studded messenger bag over her shoulder. "See you in an hour, Harp." She merges into the shuffling crowd of beige and blue and disappears through the cafeteria's double doors.

I learn two things in this moment: Margot hates the school's dress code, and I like the way my name sounds when she says it.

CHAPTER SEVEN

Mom's private study is like the Oval Office of Golden Oaks. It's circular with planked walls and a bay window overlooking the rose garden she had installed over the summer. It's infinitely pretentious with gold crown molding and a plush blue carpet that probably cost half the school's treasury funds. At least Mom's comfortable, I guess.

"Harper!" she says jovially. "Marcus, I'll call you back. Yes, *fine*, I'll tell her." Mom slams down the phone without even telling Dad goodbye. That's not unusual for her, though. When she's done with a conversation, she's done with it. "Hi, baby. How was school?"

I sink into the dark leather chair across from her. It's the most comfortable thing I've ever sat on, and it lays down flat so the sitter can recline and take a nap. I think that's why Mom bought it; I've caught her napping in here on more than one occasion. "It was okay. I found someone to sit with at lunch."

Her smile would be blinding if smiles could *actually* be blinding. My mom is a young forty-five because she frequently gets Botox to smooth out the wrinkles around her eyes. Her curly hair is the same shade of red as mine, perfectly coiffed and pulled into an elegant bun. Dad hates when she wears her hair like this because he thinks it makes her look like a flight attendant, but I like it. It softens the lines of her face.

"See, Harper?" I'm sure she doesn't mean to sound so condescending. "All you had to do was try! Who'd you sit with?"

"Margot Blanchard," I tell her. "From band."

Her mouth turns down at the corners, her brow furrowing despite the money she's spent smoothing out those wrinkles too. "The transfer student from Canada?"

"Yes."

"The one who kisses girls beneath the bleachers? We have her on camera, you know."

I wince and sink further into my chair. "Yes, Mom. *That* Margot."

"I see." She clasps her hands together on top of a manila folder. "I suppose I can move Nadia to your lunch hour."

"What? No!"

Mom's frown only deepens at my protest, her dark red lipstick smearing down into a nearly perfect half-circle. She doesn't understand—or maybe she just doesn't care—that if she switches Nadia to my lunch hour, she'll resent me for the rest of the school year. Nadia is known to hold a grudge, and being on the receiving end sucks.

Nadia spent half the summer begging my mom to play favorites, insisting she deserved one of the limited seats in the Academy's new astronomy class. But that was before we knew that lunch would be split between two periods, and the astronomy class would be during mine.

I don't want to take that away from her. Even though Nadia tried her best to get out of it, and spent the entire weekend arguing with her adviser, I know she was reluctant to do it and only willing to because of me. It's not a big deal if she looks through a telescope while I eat lunch with Margot.

Unless she discovers an asteroid, then it's a big deal, and for the rest of my life, I'll have to hear that NASA named an Earth-killing space rock after her.

"Margot doesn't have anyone to sit with, either," I explain to Mom. She raises an eyebrow like she's waiting for me to get to the point. "Switching Nadia to our lunch hour won't change that, and Margot is my friend. We're friends."

Friends.

The word feels funny on my tongue, like I've stuffed a cotton ball between my teeth or am chewing on a copper penny. I don't know if that's what we are, though, or if Margot and I are just acquaintances brought together by an asshole.

Mom leans back into her antique chair, reminiscent of the gilded thrones that look like they belong in a museum. She thinks it makes her look intimidating when it's really just ridiculous. "She's a terrible influence, Harper. I don't like her."

My cheeks heat with a blush that spreads beneath my skin. "You say that like I'm easily influenced." I try to keep the bite from my tone, but Mom must hear it, anyway. She sets her jaw and raises her chin to remind me who's in charge here, that she's the parent and I'm the child and whatever she says goes. "I can think and act for myself."

"Can you?" she asks. The question is a punch to the gut. "Everything Nadia does, you do. Remember when she first started wearing makeup? You begged and cried until I bought you makeup of your own, and it was *only* because I was afraid you'd catch pinkeye."

"That was different, Mom."

"Oh? What about the time you let that Evelyn girl convince you to drive into town with her? The one whose father is running against us for the presidency."

Us. There is no *us* in this race, but I don't dare tell her that.

I groan and pick at my fingernails. "She didn't convince me to do anything. I needed fish food and you were in D.C. with Dad."

Mom waves her hand in dismissal. "It could have waited until we got back."

"Mickey and Martha would have died. Don't you remember why the fish in your aquarium ate each other? They were starving!"

"Harper, be reasonable," she sighs and pinches the bridge of her nose. Soon she'll start complaining about the tension headache I'm undoubtedly giving her. "It's your last year of high school, sweetheart, and I want you focused on your studies. Margot barely makes Bs."

"We're in band together, Mom. And lunch and class. I see her walking around campus; I can't exactly avoid her." I grip the armrests of my chair because I know what Mom's real problem is. She's against same-sex marriage, and Margot isn't straight. "There's nothing wrong with being friends with her, and I'm friends with her. Have you ever stopped to think that maybe I could be a good influence?"

Mom blinks. "Perhaps."

I change the subject while she's subdued with thoughts of my influencing Margot. She probably thinks I can write a college essay on how I converted Margot to the hetero side. "What did Dad want you to tell me?"

Her expression brightens and she smiles again, Margot swept back into some proverbial closet where Mom keeps all things queer. "As always, he sends his love."

"His love doesn't make you smile with all of your teeth."

She purses her lips to hide them. "I know it's early, but he's already leading in the polls."

Somehow, this doesn't surprise me. Dad can be charming when he wants to be, even if that charm is sprinkled with manipulation. It's probably why he's such a popular politician. "That's good."

Mom shifts in her seat and crosses her legs at the knee. "He wants to film a commercial here at Golden Oaks. One of the focuses of his campaign, as you know, is bettering youth education."

"Then why film it here?" I ask. Mom's eyes flash with annoyance. "Golden Oaks is a private academy that most parents will never be able to afford, and nothing here needs to be 'bettered' because we're not lacking for anything. Using us as an example to further his campaign defeats his purpose. Besides, he's a booster; he donates money every year."

"That money pays your tuition."

"That money funded your office renovation."

"Harper," Mom says sternly. Her eye is twitching now. It always does when I've frustrated her. "Christ, you sound like a liberal."

"I'm just saying: If he wants people to think he's focused on education, he probably shouldn't film a campaign promotion at a private academy with a very specific demographic."

Mom rubs her temples. She'll probably go home and drink tonight. "And what demographic might that be?"

"Rich, privileged, and most of us here are white or white-passing."

"I don't have time for this, Harper." Mom rises to her feet and smooths out the wrinkles in her blazer. It's an ugly periwinkle with a pencil skirt and heels to match, and it makes her figure look boxy. "If you only came here to fight with me, you can take your leave and be ungrateful elsewhere."

It's a dismissal if I've ever heard one, as if she's talking to another student and not her child.

"I came here because you asked me to," I snap. "Not because I wanted to."

"Harper Josephine," Mom warns. She never uses my middle name unless I've really gotten beneath her skin. She hates the name Josephine, but Dad had insisted that we name me after his sister, who'd died right before they had me. "Do not make me ground you."

"Ground me for what?" I ask. "Calling bullshit on Dad's campaign, or disagreeing with your opinion on my poor cafeteria companionship?"

Mom points at the door. Her nails are perfectly manicured. "Don't you have somewhere else to be? Working on college applications, perhaps? Yale won't wait for you to procrastinate, and I expect to critique your essay before you send it off."

Rehearsal doesn't start for another hour, but I stomp to my feet and snatch up my backpack anyway. I haven't even looked at Yale's website. "Always a pleasure, Mom. See you next Monday."

It's the only day of the week she makes time for me, but even an hour is usually too much for both of us. I'd skip having to see her at all if I could.

CHAPTER EIGHT

Margot Blanchard: *What did you get for #3?*

My phone has been buzzing nonstop for the last two hours. Margot can't do math. In class today, she'd been counting on her fingers and cursing beneath her breath, eventually declaring that calculus was the Devil's language. I don't disagree, but at least I know my way around a calculator. Margot, it seems, doesn't even know how to turn one on.

Harper McKinley: *How are you supposed to learn if I keep giving you the answers?*

Margot Blanchard: *Pls harper.*

Margot Blanchard: *I'm dying over here.*

I roll my eyes to the gritty popcorn-painted ceiling. Nadia and I have plastered glow-in-the-dark stars all over it. They wink down at me with a faint green glow in the dim lighting from our desk lamps.

Harper McKinley: *You have to show your work. I can't just keep giving you the answers.*

Margot Blanchard: *Take a picture of your work and send it to me.*

Margot Blanchard: *I'd do it for you.*

"For God's sake, Harper." Nadia slams her physics book shut with such force it sounds like she's let off a firecracker. I jump and turn around to look at her, my heart vaulting into the back of my throat. Nadia glares at me from her chair; our desks are pressed against opposite walls so we can study in peace and without the temptation to talk. "Either put your phone on silent, or I'm leaving to study somewhere else. I can't concentrate with that damn thing dinging every other minute."

"I'm sorry," I say. "Margot needs help with her homework."

"Then go help her," Nadia snaps. She pulls her ponytail tighter. "In her room."

Nadia is always tense when the school year starts. She's competitive in her studies and ranked number one in our class, whereas I'm somewhere behind her in the top ten of our grade and a little less strict with my studies. Nadia calms down near the end of the semester when football is over and rehearsal doesn't eat into her study time.

"We're locked in our rooms until nine," I remind her. Study hours are between seven-thirty and nine, and they're mandatory. Every half hour, Mr. Clifford cracks open our door to make sure we're still sitting at our desks. If he catches me on my phone texting Margot he'll confiscate it. "I can't just go and help her, and you can't study somewhere else."

"Then put it on silent," she says through her teeth. "Not all of us have a father in politics."

This is new for her. It stings. Something in my chest starts to crack. "What's that supposed to mean?"

Nadia sets down her pencil. She squares her shoulders and angles her body to face me. "It means that your dad can pay your college tuition out of pocket, and not everyone has that luxury. My father struggles just to keep me enrolled here, and he works three jobs to do it. *Three*, Harper. You have no idea what that's like, how guilty I feel."

My phone dings. I ignore it. Nadia is more important than

helping Margot with her homework. "That's not fair and you know it."

Nadia's nostrils flare. "No, what's not fair is that while I'm trying to study to make sure I get a scholarship for college, you're over there texting your new best friend and distracting me. I get that I— that we—me, Bell, and Eve—aren't good enough for you anymore, but you don't have to rub it in my face. *Our* face. Faces. Whatever." Nadia sucks in a breath, and even from here I can see her hands trembling in her lap. One of her polished rings catches and sparkles in the lamp light. "That fucking dating app is the bane of my entire existence, and you've been acting all—all—not *you* ever since Margot decided to actually pay attention to you!" Nadia's tone is clipped, like she's been thinking about this for a long while and has planned every word that she's saying to me. Her voice rises, and each word feels like a stab to the heart with one of her ballpoint pens. "I'm glad you don't need financial help, Harper. But I do. Either put your phone on silent or fork up the cash for my tuition. It's not like Marcus would lose any sleep over it."

Nadia spins back around and flips open her textbook. I can see the tension in her shoulders and the way she's picked up her pen, gripping it tightly between her fingers. Clearly, she's done with this conversation, even if I'm not. We've never not talked out our problems, and it feels like this is something that's been weighing on her. I want to fix it—I'm going to fix it—but I need her to tell me how.

"Nadia—"

"Shut up, Harper."

I flinch from the way she says my name, from the pent-up anger and hurt that shines clean through in her voice. I know that Nadia won't speak now; if I call her name she'll ignore me entirely or tell me to fuck off. She's done with me, and I'd better keep my mouth shut for now.

My phone dings in my lap again. Nadia's shoulders hunch up around her ears, stiff, and I turn my phone on silent. It's all I can do to keep myself from crying.

Margot Blanchard: *What about #4?*

Margot Blanchard: *Helloooo . . . .*

A teardrop splashes onto my screen, smearing across Margot's messages until I wipe it away with my palm. Nadia and I have never argued before, not like this. She'd been fine with me this morning before class, and all I've done differently is wave to Margot during breakfast.

Harper McKinley: *Sorry. Nadia just went off on me for being on my phone.*

Margot Blanchard: *What the hell??*

Margot Blanchard: *Are you ok?*

I rub my eyes with the sleeve of my hoodie. It's pale blue with Cinderella's castle on the front of it. Nadia has the same one, but pink. We got them together at Disney World.

Harper McKinley: *She's trying to study and apparently my phone is distracting her. Sorry. Which question were we on?*

She reads my message but doesn't immediately reply.

I continue working and set my phone in my lap. Nadia won't hear it vibrate against my leg. I'm already finished with calculus and only left my paper out to walk Margot through each problem, so I take out my history book. We're supposed to have read chapter three by morning.

Margot Blanchard: *. . .*

Margot Blanchard: *I may or may not have thrown my book on the floor.*

Margot Blanchard: *Math is fucking useless.*

Margot Blanchard: *Seriously though, are you ok??*

Our bedroom door clicks open. "How's it coming, ladies?"

I drop my phone into my lap before Mr. Clifford can see it. "Fine."

"Great," Nadia grumbles. For a moment, I wonder if she'll tattle on me. "Fantastic."

Mr. Clifford hums appreciatively. "One more hour," he says. I give him a thumbs-up over my shoulder as I pretend to be engulfed by the Civil War. Mr. Clifford is an older man, maybe my mom's age, and his clothes are as stiffly pressed as his personality. "Do your best."

The door closes again, Mr. Clifford's heavy footfalls echoing down the hallway to the next room. I sigh and slouch in my chair.

Harper McKinley: *Yeah, I'm fine. I'll take a picture of my answers.*

OUR FIRST GAME OF THE SEASON IS TODAY AND BELLAMY IS A TWITCHY ball of nerves between Margot and me. This is their first time conducting the band in front of a crowd that's not a handful of teachers from across campus. "What if I mess up?" they say. Margot rolls her eyes to the tiled ceiling that's been decorated with blue streamers for game day. But I know she shares in their fear because Margot has been twitchy, too. If the drumline falls off beat tonight, it'll be Margot's fault, not Bellamy's. "What if I cue Nadia's solo at the wrong time or cut off a song too soon? What if I get the timing wrong and I'm up on beat one instead of down? What if—"

I grab Bellamy's hand and squeeze their fingers until I see them suck in a breath. "Bell, stop. You'll do great."

"Remember how Cameron Osbourne fell off the podium last year?" Margot asks.

Bellamy and I both turn to glare at her. "You're not helping, Margot."

She holds up her hands in submission, the hallway's halogen lights reflecting off her painted fingernails. She's chipped off the red and painted them blue and gold. "I'm just saying! Nothing you do will be that bad unless you—"

"Margot Blanchard, I will strangle you." I poke her in the neck for emphasis. She giggles. "Shouldn't be too hard when you're as skinny as a goddamn giraffe."

She tips back her head and places a hand over her heart, her tongue lolling out of her mouth as if she's feigning death. "Ouch, McKinley. You wound me."

Margot should talk to the theater teacher. She has a real shot of upstaging Evelyn for the school's winter program.

Bellamy drops their head to my shoulder. Cooper Smalls, who's wearing the Oak the Badger bodysuit, nearly crashes into them because Bellamy is panicking and isn't paying attention. The massive furry head tucked beneath his arm goes rolling down the hallway, but Bell doesn't notice this either. "I'm doomed with weirdos like you two in my band."

Margot and I slap their arm in unison. "Asshole," she says.

"Evelyn!" Bellamy cries when she rounds the corner across the hall, knocking people aside with her flagpole.

Her face is twisted with a scowl, and even with a sea of bedazzled students between us, I can hear her spitting curse words at freshmen.

"What are you bitching about?" Evelyn asks, whacking Bellamy with her flagpole before she kisses their cheek.

"Margot and Harper are being mean to me," they say, sidling up beside her and jutting out their painted bottom lip. They'll have to wipe it off before putting on their band uniform, but Bellamy always wears sparkly gold lipstick on game days. It's the only time we're allowed to dress up. School spirit trumps the dress code, apparently, and Margot is wearing a furry tail tucked into the back of her skirt to prove it.

"You probably deserved it," Evelyn tells them with a grin. "Hi, Harper."

She eyes Margot with open apprehension, her hand on her hip as she studies the way that Margot's arm loops through my elbow. She doesn't know what to make of it, of us, and I know what she's probably thinking: *So much for Margot being my temporary Prince Charming from the bonfire.*

I don't think the two of them have ever spoken before, but that doesn't stop Margot from smiling politely and waving at her. "Hi, Evelyn."

Evelyn tilts her head to one side, her eyes flickering to me as she stares at the shirt she knows can't be mine. There's a weird little badger on the front of it, and I guess it could be mine if it wasn't riding a unicorn. It is, undoubtedly, Margot's. "Interesting."

"What's interesting?" I ask.

"That is definitely not yours. Your mom would shoot herself in the foot before she ever bought you something with a rainbow on it."

Margot steps in as my face heats with a very unwelcomed blush. The unicorn's tail is, in fact, a rainbow, and I'm lucky I haven't seen my mom today. I'd buttoned up my cardigan, just in case, but the art room is hot and I took it off to avoid splattering it in paint. "I ordered it off Amazon a few days ago," Margot explains. "I got it yesterday, but it doesn't fit me, so I gave it to Harper. Isn't it cute?"

"Yeah," Evelyn says skeptically. "Real cute. So, what, are you two like a thing now?"

Margot coughs into her fist and I could die. It's a ridiculous assumption. "Of course not."

Evelyn taps me with her flagpole. "Good," she says with a wink. "Harrison will be happy to hear that." She looks at Margot and adds conspiratorially, "Our infamous Second Son has a thing for our wanna-be First Daughter. Isn't that right, Harp? He's constantly asking you out."

Margot's laugh is a nervous little rasp as she rubs the back of her neck. "Have you ever . . . you know, gone out with him?"

"No," I tell her, glaring noticeably at Evelyn. "Never have, never will, no desire."

Bellamy holds open the band room doors, ushering us all inside before Evelyn can snort and tell me, again, that I should go for him. Bell's eyes are full of sympathy as I shuffle through and grumble an embarrassed, "Thanks." My face is burning hotter than the surface of the sun, and Evelyn is smirking like she can hear the beat of my heart. It's kicked into overdrive in my chest, high-stepping on my diaphragm and making it difficult to breathe. Sometimes, I hate her.

Margot has let go of my arm, already swept away by the drum-line. Matt can't find his sheet music, Justin broke his only pair of sticks, and Dara has put her fist through a brand-new drumhead. Margot looks ready to kill someone.

I am thoroughly reminded that I live for this. This band and my saxophone are the only two things I've ever chosen for myself. I picked this instrument when I was ten, and took private lessons during the summer vacation before freshman year just so I would ace my audition. If anywhere in the world feels like home to me, it's not our house in Baltimore or even my dorm room, it's the band room on Friday afternoons when a hundred kids replace their expensive cardigans with sashes and plumes.

But for the first time in all my years of marching band, it's like I'm walking into chaos for the first time, like I don't belong and still need to find my place. After snagging a piece of pizza from the table at the front of the room, I don't know where to sit. Evelyn is gone, Bellamy is nowhere to be found, and Nadia is sitting with her back to me, a likely sign that I'm not welcome to sit with her and the trumpets near the piano.

"Yo, pitiful saxophonist who looks like a wandering spirit! Is she a saxophonist? Saxophoner? Yo, Harper!" Margot waves at me from the back of the room because I am indeed a very pitiful saxophonist. She's sitting in a separate circle, her friends sprawled out around her in chairs and on the floor, a slice of veggie pizza covered in spinach hanging out of her mouth. "Come sit down before you cross into Woodwind Limbo. It's dangerous territory."

I pick at a fingernail. "Are you sure?" I ask, expecting someone to tell me to get lost.

Margot rolls her eyes as she stuffs more pizza into her mouth. "No, Lady Damsel. I'd prefer you continue wandering in distress."

"We don't bite, McKinley." Sarah Lewis pats the chair Margot has pulled up between them. As Margot's cymbal player, she follows Margot everywhere on the field so she can tap her sticks against the gold plates whenever her sheet music calls for it. Sarah playfully snaps her teeth at me. "Unless you want us to."

"Jesus, Sarah. Shut up." Margot kicks her in the ankle. "Harper, get your lonely ass over here. Don't make me tell you twice."

Margot grins as I take the seat beside her, my shoulders stiff as

I lean into the back of the chair. She plucks a Dorito off my plate. "Welcome to Drummer's Paradise."

"Is that what you're calling this?" I can't keep the smile from my face.

Margot seems less frustrated now that she's surrounded by her friends, or maybe it's because she's finally eaten something that's not a salad. "Don't judge."

Sarah steals a chip from me, too, and I notice that her nails are painted the same colors as Margot's. "It's better than Trumpet Valve-y Hell and Piccolo Purgatory. At least here we don't have any squeakers."

Margot snorts and nearly chokes on her—*my*—Dorito. "That is a fucking lie."

"Have you nicknamed every section in the band?" I question, though it's very clear that they have. I just want to hear Margot name them all.

It also helps to ignore the fact that Nadia is openly glaring at me.

CHAPTER NINE

M RS. DEVEREAUX ALWAYS GIVES US THE THIRD QUARTER OFF AFTER
halftime.

Margot has shucked off her jacket and slung it over her shoulder. I'm still dressed in my stiff, navy-colored blazer, though I've popped open the button at my collar and undone the strap of my helmet.

Dad's Cell: *What's the score, Jos?*

"I can't believe Sarah went to the wrong yard line!" Margot has been ranting for a solid ten minutes about halftime. It couldn't have gone worse for the drumline, who messed up their cadences between songs. On top of that, Margot had no cymbals for most of our final number because Sarah had marched to the twenty-yard line instead of following Margot across the field to the fifty-yard line.

Harper McKinley: *I'm on break, we're winning.*

"Maybe she just got turned around?"

We're looking for her parents who are excited to meet me and introduce me to Issy. Margot has been talking about it all day, telling me how she spoke to her sister and told her there was someone who wanted to meet her. I couldn't back out now even if I wanted to.

Dad's Cell: *Hell yeah, my little badger!*

I shove my phone into the inside pocket of my overalls, then nervously tap at my keys.

Margot scoffs at me as she stands up onto her tip-toes and searches over peoples' heads. "We've rehearsed this set a thousand times," she says. "And I've even called sectionals!" Margot isn't quite as tall as me, especially not with the added height of my helmet and feathered plume. On a good day, when she's wearing her platform combat boots, Margot is at eye level with me. But right now, in her shiny leather band shoes, she has to tip her head back to look up at me.

"Were we really that bad?" she asks sincerely.

I can tell that Margot is self-conscious about her performance tonight, in need of some sort of reassurance from me, probably the kind that doesn't have to be truthful. "Honestly? I barely even noticed." I absolutely noticed, but Margot slumps with relief, so I don't feel guilty for fibbing. "I bet you only noticed because you were anticipating a screwup. But it happens, and now you know what to work on with the line."

She slings her arm around my waist and gives me a tight squeeze. "You're an awful liar, but thanks anyway, McKinley."

"Margot!"

Tucked beneath the bleachers near the food stand, a woman is frantically waving in our direction. She's hardly any bigger than Margot and is bouncing on the heels of her feet, excited to see her daughter in even half her uniform. I recognize Margot's father from several of the fundraisers I've attended in D.C. with my parents.

Standing between them is a girl who looks just like Margot. Issy's hands are folded in front of her, and she's wearing a pair of sunglasses that match her cat-eared headband. They're a sparkly purple plastic with a white bow above each lens, definitely something a seven-year-old Harper wore back in her day.

"Is there anything special about the sunglasses?" I ask, keeping my voice soft as Margot guides me to her family. I try to remember everything from the preparatory articles I've read over the last few days so I don't upset Issy.

"She's sensitive to the stadium lights." Margot's teeth cut into her bottom lip, right where there's a scar from the lip ring she sported over the summer. "Are you sure you want to do this? Now's your chance to back out."

I shake my head as my fingers click against my saxophone keys. "I'm sure."

Margot takes a breath before smiling a bright, genuinely wide smile at her parents. Her parents beam right back at her. "Hi, Mom. Hey, Dad." She gives them both a hug, then bends at the waist and smiles even wider at her sister. "Hi, Issy. I missed you."

Issy doesn't say anything, just holds out her hand expectantly. Margot pulls out her drumsticks and gives them to her. Issy gives them a little flourish, trying to twirl them between her fingers. She's a mini Margot, especially with those sticks.

"This is Harper," Margot announces, gesturing to me once she's risen. "Harp, this is my mom, Elizabeth, and my dad, Leon. And this, of course, is Issy."

"Hi," I say to all three of them. I don't remember the last time I felt this nervous, and it shows in the way my voice cracks. "It's nice to meet you."

Margot's mom wraps me up in the world's warmest hug. "It's so nice meeting you, too! GoGo has told us all about you."

"Mom," Margot whines. "Don't call me that."

Mrs. Blanchard clicks her tongue in my ear. "Margot likes to think she's all grown up," she says, and when she finally lets me go, I turn to find Margot pouting. "But she'll always be our baby."

"That's enough, Lizzy. You're embarrassing her." Mr. Blanchard's smile is reserved, the practiced kind that politicians use. He has the same dimples as Margot, the same dark hair and skin. She looks more like him than her mom, who's blonde and as pale as me. "It's nice to meet you, Harper. I know we've seen each other around, but it's great to finally say hello."

"It's hard to say hello at fundraisers," I tell him. "They're hectic." Mr. Blanchard chuckles. "That they are."

Margot tugs on my sleeve, guiding my attention to her patiently waiting sister. She's still fiddling with Margot's drumsticks. "Issy," Margot says, bending her knees until they're eye-level. "Would you like to meet my friend Harper? She has something to show you."

Issy looks up at me through her sunglasses.

"Hi, Issy." I crouch down low next to Margot, my knees aching with protest. "I like your sunglasses. I used to have a pair just like them."

The corners of her mouth twitch, as if she might smile.

"I told Harper that you want to play the clarinet someday." I've never heard Margot so calm before, so patient. I wonder if she's ever introduced her other friends to Issy. "But Harper says that those are no fun. She plays *this* cool thing instead."

I angle my instrument toward her. "It's called a saxophone," I tell her. Issy pulls down her sunglasses to get a closer look. "It's kind of like a clarinet, but bigger. And more awesome. Do you want to feel the keys? They click." I tap on them to show her the sound they make.

Issy looks at Margot for permission. She smiles and taps on one herself. "Go ahead."

Her fingers are gentle as she presses against the keys. She seems to like that they click and pokes out a familiar rhythm. "That's one of Margot's cadences," I say, surprised she's played the snare on a saxophone. She flashes me a quick little smile, happy that I've recognized her beat. "I bet Margot couldn't have done that."

"Play," Issy demands in a flat, single pitch. Margot looks shocked that she's spoken at all, gasping in a quiet breath beside me. I don't know what to say.

"Oh, um . . ."

"It's okay," Margot says quickly. She knows that if Mrs. Devereaux hears me, I'll get in trouble. We're only allowed to play when we're told, either on the field or in the stands during a touchdown. "Maybe she can play for you some other time, Issy."

Issy noticeably frowns.

"I can play a quick scale," I offer. "Just the arpeggio."

Issy leans in as the notes whisper between us, a quick seven blasts that barely last a second. She lifts her sunglasses and studies the keys as I hit them, squinting against the stadium lights. When I'm finished, Issy reaches forward with a confident hand and taps at the keys I've just pressed.

"Exactly!" I say. "That's right. You'd be an awesome sax player."

Mrs. Devereaux is calling everyone back to the stands with her megaphone.

Margot waddles a little closer to her sister. "Harper and I have to go now, Issy. We have to play."

Issy blinks at us through her glasses.

"It was nice meeting you, Issy." I smile wide until my cheeks hurt. "Maybe I can come visit you sometime. I'll bring my saxophone. How does that sound?"

Her smile is small as she nods and hands Margot her drumsticks.

Margot presses a kiss to Issy's cheek, right over the stick-on tattoo of a badger she's wearing. "I'll see you again soon, okay? I'm coming home for the weekend."

Issy nods again and clasps her hands together in front of her. "Home."

Mindful of Issy's headband, Margot ruffles her hair before standing. She loops her arm through my elbow after saying goodbye to her family, giving my arm a reassuring squeeze when her mom tells me not to be a stranger.

"Was that okay?" I ask, my voice jumping into a weird, high-pitched octave. I hope I haven't upset her, especially by offering to visit Issy. I don't know if that's something Margot wants or if this was a one-time thing that's never meant to be repeated. I don't even know if Issy liked me or if her parents were comfortable with me around her.

But Margot turns to me and throws her arms around my neck, nearly toppling us over. "Thank you."

I awkwardly pat her on the back, my saxophone digging into my chest. Her hug is as warm as her mom's, and I try my hardest not to sink into her entirely. "Anytime."

Margot and I part ways at the steps, though she doesn't have to go far. The drumline occupies the first several rows of the bleachers. Margot sits at the very bottom with her snare, surrounded by tenors and bass drums, so that it's easier for Bellamy to signal her to start a cadence. I climb to the very top, where all ten of my saxophone players are shuffling to attach their flip folders to their instruments. Cassidy Barnes can't find hers, so I give her mine, since I have my music memorized.

"Since when are you friends with Margot Blanchard?" Rebecca

asks, adjusting her reed as I squeeze between her and Cassidy. "I used to swear that you and Nadia were dating because I never saw one without the other. It's a pity you're trading her in for Margot."

Rebecca is Harrison Bentley's cousin, but she's never been invited to the White House. Not to the Christmas party, annual fundraisers, or even the Thanksgiving turkey pardoning. If it wasn't for the fact that she boasts about being related to the Second Son of the United States, I never would've known they were family. Harrison attended Golden Oaks until he graduated last year, and I never even saw him talk to her.

I wonder if she'd tried to steal some kind of chair from him, too. Or, if she had potentially made a fake dating profile for some weird, petty revenge scheme because Harrison was the Second Son and Rebecca was a second-chair nobody.

Why else would she be interested in my and Margot's friendship?

Shit.

I don't have time to consider it now. From the bottom of the bleachers, Margot taps out three quick, sharp beats on her drum. The rest of the drumline falls into a short cadence, one that begins our touchdown sequence, and I swing up my saxophone. The movement is ingrained into every part of who I am; it's time to play and everything else can wait. My fingers move methodically over the keys, every note burned into some strange muscle memory. It's as easy as breathing, maybe easier.

I've never watched Margot play before, and I realize what a terrible mistake I've made. I should have been watching her all along. She's focused, glancing back and forth between her snare and Bellamy's conducting. Her sticks move so fast and hit her drum so hard they're a blur of wood and blue electrical tape. She tapes them so that the sticks last longer, but if taking art together has taught me anything about her, I think she loves the excuse to be crafty. Tonight's sticks are a solid blue, but I've seen them striped and in checked plaid before.

Margot's brow furrows as she plays, her shoulders hunched forward as if she's protecting her snare from some devastating force of nature that'll otherwise rip it away from her. I wonder if she knows how serious she looks or if she feels the same passion I can see on her face as she beats on her drum with everything she has. It's a stark contrast to the calm she exudes around her parents and sister, a side of her I've never seen before tonight but want to see again.

The game is over soon, and we win 47–23. The band shuffles from the stands and back into the school to put our instruments away, though it's uncoordinated chaos and half of us are trampled by the football team.

"I'm leaving," Margot announces from behind me, giving my cheek a light tap with her plume. She's already changed out of her uniform and into a pair of loose-fitting sweatpants. "Just thought I'd say goodbye."

She gives me a little hug before spinning on her heels to leave, her parents outside waiting for her. Margot obviously doesn't expect me to care, to say good night, goodbye, or anything in between, and there's a sinking feeling in my gut. I don't want her to leave yet. "Text me," I say quickly. Margot whirls back around, grinning. "If you want to. You don't have to."

Her eyes are bright. She's soaking up every bit of my awkwardness and living for it. "I'll text you as soon as I get home. To let you know we got there okay. Sound good?"

I clear my throat. "Yeah. Sounds good."

She gives me a quick hug before turning to leave, and I loop my arms around her middle. Her parents and sister are probably outside waiting for her. "Good night, Harp."

I watch her weave between adrenaline-filled tuba players and tired, stumbling woodwinds. Margot doesn't seem tired at all. "Good night, Margot."

CHAPTER TEN

"I'M SPENDING THE NIGHT WITH EVELYN," NADIA FLATLY SAYS TO me when I return to our room.

I don't have the energy to fight with her. The game left me exhausted. I don't know what I've done to upset her except text Margot while Nadia was trying to study, and I've apologized a thousand times for it. She's barely said a word to me since, not a good morning, a good night, or her usual, "Have you seen my glasses?" when they're sitting on top of her head. I'm starting to get the impression that her anger runs deeper than my newfound friendship with Margot, but I don't see a point in prying. Not when she won't even look at me.

But there are tears in her eyes when I decide to look at her. Nadia is shoving things—makeup, phone charger, tablet—into her backpack with such force that I'm worried she's going to break it all. I toss my backpack onto my bed. "Nadia?"

"What?" she snaps. I flinch.

"What's the matter?" I ask tentatively. I don't know if I can handle Nadia biting off my head tonight. "Would you please talk to me?"

Nadia whirls around like my words are a physical blow. "Oh, now you want to talk?"

I cross my arms and sit on the edge of my bed. "I've been trying to talk to you for days. Don't you dare pretend like I haven't."

"Yeah," Nadia scoffs. She flings her hairbrush into her backpack. "You talk to me when your nose isn't buried in your phone because Margot is more important to you than I am."

"What?" My voice rises to echo through our tiny dorm room. Nadia flinches. "You're joking, right? You're the one who encouraged us to bond at the bonfire!"

Nadia rubs her nose in the way that you do when you're about to cry and don't want to, so your nose runs instead. Human biology is a bitch. "You sat with her during pregame," she says. "And you were with her during the third quarter. We always sit together, and we always get food during break. That's our thing, and you did it with Margot."

I want to believe she's joking, that there's absolutely no way she's serious. But she is. I can hear it in the way her voice quivers. "You haven't spoken to me all week," I remind her. "And you were with your section for pregame. Sue me for assuming I wasn't welcome."

"So you sat with the drumline?" She spits out the word like it's poison on her tongue.

"What was I supposed to do, Nadia? I'm not some wounded animal who needs to beg for your attention to survive. Margot offered me a place to sit, so I sat. And I was with her during break because her sister wanted to see my saxophone."

Nadia sniffles and rubs her nose again. "This isn't my fault."

"Well, it certainly isn't mine." My phone vibrates in my pocket. "I apologized for texting Margot during study hours. I make an effort to at least tell you good morning, and I still try walking to breakfast with you even after you've purposely been picking tables where there aren't enough chairs for me to sit. The *one* time I give you what you dish out, you take it personally."

"It is personal!" Nadia yells. "You're my best friend. Margot wouldn't even be talking to you if it weren't for that fake Tinder profile!"

My lungs start to ache and I take a breath to calm myself. "Some asshole made the profile, and Margot and I made the best of it. We're friends. I am allowed to have other friends, Nadia. If you actually sat down and got to know her, you'd probably like Margot too."

Her nostrils flare. She's angry. "Margot drinks, Harper. How do you think there was alcohol at the bonfire? Margot brought it. She keeps it stashed in her dorm room."

I grit my teeth at the accusation. She has no room to judge Margot's potential drinking habits after she'd helped me bring Nadia home drunk. "Margot wasn't drinking at the bonfire."

"Of course she wasn't," Nadia snaps. "She was too busy preying on the straight girl she hoped she could turn queer for the night."

I'm on my feet before I can stop myself. Nadia has crossed some strange, gut-wrenching line I didn't know was drawn in the sand between us. "Margot wasn't preying on me," I say. It takes every bit of restraint I have not to scream at her. "I am not some victim who turns into anything at someone else's will."

"Ask her," Nadia insists. "Ask Margot where the beer that night came from. She's not a good person, Harper. Have whatever friends you want, but pick better ones."

"Maybe I am picking better ones."

Nadia's lips part around some dramatic little gasp. "What are you implying?"

"That maybe Margot isn't the bad friend," I say. Nadia's eyes are brimming with tears that are going to roll down her cheeks soon. "Friends don't give friends the silent treatment when you've done nothing wrong, then expect you to read their mind that they still want you to sit with them at pregame. They don't get jealous and lose their collective shit when you make a new friend and don't ask for their permission first."

Nadia might not be done with this conversation, but I am. "If you're staying here, then I'm leaving. But either way, I don't want to be anywhere near you right now."

Nadia whimpers and snatches up her backpack. "You're a real bitch, Harper."

"Yeah, well, I'll own that tonight."

She slams the door behind her as she leaves.

I don't understand what just happened, why Nadia is so upset that I've befriended Margot. I've never kept anything from Nadia. If she were this upset about Margot, I've never given her a single reason to think she couldn't come and talk to me about it.

I rub my eyes and realize that I'm crying, too. I don't want fighting with Nadia to become some new normal.

My phone vibrates in my pocket. Part of me hopes that it's Nadia with a half-assed apology, but it's not. My heart sinks a little in my chest.

Margot Blanchard: *My mom fucking loves you.*

Margot Blanchard: *Issy won't stop talking about your saxophone.*

Margot Blanchard: *We made it home.*

Margot Blanchard: *Good night harper.*

Dad's Cell: *What was the final score?*

Margot's already offline, so I don't bother replying. What's another person mad at me, anyway?

Harper McKinley: *We won.*

CHAPTER ELEVEN

I T'S FAR TOO EARLY WHEN I BEAT MY FIST AGAINST BELLAMY'S bedroom door.

It flies open beneath my hand, and I nearly punch Jeremy, Bellamy's roommate, in the face. He stumbles back before I can break his nose. "Jesus, McKinley. What's your problem? Do you have any idea what time it is?" Jeremy is still bleary-eyed with sleep, which means that Bellamy isn't awake yet.

"I'm sorry," I say, making a point to look directly at his face. "Is Bellamy here?"

Jeremy spits out a "fuck" beneath his breath. "It's one of your goddamn nerds, Bell. Get up and deal with this. It's too early."

I hear them groan from somewhere inside the room. "We're not supposed to meet until noon, Nadia."

Pushing aside the sting that I clearly wasn't invited to this meeting, I clear my throat and peek around Jeremy's massive shoulder. "It's Harper, actually. Sorry, I know it's early."

Bellamy sits up and rubs the sleep from their eyes "Oh. Hey, Harp. Give me a minute to get dressed. I'll be right out."

"Are you sure?" I ask. "I can come back later."

"No, it's fine." They smile from behind Jeremy, but there's

something strained about the way their mouth twitches at the corners. "Wait here."

Bellamy doesn't leave me waiting for too long. They're still pulling on a light pink sweatshirt when they slip into the hallway a few minutes later, Jeremy storming out behind them and into the bathroom across the hall.

"Don't mind him," Bellamy says.

I rock onto my toes as Bellamy fixes their hair, scraping the strands into a loose, messy bun that flops from side to side on their head. "Do you think we could talk somewhere a bit more private?" I ask. Bellamy bites their lip. "The track, maybe the practice field?"

"Yeah, sure." Bellamy doesn't sound sure. "Is everything okay? You're not usually up this early."

"Everything is fine, I just . . . ."

Bellamy raises a manicured eyebrow. "Does this have anything to do with a certain drummer named Margot?"

Warmth spreads beneath my skin, crawling up my neck until I'm certain my cheeks are blushing red. "Maybe."

Bellamy slings their arm around my shoulders. "Let's walk."

The track is closed because the janitors are repainting the starting line, so we settle beneath the old weeping willow tree that sits on the north end of campus.

"So," Bellamy begins. "Tell me what's going on in that head of yours, McKinley. Lay it on me."

Easier said than done. I bite the inside of my cheek. Asking Bellamy what I need to ask is harder than I thought. I've swallowed the words on the tip of my tongue and now they're trapped in my throat. The question feels wrong, invasive, and Bellamy doesn't owe me an answer. But they'll answer because they're nice, because they'll want to help me understand why I'm asking.

"Harp, you can ask me anything."

I take a deep breath and welcome the warm, crisp fall air into my lungs.

"How did you . . ." I stop and choke the question back down. My hands are shaking at my sides, so I curl my fingers into trembling fists. "How did you know that you . . ."

"Harper." Bellamy grips both of my shoulders, "Breathe, okay? If you're wanting to ask me what I think you are, it's fine. Your question won't upset me. I promise."

I focus on the smell of the tree sap and the rustling of the branches as they sway around us in an early morning breeze. Bellamy is making a show of breathing deeply, wanting me to mimic their breaths, so I do.

"How did you know you were bi?"

The question rushes out before I can stop it. Anxiety sinks into every part of me, and my pulse is rushing in my ears. Bellamy pats their fingers against my cheek.

"Harper," they say. "Harp, it's okay. I think I know why you're asking, and it's okay."

I don't know when I started crying. "No, Bell. It's not okay. I need to know how you knew."

Bellamy wraps their arms around my middle and pulls me into a bone-crushing hug. "It's going to be okay," they murmur, rubbing my back as I press my face into their shoulder. "It might not seem like it right now, but it will be."

"You don't know my parents."

Bellamy tenses against me. "I do, actually. Your mom looked right at me and said that non-binary wasn't a gender, and under no circumstance was I to use the girls' bathroom. She's just look-ing for an excuse to expel me because she thinks I'm some kind of fuckin' liability. I'm surprised she hasn't called me into her office for wearing a skirt to class, or for my petition to convert one of the bathrooms into a gender-neutral one."

I squeeze my eyes shut and don't let Bellamy go. "I'm sorry."

Bellamy drops their chin onto my shoulder. "You aren't your mom, Harp. Don't apologize. But I know what Dean McKinley is like, and if either of us needs to be sorry, it's me. She's not going to make this easy for you."

A whimper cracks out of me. "I don't know what to do, Bell. I don't even know what this is."

They gently pry me away. "Tell me about Margot," they say. "How she makes you feel when you're with her."

I ball up my sleeves and rub the tears from my eyes. Margot makes me feel like someone sees me, like I'm not the dean's daughter or the girl in band whose father is running for president. It's like someone finally hears me, and thinks I'm worth getting to know beyond the sounds that come from my saxophone. That's all the tabloids have ever written about me, that Marcus McKinley's daughter is a band geek at Golden Oaks.

But I can't tell Bellamy any of this. It sounds too silly, like a school-girl crush for someone who doesn't know what this is yet.

"Like I'm glad someone made that profile."

Bellamy rubs the back of their neck. "Yeah, I guess I forgot about that. I haven't heard anyone talking about it. You still don't know who did it?"

"No." I pluck at the leaves from a nearby willow branch. "Margot thought she'd been talking to me until, well, a week ago. But I think that maybe she liked the fake me."

"What makes you think that she doesn't like the real one, too?" Bellamy asks. "Do you even know how Tinder works? Margot would have had to pick you, Harp. She would have had to swipe right on your photo."

"She said she's only on there for hook-ups and doesn't want to be tied down because she's moving back to Canada after we graduate. Besides, she hasn't said a word about liking me. Not the real me."

Bellamy scratches their cheek. "Maybe she's still getting to know you. There's a whole lot of you to like, Harp. You're weird, quirky, complex. Let Margot decide if she likes you or not. Don't assume."

They're trying to make me feel better, so I don't bother telling them how wrong they are. "How did you know you liked multiple genders?"

They take a deep breath and shrug. "It wasn't some heart-stopping revelation for me. I realized I was attracted to my roommate freshman year, and I thought that I might be gay. But then I realized I was attracted to Evelyn, too, and I knew it couldn't be that." Sometimes I forget that Bellamy and Evelyn used to date before deciding they were better off as friends. Nadia says they're too self-absorbed to realize that they love each other, and we've caught them kissing in tucked-away alcoves of the school, but I think they like what they've got going and neither of them wants it to change. "Labels are weird, you know? I like guys, girls, and I had a huge crush on Riley Anderson the summer before sophomore year. Do you remember them? I nearly shit myself when they came out as nonbinary. It was the first time I'd ever heard the word." Bellamy adjusts their ponytail. "I know it's a lot to process, but I use the term bisexual for myself because I'm attracted to people of multiple genders." Bellamy gives me a moment to think, to let everything they've told me sink in, then asks, "Are you attracted to Margot?"

"Attraction" is a funny word that feels fuzzy on my tongue. "I like her."

"That's not what I asked," Bellamy says gently. "Physical attraction and liking someone can be different. You could like her as a friend, like you do me, or you could want to kiss her and be intimate."

I tug on the ends of my sleeves. "I . . . would be fine hugging her. Her hugs are nice, I guess. But *intimate* . . ."

Bellamy tilts their head, drumming their fingers against their hips in thought. "Do you like her in the way that someone likes someone when they want to be in a relationship?"

"I don't know. I've never liked anyone before."

They hum appreciatively. Bellamy strokes their chin and scrunches up their nose at the slight stubble that's grown there between this morning and last night. "How do you feel about boys?" they ask. "Can you see yourself dating one?"

"No," I admit, feeling guilty to say it. "But I've never seen myself dating anyone before."

"I know," they say. "We've tried to hook you up with every good-looking guy with a decent personality in the band. Can you see yourself maybe dating Margot?"

The thought of dating anyone, especially Margot, is new territory. Margot and I haven't spent a lot of time together, but I try to imagine what it would be like if we did, if there wasn't a school or my dad's campaign between us.

Margot loves to draw and paint, and I can see us together while she works, see her hands splattered with rainbow acrylics and a book or three in my lap. I would watch her over the top of my book, absently flipping pages.

Dating Margot is sitting together at lunch, bantering over salads, and hoping there's no seafood on my plate. It's sharing a seat on the bus to away games, then falling asleep against Margot's shoulder on the midnight drive back. It's holding hands at the library or a craft store and not being afraid of who's watching us.

But I can't tell Bellamy any of that.

I sigh and lean against the willow tree. "Maybe."

Bellamy hums again. "Have you ever thought about kissing her?"

I forget that kissing is part of dating, a part I know Margot likes, even if I don't know how I feel about it. "Not really," I say. "Not until last night, after Nadia accused Margot of trying to turn me queer."

Their eyebrows nearly shoot into their hairline. "Nadia said that?"

I nod and pick at my fingernails. "She thinks Margot was preying on me at the bonfire."

"Jesus." Bellamy tucks a loose wave of hair behind their ear. "Anyway, how do you feel about kissing her? Your face turned a little green."

"I don't know," I say. On one hand it makes my heart race, but on the other I feel nothing at all, and I know I'm supposed to feel something. "It . . . it might be okay. Maybe. Eventually. I don't think I want anything more than that, though."

"That's okay," Bellamy says quickly.

"But what if that's all Margot wants?" I ask. "It's why she's on Tinder."

"Then fuck Margot," Bellamy answers. "Not literally, obviously. If you don't want to." Their phone chimes and they pat their pockets to remember which one they put it in. "How do you think you identify? Lesbian, bisexual, straight, something else?"

I watch them scroll through their phone. "I don't know," I say. It feels ridiculous to admit that I don't know what I am, where I fall on this weird spectrum of sexuality and gender. "How do you think I identify?"

Bellamy is typing out a message. "I can't decide this for you, Harp. I'm not inside your head to know how you feel or what you do or don't want." Their phone dings again and they sigh. "I hate to cut this short, but it seems that Nadia and Evelyn have invaded my room, and Jeremy is ready to murder them."

"Oh," I say softly. I don't want them to go. "What are you guys doing today?"

Bellamy freezes, remembering that the four of us usually hang out together on the weekends. "Nadia's mom is taking us into town," Bellamy tells me carefully. "To shop, or whatever. Nadia didn't really say, but I wanted to get off campus for a while."

"Oh," I repeat. "I won't keep you, then. Go have fun."

Bellamy scratches the end of their nose. They fidget whenever they're nervous. "Nadia's just upset that you're spending so much time with Margot." Bellamy rolls their shoulders. "Just give her some time to come around. I think she thinks you're replacing her."

"She's barely spoken to me all week, Bell, and the three of you don't even wait for me in the morning anymore. Or save me a seat at breakfast."

At least Bellamy has the nerve to look guilty about having put their backpack in the only empty chair at their table yesterday.

"It's complicated, Harp. Nadia is going through some shit right now, but you know she'll get over it eventually."

I should ask what she's going through, what she's told them and not me, but I can't find it in me to care. Not when she's turned Bell against me.

"So you and Eve are just going to ice me out until she does?"

"Don't put me in the middle, Harper."

"What middle?" I ask. "You've already picked a side."

Bellamy's phone chimes again. Their face flashes with a barely subdued annoyance, their nose crinkling and mouth pinching at the corners. "I don't have time for this, Harper. I have to go before they come looking for me."

"Whatever," I snap tearfully. But Bellamy doesn't deserve to see me cry. Not over this. "Go and have fun, but keep your big mouth shut. I'm sure it'll be all over school if you tell Eve and Nadia what I told you."

Bellamy's swallow is audible. Their moss-colored eyes are glassy with what I think might be tears of their own. "I would never betray your trust, Harper. You know that."

"Do I?" I don't care if it's a low blow, if I've always told Bellamy I trust them.

They shake their head and take a step away from me. "This is why Nadia isn't speaking to you, you know. Because you take everything so personally." Bellamy's phone vibrates in rapid succession. Someone's calling them, and I bet I know who. "I have to go, but your secret is safe with me. I'll see you in class on Monday."

Bellamy answers their phone and leaves me standing beneath the willow tree, the weight of our twisted, boarding school world sitting unfairly on my shoulders.

I don't know what any of this makes me, where I stand with my friends, or where I fall on the maybe-queer spectrum. But I know I like Margot, and we all have to start somewhere.

CHAPTER TWELVE

L UNCH TODAY IS THE ONLY THING I'VE BEEN LOOKING FORWARD TO since Saturday morning, and not because I skipped breakfast to avoid the embarrassment of having nowhere to sit. Margot is slouched in a chair at our table in the back of the cafeteria, a dark gray hood pulled over her head. Her eyes are fixated on her phone, her brow furrowed, and her bottom lip caught between her teeth.

"Hey," I say, taking the empty seat across from her. It's the only chair left at the table.

Margot doesn't look up at me as I sit. "Hey."

"Is everything okay?" I ask. She looks like she hasn't slept, and her uneven hair is swept into a messy bun beneath her hood. I wonder if Margot thinks I blew her off on Friday night when I'd been too busy fighting with Nadia to text her back. She's barely spoken to me since I messaged her on Saturday morning to tell her about the fights with my friends.

"My weekend sucked," she tells me. Her phone vibrates against the corner of her lunch tray. She immediately scoops it up, scrolls, and winces at whatever is on the screen. "Do you remember Emily McDaniels? Graduated last year, was in the color guard, total bitch?"

"Vaguely," I say. Total bitch describes most of the color guard.

"Why?"

"I dated her." Margot pauses to type out a message on her phone, her tongue poking between her teeth in concentration. This new information about Margot's love life doesn't surprise me. I feel like I remember her kissing Emily beneath the bleachers of an away game last year, though I hadn't known they were official. "Anyway, we broke up at the beginning of summer because she was going away to college."

"Okay . . ." I tilt my head as Margot sets her phone back down. "What about her?"

"She texted me Saturday morning."

There's something in Margot's voice, some hopeful longing that makes everything inside of me sink. Margot misses Emily; I can see it all over her face. I've read every bit of this—of us—all wrong. "Yeah?" It's a struggle to keep my voice from cracking.

"She's back in D.C., said she hated New York, and that college isn't right for her now." Margot clears her throat and clutches her phone with both hands. "She asked if we could hang out after class sometime."

"What'd you say?"

Margot shrugs and slouches further in her chair. "That I'd think about it."

"Well, what do you want?" I ask, pushing away my lunch tray. I don't feel hungry anymore.

"I don't know," Margot sighs. "We were kind of bad for each other, I guess."

"What do you mean?" I'm not sure if I want to know, but if Margot needs to talk, I'll listen.

Margot doesn't look great, especially with the circles that hang beneath her eyes like bruises. "Emily drinks. Or she used to. I don't know if she still does." I know I should ask her about the beer at the bonfire last weekend, but if Margot says it was hers, it'll mean that Nadia was right. "I mean it was fun. Sometimes. I used to drink too, but you knew that. I told you the night of the bonfire when Nadia was shitfaced."

I nod. "You did."

"Anyway, she graduated and we broke up, so I quit drinking. It's kind of a downer, you know? Or, well, I guess you wouldn't." Margot rubs her temple. "It's been nice being clear-headed, and I can't be clear-headed when Emily is around. Even without all the alcohol. She makes me feel so foggy. Like my head's underwater and I'm drowning, but not in a good way."

"So why would you meet up with her?" I ask. "You don't seem like you want to."

Margot uses her teeth to open a packet of dressing and pours it over her salad. "She says she misses me, but I don't know if I miss her. I've tried not to think about her. But maybe if I see Emily, it'll help me figure it out."

"Maybe."

Margot watches me open my water bottle. "Are you feeling okay?" she asks. "You haven't touched your food yet, and I didn't see you at breakfast or dinner last night. You should eat something, Harper."

"I'm not hungry," I tell her. Margot's brow creases with concern. "I guess I don't feel well, either."

"Should you see the nurse?" Margot asks. "I can walk with you. Is it your asthma?"

I shake my head and will my hands to stop shaking. "No, it's not that."

Margot slides around the table until her chair knocks against mine, dragging her lunch tray with her. "You look a little flushed." She presses the back of her hand against my cheek. I'd swat her away if she didn't still look so concerned. "You don't have a fever."

"I'm fine, Margot." I nudge her hand away and hope that no one saw her touching me. "How would you know if I had one, anyway?"

"You'd feel hot," she says dryly. Margot's phone vibrates on the table, and she nearly falls out of her chair as she lunges for it. I turn my head as she scrolls. "Ugh."

"Everything okay?" I shouldn't ask because I don't know if I want to know the answer.

"Emily wants to come to the game on Friday."

CHAPTER THIRTEEN

MOM'S OFFICE IS TOASTY TODAY. I SEAL IN THE HEAT FROM HER ELEC-tric fireplace as I close the door behind me. "Just a second," she murmurs, squinting in concentration at her computer screen. I can see the email she's working on in the reflection of her glasses.

I sit in the chair across from her, the comfy one that reclines, and I'm tempted to flip it back and take a nap in it. "I can come back."

"You should be in class," she says. "Care to tell me why you're not?" She crosses her legs at the knee and turns to give me her full attention once she's sent off her email.

I slouch in my chair and hope she can't tell that I was crying in the bathroom before I came here. "I—I . . . I'm not feeling well. I was wondering if you could, uh, excuse me from my afternoon classes. Just for today. I promise I'll go tomorrow, I just really want to go lie down."

Mom frowns, and concern cracks her icy exterior. "That isn't like you. What's wrong? Is it your asthma? Are you taking your medi-cine?"

"Stop," I say tiredly. Mom purses her lips. "It's not my asthma, and I am taking my medicine. I just feel sick. My stomach aches and it feels like I'm going to throw up."

I can never tell Mom that Margot is the reason I feel this way or that breathing is a little easier when I'm around her, especially since I don't know what liking her means. How do you come out to your homophobic mother when you don't know what "out" really means for you, just that you like Margot Blanchard?

Mom rises and skirts around her desk to stand in front of me. "You didn't eat breakfast this morning," she says. She forcefully places her hand against my forehead. Her fingers feel like ice. It's not the same as when Margot checked me for a fever, the back of her hand gentle and warm against my cheek. "You don't feel hot. Did you eat lunch?"

"A little," I lie. "How'd you know I didn't eat breakfast?"

"Parents are notified when their child doesn't enter their student number at the register during mealtimes." Mom smooths the wrinkles in her blazer. "Did you oversleep? I saw that Nadia was at breakfast. Did she not wake you?"

I fiddle with my cardigan sleeve, pulling at a loose thread until Mom slaps my fingers. "Nadia and I aren't really speaking right now. But no, I didn't oversleep. I just wasn't hungry."

She raises an inquisitive eyebrow. "I see. Do I need to talk with her mother?"

I don't know if our friendship is salvageable at this point, but it won't be if my mom calls Nadia's mom and manages to get her in trouble. This whole thing is my fault, anyway.

"We argued," I say. Mom crosses her arms, a silent demand for a better explanation. Of course, she wants all the details. "She's mad that I sat with Margot before the game on Friday, but she'll get over it. Do not call Rosalia, please."

Mom studies me in that overly critical way of hers—her mouth pinched and brow furrowed until her eyes are nearly squinting shut.

"I'll write you a note excusing you from your afternoon classes," she says eventually. "But you can't go to rehearsal tonight, either. If you're too sick for class, you're too sick to play."

There's no point in arguing. I'm not feeling up for rehearsal, anyway. "Thank you."

A heavy sigh escapes from her, one that's long and drawn out like the weight of the world is on her small, dainty shoulders. I guess maybe it might be with Dad running for president. Mom will inherit a country if Dad wins the election. "We're filming your father's commercial next Saturday," she says. "He'd really like you to be a part of it."

"I really don't think that me being in the commercial is a good idea," I tell her, and not only because I don't like his platform. "Don't you remember what happened the last time he tried to involve me in his campaign?"

Mom stifles a surprising laugh behind her fingers. "You vomited on stage during a rally," she recalls. "Right in the middle of his speech. I tried to tell you not to eat all that pizza, but you insisted. You were twelve, and it was right after . . ."

"Right after you pulled Christian from Golden Oaks."

She doesn't like to talk about Christian, but I can see it in her eyes that she misses him. No amount of Botox will ever smooth away the wrinkles that crease her forehead whenever she hears his name. Christian hasn't called in almost a year, and last we knew, he was stationed at Fort Myer in Arlington. He doesn't respond to the update messages I send him once a month, but he reads every single one of them, so at least it's confirmation he's alive.

"Yes," Mom murmurs. "You were still upset with us for sending him away, and your father thought that you'd made yourself puke on purpose. He grounded you for a month."

"He was still reelected, and the timing was purely coincidental." Mom nods and starts to fiddle with her skirt. "Do you think that maybe you could call the base in Arlington? Maybe Christian could drive up and be in the commercial, too."

Her spine visibly stiffens, and almost immediately Mom's cold again. "No, Harper. I can't. If Christian wanted to be a part of this family, he would reach out on his own."

"What if he's waiting for one of us to reach out instead?"

"If memory serves me," she says, crossing her arms the way she does when I've thoroughly pushed her buttons. "You've tried messaging him online, and Christian can't be bothered to reply to you. I will not force him into our lives if your brother can't bother to meet us halfway. Besides, I need you focused, and Christian is a terrible influence."

"Can you please stop implying that I can't think for myself? First Nadia, then Margot, and now Christian?" I start to pick at my finger-nails, tearing at a cuticle until it bleeds. "Think whatever you want about Margot and Nadia, I guess, but Christian would have never tried dragging me down the path he was on."

"You were a child," Mom points out, as if addiction and mental illness discriminate against age. "It'd be different now. You're older, the same age he was when I found all that alcohol in his room."

"He wouldn't want that for me," I insist. "Don't you miss him?"

She swipes a hand through her perfectly coiffed hair, flattening the curls on top of her head. "Of course I do, Harper. He's my son. But staying away is his choice."

"Can't we just . . . storm the base or something? Demand to see him?"

Mom's laugh is sad and tinged with a motherly longing. "No, sweetheart. That's likely a form of terrorism. Again, it's Christian's choice. He doesn't want to see us."

"Maybe he thinks you're still upset," I say. She sighs, shuffling behind her desk to sit down. "You told him to get out on Christmas Eve, and it's the last we saw or heard from him."

"Harper," she laments. "He showed up drunk and fell into the Christmas tree. Of course I kicked him out. I didn't want you to see him like that."

Mom did more than tell my brother to leave that night. She cursed and screamed and said that he'd been a mistake and that she didn't know where she'd gone wrong. Mom's cried every holiday since when Christian doesn't show up or call. I don't think I need to remind her.

"Let's talk about something else," she suggests, clearly done talking about my brother. She taps her manicured nails against the top of her desk like she's thinking hard about a new discussion topic. "Homecoming is in a few weeks!" she decides on.

I grimace and drag my fingers through my hair. "Unfortunately."

Even with the way her computer screen is angled, I can see that she's bringing up her calendar. "Hmm. Your father and I are both free on Saturday the 28th. We could pick you up and take you dress shopping! We'll need to find you a dress for dinner at the White House, too."

My spine stiffens against the comfy recliner. "What dinner at the White House?"

She blinks at her screen before looking at me. "Didn't your father tell you?" she asks like it's not obvious that he clearly hasn't. "President Shannon invited us to the banquet for Prime Minister Gallagher's arrival in November."

"Why do I have to go?" I complain. "Didn't we just establish I don't do well at political functions? I'd rather not puke on a foreign dignitary's shoes and start a war with Canada."

"Harper," she says, trying not to smile. "This invitation means a lot to your father and me. We want you to be there with us. We're a family, baby, and we want the world to see that."

We want voters to see that, she doesn't say, but I know it's what she means. To her, the world doesn't exist outside of U.S. politics.

"I'm thinking," she says, "that green would look beautiful with your complexion. Have you thought about who you're going to homecoming with?"

Her question is a punch to the gut. I usually go as a group with my friends. "No," I tell her honestly. "I'm thinking about maybe not going this year."

"It's your senior year, Harper. You have to go! Perhaps you could invite Harrison as your date? I see the way he looks at you whenever the two of you are in a room together."

Everything inside of me hardens to an icy discomfort as Mom keeps scrolling through dresses. "He graduated," I say tightly. "He's alumni. You don't let alumni attend formals."

She shrugs one shoulder as she clicks her mouse and leans into the computer screen. "Harrison is a polite young man," she comments. I don't know how he's managed to trick her. "Good-looking, too. I'd love to see you end up with someone like him. I can make an exception for homecoming."

I start picking at my fingers again, ripping apart my cuticles until they bleed. "I don't want to bring Harrison."

A protest is on the tip of her tongue when her phone starts to ring. "I'm sorry, baby. I have to take this."

"It's okay," I say quickly, bending to pick up my backpack. "I should probably lie down, anyway. You know, since I'm sick and all."

"I'll email your teachers when I'm finished. Get some rest.

I expect you in class tomorrow morning. Have you finished your essay? My colleague at Yale is still expecting it."

I try not to flinch as I salute her and say, "Copy that, future FLOTUS. I'll work on it."

She doesn't have to know that I won't, or that I haven't even started any essays. I've spammed every email that comes from Yale because Mom's already given them my address.

Mom nearly chokes into her phone. "You are a goddamn heathen. No, no, not you. I'm so sorry." She glares at me and points at the door, her usual dismissal when she's done with me.

I leave her office, smiling for the first time since Saturday, and now I don't feel quite so achy. Mom might have made an ass of herself to whoever's on the end of the line, but at least we weren't at each other's throats. That's a first.

CHAPTER FOURTEEN

DEAR CHRISTIAN,

I know you won't reply, but I need to know if you're okay. Because I'm not okay, and if you're also not okay, then we can both be not okay together.

I guess what I'm saying is that I need you. I could really use your help to figure some things out because I don't know what I'm doing anymore. I don't know how to navigate this political minefield that Dad's dragged me and Mom into the middle of.

Mom's still shoving Yale down my throat, too, every time I visit her office. She couldn't get you to be a doctor, lawyer, or politician, so now she's trying to force it on me. So, thanks. What do you think she'll do when she finds out I haven't applied? That I don't want to apply? We toured the campus this past summer and it felt suffocating. I'm not cut out to be a doctor; I can't even take care of myself. I can't be a lawyer because I cry when I'm yelled at and poli-sci might eventually get me assassinated.

That's not even the worst part, though. Not really.

Someone set up a Tinder account and pretended to be me for half the summer (poor choice, if you ask me). I don't know who did it or why they'd do it to me, but now I'm all confused. They were talking to *this girl from the drumline, sending her all kinds of risqué messages. I haven't asked to look a them, it's too embarrassing, especially since I didn't send them. But her name is Margot and I think I might like her. I don't know what to do about it.*

We've been hanging out ever since she confronted me about the Tinder profile. She's really the only friend I have right now because Nadia and Evelyn aren't talking to me and Bellamy has taken their side. They're mad and think Margot is replacing them. But we eat lunch together, spend pregame together, and I've already met her parents and little sister. Her dad is that Canadian ambassador that Mom and Dad don't like. How's that for some queer crisis drama? It's like a real-life Romeo and Juliet, except we're both Juliets.

I've never liked anyone before. Not really. But fuck, I think I like Margot. A lot.

I've tried to say it out loud. To sit and think and make sense of it. But I'm scared. I'm scared and I don't know what liking her means. If Mom finds out, she'll send me away like she sent you away, and then I won't have anyone.

Whatever. Story of my life.

I took a quiz on BuzzFeed called "How Gay Are You?" just before I started writing this. The outcome was a resounding, "You're on the fence." What does that even mean?

I'm going to send you some articles I found because your continuous lack of response leaves our messages pretty empty, so I can find them again. I can't risk bookmarking them.

"The ABC's of LGBT: Lesbian, Gay, Bisexual, Transgender, and More."

This one is better, sort of. "Lesbian" might work for me; I like Margot and have never liked a boy before, but the definition is literally, "lesbians prefer sex with other women." What the fuck does sex have to do with it? I just don't think that it's an accurate representation.

"Sexual Attraction vs. Romantic Attraction: Sex Ain't Everything, Folks"

If you read any of what I'm sending you, let it be this article. It's liberating, or something. Basically, it says that you can be attracted to/love someone without wanting to sleep with them. And I feel that. With Margot, I just want to be with her? Spend time with her?

I like Margot, and I wish she liked me, too, like in a romantic way? I want to spend time with her, but not necessarily in bed. The article calls it "asexual," and wow. I relate. I don't understand why that's a thing, anyway. Why does most everyone else need the physical part of a relationship to coexist with the romantic part? Why can't they just be separate, or why can't you have one without the other without everyone else thinking there's something wrong with you?

I've seen Margot kiss other girls at football games, so maybe it's a good thing she doesn't like me back. What if she wants something I can't or don't want to give her? Some people who are ace might like that stuff, like being touched or going beyond the fence to first base, but not me. It's not for me.

Not that I know what she wants, just that it's not me.

You probably won't read all of this, anyway. Hold the articles, don't reply, and know that I think you're an asshole. I fucking miss you, but I'm over being treated like I don't exist by everyone else, including you. I miss you and I need you and I love you and you said you would always be here for me, but you're not, and I don't know what to do.

Fuck, Christian. Just say you're alive and okay because sometimes I don't want to be and I'm not.

Love you.

Hate you.

You're an asshole.

Harper

I stare at the text box, the blinking cursor, and the green dot that means my brother is online. In his profile picture, Christian looks happy. Happy without Mom, happy without Dad, and happy without me.

Tears burn in the corners of my eyes as I delete the entire message.

Christian doesn't even care anymore.

Dear Christian,

I know you won't reply. I hope you're doing okay.

Love,

Harper

CHAPTER FIFTEEN

ESTWOOD SCHOOL FOR THE ARTS IS A TWENTY-MINUTE BUS RIDE, and Cassidy Barnes, a freshman without anyone else to sit with, is crammed into the bus seat beside me. Somewhere between having to hear about her grades and how her period cramps are making her want to cry, I tune her out and make a mental note to bring headphones for next week's away game at Crescent Hill.

Pregame is quick and easy since we're not the home team. It means less time on the field, which is great because I'm the leader of two separate lines going both ways down the field. If I mess up and don't hit my mark on the fifty-yard line when I'm supposed to, a hundred other people don't either.

On the far end of the field, gathered in a semi-perfect square just inside the end zone, we stand at attention and wait for Westwood's band to join us. Together with Westwood's band, a small fifty compared to our monstrous one-hundred, we play the National Anthem while a pitiful-looking flag billows on a weak breeze behind us. It's a mess. Our bass drums are out of sync with Westwood's, and Nadia's trumpet cracks as she shoots for a solo note she can't reach. When we finish, we march off the field, trying not to glare at the enemy band woven between our pregame block, and settle into the low-sitting bleachers in the end zone.

"Yo, McKinley!" Margot is waving her sticks from three rows down, grinning as she bounces in the grass. She doesn't need to yell, but she yells anyway because she's hyped-up on adrenaline. "Look how close we are! Move to the end and I bet we could talk all night."

"Sorry, Margot. I think I'm okay right here. I don't like sitting on the end."

Margot's frown pulls at something in my stomach, a string that feels attached to a rib bone. I hate that look on her face. "Oh. Never mind, then. Sorry." Sarah plops onto the bench behind Margot's drum and says something I can't quite hear, but I see Margot wince before she turns her back to me and sits down. Her shoulders slump as she slouches over her snare.

We're winning by a touchdown at halftime. Because we're the visiting team, our band plays first to a crowd that's not watching. It turns out to be a good thing, though, because the stadium lights are blinding tonight.

A freshman marches into a bass drum, and I pray it's not one of mine when everything goes to hell. Zander topples into the grass, his mallets flying, and one hits Sarah while Margot trips over the other. After that, it's like a line of dominos tumbling across the field, one shiny drum and feathered plume after the next. In a matter of long, drawn-out seconds that inch by in horrifying slow motion, we're completely derailed because half our drumline is in the mud.

Bellamy is screaming from the podium, flapping their arms like they're trying to take flight. Margot is screaming, too, and since we're no longer playing and the band is scrambling off the field, I turn on my heels and look back at her. She's knee-deep in the mud, her helmet twisted sideways with the strap going halfway up her nose. Sarah is gripping her by the elbow, trying to haul her upright, but Margot is too busy yelling. I think she might be crying.

"Where the fuck are my sticks?"

Sarah finds them before Margot, snatches them up, and shoves them into Margot's hands. "Get up, Margot! Christ, start a damn cadence! Get us off this field!"

Margot's face is shiny with sweat. Her neck muscles are taught, making it appear as if the tendons might snap. She's screaming, straining to get the words out, and struggling to get back up, hopping on one foot to avoid putting pressure on the other. I wonder if she's twisted her ankle, and I hear her cry out when she tries putting her foot down in the grass. I shuffle a tentative step toward her.

Sarah curses and picks up Margot's drum, slipping the harness on over her head. She slings her arm around Margot's waist and grunts beneath the added weight, trying to guide her forward. "Don't just stand there, McKinley! Help me!"

I blink out of my stupor and jog over, weaving between lost freshman and the seniors trying to salvage halftime. Sarah has deposited her cymbals on top of Margot's drum, and Margot is hissing through her teeth like an angry cat. "I don't need any help."

I think she means she doesn't need *my* help, because she's leaning heavily on Sarah, but I don't care. I slide beneath Margot's arm and pull hers up over my shoulder, gripping her hand so she doesn't have a choice but to accept my help. "Come on," I say, twisting around my mouthpiece so my reed doesn't snap on Margot's sash. "Don't be stubborn. Let me help you."

Margot is cursing as she limps across the field, hanging between me and Sarah. It's reminiscent of trying to drag Nadia home, but at least Margot is making an effort to walk. Both Mrs. Deveraux and Margot's father rush into the grass when we're close enough to the track, and our director takes Sarah's cymbals and Margot's drum before either is damaged. Apparently, instruments are more expensive than Margot's likely trip to the emergency room.

Mr. Blanchard scoops her up like she's little more than an infant. "Are you all right?" he asks, carrying Margot to the bleachers. Sarah and I scramble after them, weaving between crying musicians and the band moms fighting to regain order. "What happened out there?"

Margot prattles off in French, her father nodding indulgently as he sets her down on the bench at the bottom of the bleachers. He rolls up the pant leg of her jumper. "*Merde*—ow!"

"It doesn't feel broken," Mr. Blanchard says. He twists her foot from side to side and pokes and prods at her ankle. It's already starting to swell. "Can you wiggle your toes?"

"Yes, I can wiggle my toes." Margot wiggles them so hard I can see them moving in her shoe. "It's fine. Stop coddling me so I can get my line back together. Christ, where's my snare?"

"Mrs. Devereaux took it," I say, if only to ease the visible anger beginning to seep out of her. Her eyes are full of tears, but I think it's because she's pissed, not because of her ankle. "I can go find it if you want—"

"Margot!"

Emily McDaniels tears around the bleachers, her sequined jacked shining beneath the stadium lights. She's tall and conventionally pretty, her long blond hair twined into a braid with a piece of sparkling gold ribbon, the same kind Margot wears around her wrist on game days. Of course she would be here to comfort her, rambling on in French. Apparently, Margot likes girls who speak her language.

But maybe now isn't the right time for Margot to be finding their old spark. "Wrong French, but it's good to see you too."

I tap on Sarah's shoulder as Emily throws her arms around Margot. "I'm gonna go," I say, hoping that Sarah doesn't hear the crack in my voice. "To find her snare or something."

Sarah takes my arm and pulls me away from Margot's reunion with Emily. Her lips purse into a puffy pout as her fingers drum against her leg. "Look," she says, sounding exhausted. "Thank you for helping me with Margot. She's a stubborn creature when things don't go her way, and halftime was a train wreck. If we hadn't dragged her off the field, she'd have stayed in the mud until the band came back."

"I didn't help her off the field because I'm concerned for her reputation," I say. Sarah snorts and takes off her helmet. "I helped because I was afraid she was hurt."

She swipes a hand through her short, curly blond hair, flattened from her helmet. "Look, Harper. Margot is my best friend." We look over to find Margot holding Emily's hand, her thumb tracing shapes against Emily's open palm. Sarah scoffs at them. "Emily McDaniels is a dumpster fire. I don't like what she does to Margot, how Margot acts when she's around her."

I tap against the keys of my saxophone, my heart starting to stall in my chest. I don't know where Sarah is going with this, but my hands are shaking and it's getting a little harder to breathe. My inhaler is back on the bus, in my saxophone case. "Okay . . ."

"Don't get pissed and tell her I told you, but Margot told me about the profile."

"What?"

Sarah grips my wrists, tugging me close before I can let loose on Margot. She'd sworn to me she hadn't told anyone, that she'd deleted the conversation from her phone or the app or however that works. I should have known that Margot hasn't been honest with me, not entirely. No one ever tells me the whole story anymore.

Sarah gives me a solid shake. "She was confused. She needed someone to talk to."

"She promised," I say. My voice cracks from the rage coiling between my ribs, and I tear myself from Sarah's grasp before she can try shaking more sense into me.

"She told me about it before she even talked to you," Sarah tells me. "Jesus, Harper, she likes you. At least she did before you ghosted her all week."

"Ghosted her?" I rasp. My lungs ache, and I can't tell if it's from the rage that's building up inside of me, or if it's my lungs betraying me. Perfect timing. "Margot's been ignoring me all week! She's been too busy texting Emily to find out whether or not she even misses her."

Sarah shoves her hands into the pockets of her overalls. "See, this is why I don't do relationships. They're pointless and messy and all anyone does is break each other's hearts. Here." Sarah hands me an inhaler. "I have asthma, too. Just use it."

It would be pointless to tell her no thanks when I can't breathe. I wipe off the mouthpiece with the sleeve of my jacket and bring the inhaler to my lips. "Thanks."

Sarah plows ahead and doesn't watch as I take a puff of her albuterol. "Anyway, Margot likes you, and I kinda think you like her, too. I don't know. You're hard to read."

I cough around Sarah's inhaler. "Tactful."

She grins with the slightest bit of deviance. "You're not denying it."

"I'm having an asthma attack," I say, handing her inhaler back.

"Look," Sarah says, pocketing her inhaler. It's a lower dose than I'm used to, but it doesn't feel like my lungs have turned inside-out anymore. "All I'm saying is that if you like Margot, you need to do something about it before Emily can weasel her way back into her life. No one likes Margot when she's with Emily, not even Margot."

Contemplating if discussing how I feel with her might be worth it to either of us, I turn to look over at Margot and find her kissing Emily on the mouth.

Margot's hands are curled into fists around her drumsticks, and Emily's fingers are tangled through Margot's cropped hair. Her dad has turned his back to give them privacy, but he's shaking his head. I don't blame him.

I wonder if I might need Sarah's inhaler back. No matter what she says or how much she begs me to talk to Margot, I think I'm too late.

She never would've picked me, anyway. I could never be what Margot wants.

We win the game 32–28, and I don't say another word all night.

CHAPTER SIXTEEN

WHENEVER MY DAD IS IN TOWN, WE HAVE THIS TRADITION THAT HE picks me up from school and we drive over the border into D.C. There's an ice cream shop tucked into the outskirts of the capital that serves twenty different flavors of homemade ice cream. You'd never know it was there unless you *knew* about it, and my dad knows where all the best places are.

"Does it taste okay?" Dad asks.

"Tastes great," I say, smiling around my spoon as I shovel a piece of chocolate into my mouth. "Just like I remember. I don't think this place ever changes."

Dad fishes out a marshmallow from his sea of chocolate soup. "You're quiet today, Josie. That's not like you." Only my dad and Christian ever call me Josie. "Are you having trouble in school? Your mom said that you and Nadia aren't getting along."

Dad's best quality is his ability to put you at ease, even if he might be interrogating you. His voice is soft, wanting me to know that the choice to talk is mine, but he would prefer it if I do. Unlike my mom, he's warm and welcoming and ready with a hug if I ask for one. He's not like this with everyone; only I get to see this side of him—this willingness to give you the world if you're someone he actually cares about.

I hate that he went into politics, that he traded school concerts for an office in D.C. I hate how debates and fundraisers and personal agendas have hardened him to everyone but me. I think that's why people like him, though. He's fierce, unflinching, and he doesn't back down from a challenge. But sometimes, I wish he would lose; reelection, the presidency—anything to get him out of politics.

This is the first time I've seen him in two months, and it feels like losing Christian all over again, only Dad's addicted to his work and my mom can't send him away for that.

"Josie," Dad murmurs. I blink out of a daze and look up at him. His eyes are my same shade of blue, but sometimes they look green when he's worried. They're the color of fresh-cut grass today. "You know you can talk to me, sweetheart. About anything."

I feel guilty because this isn't true. In climbing Capitol Hill, Dad is too submerged in the cesspool of Republican politics. A queer daughter is a career killer.

"Nadia and I aren't talking right now. It kind of makes for a crappy living situation."

Dad hums considerately. "Have the two of you sat down to try working it out?"

"No," I say. "Nadia's not interested in working anything out."

He frowns and scoops out a marshmallow. "What are you fighting about?"

I tell him I became friends with Margot, and Nadia is upset because I disturbed her study time and sat with Margot during pregame. Dad leans forward and listens, assessing every word.

"I think Nadia is just being a teenager," he determines, "which is fine, given the fact that she is just a teenager. You need to give her space and time to adjust to a new normal, which is your friendship with this Margot girl. Nadia will come around when she's ready."

The little bell above the front entrance dings as the door opens. Dad pulls back his shoulders, and I notice he's looking over mine. "Josie, I need you to be calm," he says, wiping at his mouth with the sleeve of his suit jacket.

My heart kicks into my throat. I make a note of every exit in the shop, every table I can flip over and use as a shield. Dad has taught me to be prepared for these things. You don't tell a person they need to be calm unless they have a reason not to be. "Dad, what's going on?"

He takes a breath and puts on his politician's smile. "Harper," he says nervously. "Gideon Bentley is here."

I think I might need my inhaler. "The vice president?" I ask. "Of the United States?"

Dad dips his chin and pats the top of my hand. It's meant to look sympathetic, but I also know it's his way of apologizing. If Gideon Bentley is here, in this ice cream shop in the middle of nowhere D.C., then all of this has been planned. "Yes, Josie. You've met him before. He's here with Harrison."

The middle-aged woman sitting near the window with a book; I haven't seen her turn a single page since we sat down. She's Secret Service. I have no doubt there are more of them that I can't see; in the bathroom, behind the counter, in a storage closet. All of this has been planned, from Dad and I coming in to Gideon Bentley showing up with Harrison unannounced.

"Did you know about this?" I ask, but of course he did. It's the only reason we're allowed in here, and it's why the owners of the shop personally served us our ice cream. They're serving Gideon and Harrison, too, who are sampling flavors at the front counter.

"Josie, sweetheart, this meeting is important, okay?" His smile is still perfect, still practiced and polished and full of shit. "Gideon and I have things to discuss."

"What things?" I demand. "You have an office for a reason, Dad. Why would you invite Gideon and Harrison here?"

He doesn't have to answer because I know why Dad invited them here. It's a publicity stunt. The headlines tomorrow will tell the world there's likely an endorsement in the future, that Vice President Bentley was seen in public with Senator McKinley and their children. There's probably someone outside with a camera, ready to document all of this.

"Hello, Marcus."

Gideon Bentley's voice makes my skin crawl.

"Afternoon, Gideon." Dad makes room for Gideon and Harrison to join us. "You find this place okay?"

Gideon drags up a chair, the metal legs scraping over the sparkling grout floor. He sinks into it with a groan. "Hell, Marcus. It's only ten minutes from the House. I could have walked here if my knee wasn't shit." He turns to raise an eyebrow at Harrison, who's standing at the edge of our booth with an ice cream cone. "Well go on, boy. Sit down."

He plops down with a sigh. "Hi, Harper. Didn't know you were gonna be here."

I stir my melted ice cream. "Likewise."

Gideon leans around him and smiles at me. "Hello there, Miss Harper. I swear, Marcus, she gets prettier every time I see her. Good thing she takes after the wife, am I right?" He claps Harrison hard on the back. "This poor son-of-a-bitch looks like me."

Harrison looks like he wants to chuck his ice cream into the nearest trash can and leave.

Our fathers launch into a colorful discussion about the upcoming Republican debate, Harrison and I forgotten in the far corner of our booth. He turns to me and heaves another sigh, licking the strawberry ice cream that's dripping from his waffle cone. "Sorry about him."

"Why?" I ask quietly, smashing a chocolate chip with my spoon. "He's a creep, and you literally asked me to sleep with you at the Easter egg hunt last year."

To Harrison's credit, he winces. "I . . . yeah. I'm sorry about that."

Gideon leaps out of his conversation with Dad and dives into ours. "I hear Miss Harper'll be making her television debut soon," he says with a smile. Gideon looks like he cannot wait to see the commercial we filmed this morning, and not because he plans on endorsing my dad in the election. "Did you have fun today, Miss Harper?"

"No," I tell him dryly. Dad kicks my ankle beneath the table. I can see the pinching of his mouth, the slight pursing of his lips. If we were alone, he'd tell me not to ruin this for him. "I don't like being in front of cameras. They make me nervous."

Gideon spits as he laughs, right onto Harrison's arm. The Second Son of America winces. "Well, darlin', it's something you're going to have to get used to. When your old man here wins the election, you'll never know a moment without the media."

His words crash into me with a weight I'm not expecting.

I want to excuse myself from the table, bolt into the nearby bathroom, and splash my face with water that's cold enough to ice out the panic coursing through me. My hands are starting to shake, my lungs beginning to seize with a warning: They will betray me if I can't calm down.

Harrison touches my arm as if he knows I want to run and this

is the only way he can stop me. "Don't," he murmurs, angling himself between me and the window. "There's someone with a camera
outside. My dad hired him. If you run away, they'll see it. Don't do
that to yourself."

"Camera?" I rasp. I don't know what's gripping me more: fear
that I've been watched this whole time, or anger because my dad
has dragged me into the middle of his agenda. He never wanted
to spend any time with me, just remind the public that I existed.
"Have they been here this entire time?"

Harrison bites his lip. "I'm sorry. I thought you knew."

"Why are we even here?" I ask him. I'm gripping my bowl so
tight that its shape is starting to bend into a pointy oval. "Me and
you. Why are we here?"

"Because America likes families," Harrison says. "And this outing is a pre-endorsement for your dad. Them, their kids, an ice cream
shop that looks like a 1950s diner—the media will eat this up."

"So, what, we're here to make them look good?"

Harrison sighs and bites into his waffle cone. "Every kid in politics is a pawn, McKinley. It's best you learn that now. This won't be
the last time your dad drags you out to make him look good."

CHAPTER SEVENTEEN

BREAKING: *Possible Endorsement as Presidential Hopeful Marcus McKinley Seen Accompanying Vice President Bentley and Children at Ice Cream Shop.*

BREAKING: *Who's Endorsing Who? Harrison Bentley's Possible New Romance with Harper McKinley, Daughter of Presidential Hopeful Marcus McKinley.*

NEWS: *Who Is Harper McKinley? Everything You Need to Know About Harrison Bentley's New Ivy-League-Bound Love.*

RT *@GuardBabe101: @TrumpeterJuliette @CommanderBellP have you guys seen this shit? @harpermckinley you switched sides awful quick! Has he shown you his private plane yet? ;)*

The articles don't stop coming, and so many people have tagged me on Twitter, I've deleted the app from my phone. TMZ, CNN, and even BuzzFeed are reporting on my weekend out with Dad, the vice president, and Harrison. The four of us are shown together in the ice cream shop, and Harrison's blurry hand resting on my arm sparked rumors of our relationship. I want to shatter my phone into a thousand pieces or break Harrison's fingers for touching me.

Even the band room doesn't quite feel like home today. Mrs. Devereaux is watching me from her office window as I piece together my saxophone. I adjust my reed a dozen different times just to give my hands something to do, to spare my cuticles from being torn into bloody stumps. My saxophone and my ability to play it are the only things left in my control. At least the tabloids got this right.

My phone vibrates on the raised edge of my music stand. It's probably another message from Mom, who's been sending me new articles all day. I flip my phone screen-down without checking it. I don't care about another damn tabloid. I don't care that everyone in America thinks I'm dating Harrison or that the media thinks we won't last. I have more important things to worry about. I concentrate on the sheet music Bellamy placed in front of me, a piece for next week's new halftime show.

Bellamy bites their bottom lip and hovers behind my music stand. "Hey, Harp."

I don't let myself look up at them, afraid I might start crying if I do. It's the first time they've spoken to me in two weeks. "It's not true," I say. I know that's why they're here, why they're lingering behind my stand. "Not about Harrison."

"I know," Bellamy says softly. "I just . . . I wanted to make sure you were doing okay. I know you didn't want any of this, and I know how much you hate Harrison. Your dad's such an asshole for dragging you out in front of cameras like that."

"I'm fine, Bell." I think I've taken a page from Margot's book because I don't want Bellamy's sympathy. "I still need to warm up, so . . ."

Bellamy knows it's a dismissal. They sigh. "All right, I get it. Text me tonight, okay? Let me know how you're doing. I'm worried about you, Harp. You skipped class today. Everything's gonna be okay, you know? Something else will come along for everyone to obsess over and—"

"I said I'm *fine*, Bellamy." If they hear the break in my voice, they do me the favor of not mentioning it. "I don't want to talk right now, Bell. Please. I need to warm up."

Their swallow is audible as they sigh again and sulk away, walking sideways between each row of chairs to finish passing out our music. I feel them periodically looking back at me.

Our newest number is "My Songs Know What You Did in the Dark" by Fall Out Boy. We spend our entire two-hour rehearsal learning the upbeats, the downbeats, the rests, crescendos, and slurs. It's messy and chaotic. We've barely put a dent into playing it straight through when Mrs. Devereaux calls rehearsal to an end. I feel better having lost myself in the music, where the tabloids and politics and my dad's betrayal can't reach me.

That is until Mrs. Devereaux asks, "Does anyone want to challenge for a chair?"

Rebecca's hand flies into the air, waving frantically like Mrs. Devereaux can't see her. She's gone nearly a month without challenging me, and I've made the mistake of starting to believe that she'd finally given up on ever taking my chair. But Rebecca's grin is confident as she turns to me and smirks, her eyes burning with a fierce determination that makes everything inside of me sink. Normally, I would have the same confidence, but at this moment, I don't.

Mrs. Devereaux sighs. "Yes, yes, Rebecca. Which song would you like to play this time?"

Rebecca isn't cocky enough to challenge me on a song we just learned, so I watch her turn the page in her flip folder. "Heathens," she says, settling on the sheet music. We haven't played the song since our disastrous halftime two weeks ago when Cassidy knocked into Zander and Margot sprained her ankle and Emily kissed her. Rebecca has likely been practicing it ever since Mrs. Devereaux pulled it from our set list.

Bellamy takes Mrs. Devereaux's place behind the podium. Rebecca, as the challenger, gets to play through her chosen song first. We all play alone for challenges, Mrs. Devereaux standing at the front of the room while Bellamy conducts so she can listen. She's barely paying attention to Rebecca, who flies too fast through "Heathens" but otherwise plays it perfectly.

Rebecca doesn't miss a single note. She hits every rhythm and slide, pauses for a breath at every rest. Her speed will be blamed on her nerves; everyone in the room is watching her, and they clap when she finishes. It's the best she's ever played. Even Mrs. Devereaux looks mildly impressed by her performance.

I know this song. Nadia and I have rehearsed it in private with Bellamy. But I can't remember any of the notes, and I *always* memorize my music. There are too many things in the way, too many thoughts for me to sift through. I can't find the melodies or the rhythm, even if I'd just listened to Rebecca play it flawlessly. My hands are shaking as I turn the pages in my flip-folder.

"Are you ready, Harp?" Bellamy asks. They look nervous as they wait for me to settle, while I fidget with my flip-folder and adjust the height of my music stand. I nod and swing my mouthpiece up.

Bellamy counts me off, and I miss my cue entirely; I come in on beat three instead of one. They try to slow down to give me the chance to catch up on the next measure's downbeat, but my palms are sweaty and my fingers fumble over the keys. I miss every note that Rebecca played to perfection. I miss slides and misread rhythms. I barrel through rests and play soft when I'm meant to play loud.

No one claps when I'm finished. Bellamy cuts off the song and slowly lowers their hands, their fingers twitching at their sides. They're disappointed, maybe a little angry that Rebecca has picked today to challenge me. My sheet music is a blur on my stand, smudges of black along lines that bend and break through the tears hanging heavily from my lashes.

I don't need to be told that I've lost, but Mrs. Devereaux clears her throat anyway. "Harper," she says carefully. She takes a breath and shoos Bellamy from the podium. They flop into a chair in the corner of the room near the piano. "Do you want to try again?"

"No!" Rebecca shouts. She's on her feet, pointing at my chair until she's red in the face and huffing to gasp in a breath. "You've never let me try again. I won that chair fair and square!"

"The hell you did." I don't need to turn to know that Margot is on her feet, too. Her crutches clatter to the floor, and her chair scrapes over the dirty white tile as she stands. I can hear her grunting from the effort and wish she would sit back down. "Today was an off day for her, and you knew it. There's no other way you would have won that challenge."

"Ladies," Mrs. Devereaux says sternly. The vein in her temple is pulsing as she taps her baton against the podium. "Sit down, Miss Blanchard. This doesn't concern you. Harper, if you'd like to try again—"

"No," I say quietly. Everyone in the room turns to look at me, and I wish more than anything I could just disappear into the chair that is no longer mine. "I don't want to try again."

Mrs. Devereaux frowns at me, leaning over her podium and peering between the clarinets that separate us. "Harper, that wasn't your best performance. I've heard you—"

"I don't want to play it again," I repeat. I twist off my mouthpiece for emphasis. "Rebecca can have the chair. I don't care."

Mrs. Devereaux sighs heavily. She wants me to change my mind, but I won't. Rebecca issued a challenge and outplayed me. I don't deserve this chair. It doesn't matter how "off" today might be for me, she won it fair and square and I'm not going to take that away from her.

No one else wants to challenge for a chair, so Mrs. Devereaux tells us to put our instruments away. In record time, I jam my saxophone back into its case with trembling hands and a growing need for my inhaler. I never want to come back into this room.

"Harper!" Nadia grabs my arm and spins me around the moment I step outside. She's furious. "What the hell was that? You practically gave her your chair!"

I yank myself free as Bellamy joins us in the parking lot, their contoured cheeks flushed a dark scarlet like they've rushed from the band room just to help Nadia corner me. But I can't handle the two of them ganging up on me, not tonight. Not when neither of them has spoken to me in weeks. "She won the challenge. She earned it. Leave me alone, Nadia."

"I've heard you play that song, Harper. Did you lose on purpose?" She crosses her arms and blocks my path to the practice field, to our dorm room, to my inhaler. I wonder if my extra one is still in the backpack slung over her shoulder. "What is going on with you? Is it Margot? The Tinder profile? The tabloids? For God's sake, Harp, you're better than this. Rebecca doesn't deserve first chair!"

I can't breathe—don't want to breathe. Nadia is rattling off assumptions faster than I can make sense of them. "Nadia, please," I beg. "I can't do this right now."

Bellamy shoves between us and gently grips my shoulders. "Harp, hey. It's okay."

"I need my inhaler," I tell them. My chest is tight, like my lungs have inverted, twisting themselves into knots. "Now. It's in our room."

"All right." Bellamy slings a steadying arm around my waist. "Nadia, move. You can pretend you're concerned when she's sitting down and breathing. Your melodrama isn't my priority."

Nadia blinks and steps aside. "You know I'm concerned," she says, and I know she means it. "I just want to know what's going on. If this is about the Harrison thing, literally no one believes it."

Bellamy's nostrils flare. "Why?" they demand. "Because Harper's not capable of dating someone high profile? Get a grip, Nadia. You're only pissed it's not you. Let's go, Harp."

I lean into their side as Bellamy guides me through the practice field. "You didn't have to do that," I say, even though breathing is a little easier when I have Bellamy's support. I realize now how much I've missed them. "She'll tell Evelyn."

They grit their teeth and hold me just a little bit tighter. "They can both go to hell for all I care. I'm done shutting you out because they want me to. I'm done with both of them." Bell's voice becomes pained as they add, "I am so, so sorry, Harper. I should have never listened to either of them."

I smile even though I'm wheezing, even though everything hurts and I lost my chair and everyone thinks I'm dating Harrison. "Apology accepted," I say. "It's good to have you back, Bell."

They press a kiss to my cheek. "It's really good to be back, McKinley."

CHAPTER EIGHTEEN

M Y LAPTOP IS OPEN ON MY DESK, THE TARDIS FROM *DOCTOR WHO* whirring as Nine and Rose race across the universe to defeat a hoard of Daleks or something. My back is to the screen and I'm not really listening to the dialogue.

No one except Bellamy has bothered to come by and check on me. Not my mom, not Mrs. Devereaux, nor any of my other teachers, though it's only been two days since I stopped going to class. Nadia has finally stopped asking if I'm going to get up and be productive, if I'm going to shower, change my clothes, or brush my hair and teeth. My answer is always "eventually," but apparently eventually isn't soon enough because before Nadia left for class this morning, she threw a toothbrush onto my nightstand. "At least brush your damn teeth," she'd snapped. "I can smell your breath across the room."

It's still sitting where she left it.

I haven't gone to rehearsal since I lost my chair on Monday. I haven't checked my student email or looked at my phone to catch up on the latest McKinley gossip. Bellamy stopped by late last night to tell me it was starting to die down and that the tabloids have already moved on because one of the Kardashians is pregnant.

Well, it's not why they'd stopped by, but the news came as a relief regardless.

My phone is nearly dead when it vibrates beneath my pillow, a dull buzz against my cheek that comes after the rain has stopped and I've rolled over to look at my computer screen.

Dad's Cell: *I know, Josie. But your mom's already pissed that I excused you from class without talking to her first. You have to go tomorrow, I'm sorry.*

I let out a wheezy sigh. It's only taken him an hour to respond since I asked if he could excuse me from school again.

Harper McKinley: *Everyone's talking about those pictures, Dad. They all think I'm sleeping with Harrison.*

Dad's Cell: *You can't let what other people think get you down like this, honey.*

Harper McKinley: *So I'm supposed to just be okay with all this? You didn't even talk to me about the Bentleys meeting us at Rizzo's. Did Gideon tell you he'd hired a photographer?*

It takes him a long while to respond again, and when he does, I'm already two episodes deep in the Tenth Doctor's first season.

Dad's Cell: *I'm sorry, Jos. I'll make it up to you.*

Harper McKinley: *I lost my chair, Dad. My second chair beat me in a challenge.*

Dad's Cell: *You'll get it back. I know you will. Just lie low for a while, okay? Go to class, do your homework, and keep yourself out of trouble. It'll blow over.*

Harper McKinley: *How am I supposed to lie low and go to class? Can't I just have one more day? Please?*

My phone dies before Dad can reply, but only after I've already waited thirty minutes for a response. He's probably too busy roaming the Capitol and sweet-talking other senators into endorsements.

Priorities, I guess. I haven't been one since I was twelve.

The Doctor and Rose are being chased by Cybermen when my dorm door opens with the faintest click. It's far too quiet for Nadia to be the one opening it, so I assume it's Bellamy coming to check on me during lunch. They don't sit with Nadia or Evelyn anymore. They don't even speak to or text them, which Nadia and Evelyn have both bitched about on Twitter. Instead, they eat in the library, then dash back to the cafeteria before lunch is over to buy something else using my student ID number to make it look like I've been eating. It's the only reason Mom hasn't stormed into my room and dragged me out of bed by my hair.

But Bellamy doesn't need crutches to walk, nor is their foot in an inflatable boot dragging through the threshold and onto the carpet.

"Nadia gave me her key," Margot announces by way of greeting. Everything inside of me hardens to ice. "I hope you don't mind. Oh, *Doctor Who*! Which episode are you watching?"

I don't know why she's here, and I definitely don't know why Nadia would give her a key. Maybe Nadia is tired of dealing with me and she's recruited Margot in the hopes she can talk some sense into me.

Maybe, if I lay here quietly and pretend I haven't heard her, she'll think I'm asleep and leave without me having to ask. Or maybe she'll sit at my desk and watch *Doctor Who* uninvited since she's paused near the bedroom door and is already watching it from behind me.

I don't have the energy to face Margot today—to face her ever. We've barely talked since I read all of those articles, since she told me about Emily and sprained her ankle at halftime. Another away game has come and gone since then, and I've stopped sitting with Margot and started eating lunch in the library.

Margot sighs and hobbles over to my bed. I think she's being loud on purpose, in case I'm actually sleeping and her entrance hadn't startled me awake. "You can pretend I don't exist all you want," she says. "But can you at least give me permission to sit down? My ankle hurts, but like, boundaries are a thing and I respect them. I'll leave if you really don't want me here." I imagine her biting her lip, stretching the small scar from her summer piercing. "I might actually need to sit down, though. Just for a minute. Can I?"

I nod against my pillow because she came all this way on a sprained ankle and crutches, no less. The least I can do is let her rest before I ask her to go.

But I don't ask Margot to leave. There's a part of me that misses her company.

She plops herself down onto the edge of my bed and sidles up behind me on the small, lumpy twin mattress. She steals one of my pillows and props up her foot before settling her back against the headboard, and I let her relax to the sound of the rain on the window.

"You don't have to talk to me," she murmurs after a while. She sounds tired. Her voice is unusually soft, softer than the volume on my laptop or the sound of her steady breaths. It's the same hushed tone she uses with Issy, I realize, calm and gentle and everything I don't deserve from her. "But can you listen to me for a minute? Then, if you still want me to, I'll leave."

"Why are you here, Margot?"

She sighs, and I can picture her shoulders slumping down in the way they do when she's upset. "Because I'm worried about you, Harper. I know you're not okay. Please, can you listen? I promise that's all I'm going to ask of you."

I nod against my pillow, which smells faintly of sweat. I owe

Margot at least that much.

"You can't tell anyone any of this, okay?" Margot sounds uncertain, vulnerable in a way that I've never heard her sound before. The sheer insecurity on her face makes me want to reach out and hug her, to take her hand and squeeze her fingers and swear to her she can tell me anything. "And you can't feel sorry for me, either. That's not why I'm sharing this with you."

This is why I don't touch her. I know she hates my sympathy.

Margot's not looking at me even though I've rolled over to face her. She's grinding her teeth and drumming her fingers against her thigh in a rhythm that sounds like it's from a cadence. She's conflicted. I can see it in her eyes and the tightness of her jaw and the crinkled bridge of her nose. Margot doesn't want to tell me this, whatever she's come here to say, but she's going to do it anyway.

"I won't tell anyone. Ever."

Margot takes a shaky breath. She's always waiting for me to say something, and maybe, somehow, giving her permission to confide in me was it. "I used to do some really shitty things when we first moved here." Margot finds a loose thread on her skirt and twists it around her index finger. "I was so angry that my dad uprooted our family just so he could take this job. We didn't sign up for it, you know? I thought it was selfish, and I thought my entire life was over because I had to leave all my friends. Christ, it sounds so ridiculous now."

Her face hollows with some kind of grim determination. Margot swallows and rips off the thread. "I used to, um . . . I used to self-harm for a while when we first came here."

I prop myself up onto my elbow, sprung into a motion that jars us both by the need to check every inch of her. I want to hunt for fresh wounds and old scars that I can touch and smooth over with my fingertips. I want to hold her close and stop this cataclysmic breaking feeling in my chest. But I do not do that—would never do that. Margot is trusting me with this part of her, this chapter that she clearly doesn't like people to read. She's always felt so unshakeable, like nothing in this world could ever break her, and I wonder if she's ever told Sarah or Emily about this.

I say nothing and let her finish. Margot needs to talk as much as I need to listen.

"I was really angry and really sad, and those feelings were consuming, like a black hole or some shit. I wanted to feel literally anything else." Margot holds out her hand, placing it palm up on her knee in offering. She'll never ask me to hold it, but it's there if I want to take it. My fingers inch toward her as she continues, "I'm not telling you this because I think it's something you might be doing, or even something I think you might consider doing, because I don't. But I also don't know what you're going through, what it's like to have loser friends or to lose my chair, or to date a creepy politician's son." Margot studies my hand as I slide it across the bed. "But I know that when I felt the way you're feeling, I wish I'd had someone to talk to."

I slip my hand into Margot's, and her fingers curl around mine. Her skin radiates this soothing warmth, combating her calloused palm, and all I want is to sink into it, into Margot. I've been cold and shivering for days, even beneath my blanket. But Margot takes that all away and makes me feel warm from the inside out. The sunshine to my dark side of the moon.

"Thank you," I tell her quietly. "For trusting me."

Margot traces her thumb across the top of my knuckles and smiles. "Thanks for listening."

"I, um." My mouth feels dry as a desert. As always, I don't know what to say to her. "You don't still do that, do you?"

She flexes her sprained ankle and finds a new thread on her cardigan. "No," she says. Her voice is soft again. "My parents found out and got me help. I went to therapy for a while, off campus on the weekends, and was on some medication that worked for me. I, uh, also found some other ways to cope." With the hand that's holding mine, Margot draws shapes on my palm with her index finger. A heart, a star, and something I think is meant to resemble the TARDIS. "I assume you know that the alcohol at the bonfire was mine."

I don't let Margot hear the air as it whooshes from my lungs. "Nadia told me."

She sighs. Margot's shoulders cave in around her, her infamously bad posture like poor muscle memory. I'm surprised Mrs. Devereaux hasn't strapped her into a chair to try fixing it. "I was trying to get rid of it at the bonfire."

I bite my lip. "Is that why you helped me carry Nadia home? Because she was drunk off your beer?"

Margot winces. "Yeah. I, uh, felt responsible, I guess. And I knew you couldn't have gotten her there on your own, and I don't—had something happened to either of you, I . . ." Margot's eyes shutter. "Emily dropped it off to me when the band moved back to campus. I wanted it gone so I wasn't tempted to drink it."

I know I shouldn't ask, Margot owes me nothing more than what she's already offered, but I can't stop myself; I have to know. "Why are you even with her?"

Margot's eyes pop open wide. "I'm not. God, Harp, is that why you've been ignoring me? You thought I was back with Emily? Oh my God, why didn't you just ask me?"

I drop off my elbow and bury my face into the satin fabric of my pillowcase. Margot grumbles in French as she tugs at my shoulders, trying to flip me back over, but I've pulled the blanket over my head to hide my utter embarrassment. "Harper Middle-Name McKinley, you'd better look at me you frustrating little shit! Wait, what *is* your middle name? I need to know so I can call you by it whenever I'm annoyed with you."

"Go away, Margot."

"Mine's Amaya. Now tell me yours." She pulls on the blanket, but I've tucked it in around myself to weigh it down. Margot Amaya is pretty. I wonder if she's named after anyone like I am. "Oh, come on. Just tell me. Sprained ankle or not, I can still kick your ass with it."

"If I tell you, will you go away and pretend this conversation never happened?"

Margot snorts. "Not a chance, McKinley. Is that really why you stopped talking to me? You thought I was back with Emily?" She must see me shrug beneath the blanket because she sighs, settling back down with her hand resting gently between my shoulders. "I'm not. I mean, like, we're not together. I don't—I don't want to be with her. She represents a crappy part of my life that I don't want to revisit."

"You kissed her at the game, though," I say. "What was I supposed to think?"

"Can you look at me?" Margot asks, tugging at the blanket again. I know I'm being childish. She deserves my full attention after the way I've assumed so much about her, the way I've treated her. But I can't look at her. My face is hot with shame and is probably pinker than the rose gold comforter I'm hiding under. "Please, Harp?"

I pull back the blanket just enough to peek out at her. "I'm looking."

Margot rolls her eyes, but her mouth twitches with the

beginning of what could be a smile if she wasn't so annoyed with me. "Good enough, I guess. But yeah, I kissed her at the game. I needed to see if it felt the same sober as it did when we were drunk. Emily and I were never really together unless beer was involved."

"Did it?" I ask. "Feel the same?"

Margot shakes her head. "No."

There's a part of me that's overjoyed, albeit a bit selfishly, to know that Margot doesn't feel what she used to for Emily. But the other part of me feels empty, as if a hole has opened inside my chest. Even if Margot doesn't like her, and even if, by chance, she happens to like me instead, there's nothing either of us can do about it.

I pull back the blanket a little more. "I'm sorry."

Margot slides a little farther down the headboard, her face twisting with pained frustration as she grunts and adjusts her booted foot. "I really wish you'd just talked to me about this, Harp. I couldn't figure out what I might have done to upset you." Her head lolls toward me once she's resting on my pillow. "Can I ask you a personal question? Feel free to say no."

She's not going to beat around the bush, and I take a deep breath because I think I know what she wants. But I don't know if I know how to answer her. Not yet. "Go ahead."

Margot stretches out beside me, sinking until we're eye-level. At least she'll do me the favor of literally keeping this between us, but she might give me a heart attack in the process. My stomach flips from how close she is, how I can see flecks of green in her dark brown eyes and the scar from what looks like an old nose piercing. Something about it feels too intimate, as if I'm seeing these little details that no one ever notices because no one ever gets this close to her. "Do you even like girls?" she asks. Her voice is hardly above a whisper. "Or am I the lesbian who's got a hopeless crush on my straight friend?"

I want to disappear beneath the blanket again, but Margot deserves better than that.

Of all the people at this school, of everyone she likely met on Tinder, I don't know why she'd want me, why she'd like someone that everyone else stays away from. It shouldn't come as a surprise, not when Sarah already told me that Margot likes me, but it feels different coming from her.

"I—it's complicated." My airway squeezes shut, muffles my voice, but Margot is the definition of patience. She lays and waits and watches me, monitoring my breaths like she has my asthma down to a science. Maybe she's using Sarah as a reference, knows what to look for to know if I need my inhaler. "I don't . . . I don't know what I am. Not really. I mean, I've been googling things and reading posts on Tumblr, and I'm trying to learn queer terminology because I don't know what any of it means, and—"

"Hey." Margot's hand searches beneath the blanket, patting the mattress until she finds me. My breath catches in my throat. Margot has touched me before, patted my arm and fiddled with my hair in art class, but somehow this feels different, more nerve-racking than comforting, probably because she's lying in my bed, something no one else has ever done except for Nadia. "You don't need to have all the answers, Harper; it's complicated. Sometimes we don't fit neatly into any one category. Look at Sarah. She's pansexual and poly and has this thing with two other girls in our grade, and that's okay. Weird, because neither of them like me, and it's awkward when she invites them over, but okay."

I suck in a breath and try to grip Margot's fingers, my own sweaty and trembling, then twist them between hers because I want to know what holding Margot's hand feels like. She doesn't seem to mind. "I like you, though," I say. Margot's eyes light up, brighter than I've ever seen them. She gives a little wiggle and bites her lip to contain what I think is a grin. "What does that mean?"

Margot snuggles into my pillow, still fighting a smile, her fingers curled between mine. "It means whatever you want it to mean," she says. "I kind of had a feeling that you might, you know, like me at least a little bit. Especially when you ducked beneath the blanket the second you brought up Emily." Margot reaches up and playfully flicks my nose. I yelp and swat her away. "But after you ghosted me, again, I thought that maybe I was wrong."

I sink a little farther beneath the comforter. "I'm sorry," I tell her, and I hope she knows I mean it. "I thought I was wrong. I thought maybe, at first, you might like me. But then you were so torn over Emily, and I didn't want to get in the way, so I just . . . you know."

"Distanced yourself?"

I nod. "Yeah."

Margot is staring at our hands, at the way they bend and curl and her dark skin melds into my freckled pale. She traces her thumb against mine. "You were right, Harp. I'm sorry I misled you with Emily. I should have talked to you, too, I guess."

"What, um, are we supposed to do about this?" I ask. Margot raises an eyebrow, so I give her hand a little squeeze. "Are we, uh, anything? Or am I still reading this all wrong?"

Margot shakes her head and shuffles a bit closer. My heart jumps into my throat as she presses her booted foot against my socked feet. "I think we need to take our time figuring out what this is or what it might be," she says carefully. "Stop ghosting each other, spend time together, that sort of thing. I think you also need to take time to get out of your head a little. You're still worried about the Tinder profile, which hasn't been active for weeks by the way, and you're worried about the tabloids and whatever they're saying about you and Harrison."

I let out a sound that makes my chest ache, something between a whimper and a whine. "None of it's true."

"I know," Margot murmurs. "I saw the pictures. You looked miserable. Why was he touching you, anyway? I wanted to break his hand."

"Publicity, probably," I tell her, but I don't necessarily think that's true. Harrison seemed genuine at the ice cream shop, like he'd been trying to look out for me.

I know Margot won't buy it, though.

"Anyway," Margot scoffs. "I never believed it for a second. Harrison is an arrogant prick, and you're only into semi-arrogant drummers."

I roll my eyes to the ceiling. "You really can be insufferable, you know."

She snorts and rolls onto her back, though she keeps her hand firmly in mine. "I'm really, really good at rushing things, Harp. And I don't want to do that with you." Her voice has gone soft again as if she's confiding another dark secret. "I want to try, though, and maybe do this right. If that's what you want, anyway. I know your parents are, uh, your parents."

I wince and study Margot's face. She's staring at the ceiling, her dark eyes darting back and forth between the glow-in-the-dark stars plastered above my bed. Margot will end this now if I ask her to, but she looks like she's praying it never comes to that. "What about Canada?" I ask. "I thought you didn't want to be tied down?"

"Maybe I changed my mind," she answers.

"Maybe my parents don't have to find out."

Margot's eyes crinkle at the corners. "I knew there was a bit of rebel in you somewhere. I like it." She turns her head and looks at me. "To potentially dangerous secrets?"

"And to Nadia, for giving you her room key."

Margot snorts and buries her face into my pillow. "I didn't really give her a choice. I threatened to have my basses run her over on the field, and she was more than happy to hand it over. Now, come on." She shoves against my shoulder to try and roll me over. "Let's watch *Doctor Who* and shit-talk Harrison Bentley, and then tomorrow, we're getting you back to rehearsal before Devereaux benches you for Friday."

I supply her with the quietest giggle, one I hope she realizes is genuine. "Sounds good."

Margot's grin is blinding.

CHAPTER NINETEEN

THE BAND ROOM HAS YET TO FEEL LIKE HOME AGAIN.

It doesn't feel like I belong here. It doesn't feel like this band is my family and this room is where I go when I need to be surrounded by the familiar—familiar walls, familiar faces, familiar sounds—a room where I'm part of a whole and no one cares about who makes up the bigger picture, just that the picture exists. But it's different now, all hushed whispers and curious eyes and a chair that isn't mine.

Rebecca is slouched against the back of my old chair, her face smug as she idly taps against her saxophone keys. Mrs. Devereaux is working with the flutes, nailing down their feature in next week's halftime show, and Rebecca doesn't care enough to look over the sheet music that Bellamy passed out to us. We won't be rehearsing it until next week when we finally retire "Bad Guy" by Billie Eilish and replace it with "All Along the Watchtower," but she's made herself comfortable and is confident that no one will challenge her.

She's right.

I've been fumbling through our music since the start of rehearsal, my fingers slipping down and pressing keys that aren't meant to be pressed. My saxophone honks out each note, slides through rests, and lingers too long at every downbeat, a far cry from the smooth, rich sound I'm accustomed to. I wonder if someone has tampered with it, or if they've plucked off my keypads or shoved something inside the bell. But it's not the instrument that's broken, it's the player, and I'm huffing into the mouthpiece as if I've forgotten every aspect of breath control.

My reed is chipped too, which doesn't help.

Mrs. Devereaux returns to her podium at the front of the room and sighs. The clock reads 7:56 p.m.; there's not enough time for another run-through of our set list. "Anyone want to challenge for a chair?" she asks. The look on her face is damn near begging us to keep our hands down, so we do, keeping our chairs as they are. Mrs. Devereaux sighs again, relieved. "Good. Pack up your shit and get some rest tonight. Harper, can I see you for a minute?"

My insides twist into something foreign, something painful and aching that sucks all the air from my lungs. No one gets called into Mrs. Devereaux's office unless she's planning on taking away their marching privileges. There's a game on Friday and since I've already missed two rehearsals this week, she's within her rights to tell me I'm not allowed to play.

Suddenly, Bellamy is at my side, hunching down with their hands on my knees to keep balanced. "Hey," they say, taking my saxophone case and sliding it beneath my chair. "Devereaux knows you've had a rough couple of days, okay? And I put in a good word for you this morning. She gets it, Harp. She's gonna let you march on Friday. The band needs you."

My hands are shaking as Mrs. Devereaux knocks on her office window, motioning me inside from behind the glass, and twists the blinds shut. "But what if she tells me that I can't march?" I ask. "I'll have a fucking breakdown in front of everyone."

"So have a breakdown!" Sarah says cheerfully, coming up behind me to wrap her arms around my shoulders.

Margot grips the collar of Sarah's leather jacket and hauls her back so she can take her place. She leans her head against my temple and gives me an encouraging squeeze. I find myself sinking back into her. "Bellamy's right, Harp. You're a good musician and we need you. Shit, I take half my cues from you. And Devereaux knows that, just like she knows you're going through a lot right now. She's not gonna put you out after four years just because the media is toxic and you needed a minute to breathe."

"Exactly," Bellamy agrees, smiling wide as they rise to their feet and offer me a polished hand. Their fingernails are neon green today. "Come on, McKinley. I'll go with you. The longer you wait, the less likely she is to be reasonable. She didn't cuss out the drumline today, so I'd say she's in a fairly good mood."

I tuck myself into Bellamy's side as we weave across the band room, skirting around tubas and ducking beneath swinging trombone slides. Bellamy tells them all to put their instruments away, that the trombones can't sword fight, and the tubas can't play with someone's head inside the bell. "You'll bust his fuckin' eardrums, Leah. Christ. Put it away."

Sometimes I wonder if Bellamy misses being one of us, or if they regret trading in their clarinet for a podium at halftime. Most of the time, the band doesn't listen to them and will only come to attention when Mrs. Devereaux screams "Band, ten-hut!" until her face is red. But being our field commander means everything to them. They've been training for this since first seeing the marching band five years ago. "I'm gonna do that, Harp! I'm gonna be drum major!"

"Field commander," Nadia had corrected them, sitting with her chin in the palm of her hand in the middle school's gymnasium bleachers. Golden Oaks' marching band had come down from the high school for the sole purpose of recruiting incoming freshmen, but I hadn't needed to watch a small scale performance of their halftime show to know that I wanted to be a part of it. Bellamy hadn't needed it either, and our names had been the first ones on the sign-up sheet. Nadia's had been last, determined to ditch her band geek status until she'd realized that Bell and I would be at football games without her.

"Ah, Harper!" says Mrs. Devereaux, yanking me from the memories of an easier time and into the cluttered walls of her office.

All I can focus on is the chair, this strange blue thing she's dragged out of storage for me to sit in while she talks to me. I don't like it. How many people have sat in it that never got to march again?

Mrs. Devereaux kicks it out a little farther with her foot. "Take a seat," she says, then looks up at Bellamy and raises a bushy eyebrow. "Beat it, Parker. You can have her back when we're done."

Bellamy bites their lip, lingering in the doorway as I sit down on the very edge of the chair. "I'll be right outside, Harp. Okay? Margot, too. We'll walk you back to your dorm."

"Close the door on your way out," Mrs. Devereaux says, tapping her fingers against the top of her desk until Bellamy finally disappears, the door clicking shut behind them. Mrs. Devereaux lets out a sigh as she slumps against the back of her swivel chair, a rare moment of what I think might be peace. "Harper, Harper, Harper. What is going on with you, kid? Four years and you've never even been late to rehearsal, and now all of a sudden you miss two?"

It's the disappointment in her tone that has everything flooding out of me all at once.

"I'm sorry. I'm so sorry. I know I missed rehearsal and there's a game on Friday and—and I know you have rules and that you have them for a reason but I really, really need to march. Please. I'll never miss rehearsal ever again and I'll always be early and stay after. I know I fucked up and that I should have just come but—but did you see those articles? About my dad and me? About me and Harrison Bentley? They're not even true! But people were talking and staring and Rebecca won my chair and . . ."

"Harper, honey, calm down—"

"And I know I don't deserve to stay in band, but it's all I have and I'll do anything you want if you let me finish the season. It's almost over anyway and I promise I'll do better and . . ."

Mrs. Devereaux studies my face with a thoughtful expression, her eyes crinkling as she pinches her chin between her thumb and index finger. I feel myself shake harder beneath her stare, so hard that my teeth start to rattle. "You graduate in, what, seven months? Eight?"

I blink at her, momentarily too confused to focus on the clacking of my teeth and the twisting of my organs. "Uh. Yes?"

Mrs. Devereaux gives me a little smile. "Do you know what you're doing after high school? Where you might go to college?" She doesn't pause to let me answer—not that I have a good answer anyway—so the question must be rhetorical. She likely doesn't care. "I, personally, can see you ending up somewhere small, less prestigious and flashy. You'd do well on a larger campus, of course, but I think you'd thrive somewhere hidden away. Have you thought about it?"

No, I want to say, I haven't, and I don't understand what college has to do with whether or not she lets me march on Friday. "My parents want me to go somewhere like Yale or Harvard, somewhere close, but—"

"I'm not asking about where your parents want you to go,

Harper. I'm asking you where you want to go, what you want." Mrs. Devereaux leans back in her chair. "What about your academics? What do you want to study once you get there?"

"My parents want me to study law, or political science, or—"

"That's not what I asked, Harper."

I let out a sigh that's halfway between frustrated and anxious. It rattles my lungs because asthma's a bitch and I don't like being put on the spot like this. I don't like questions I don't know the answers to. "Why are you asking me?" I ask, wrapping my arms around my middle. I sit up higher in the chair, shifting uncomfortably to cross one leg over the other. "What does any of this have to do with marching band? I just—I want to march on Friday, Mrs. Devereaux. And I don't want you to kick me out of band."

Mrs. Devereaux frowns. "I've said nothing about not letting you march."

This time it's a whine that slips out of me. My brain and well-being can't take this. "Then why am I here?"

"Because there's something that I want you to understand," she says and closes her dot book after sticking a pen inside to mark her page. "What's that old saying, something about kids being a product of their environment? It's a load of horseshit, really. Especially for you."

My brow furrows as I frown at her. "What's that supposed to mean?"

"It means that, when I asked you about college just now, your first instinct was to tell me about what your parents want for you. 'My parents want me to go here, my parents want me to study this.' And if you want those things too, that's fine. I think you'd make a great lawyer or a non-corrupt politician. But I didn't hear you say I." Mrs. Devereaux reaches over the desk to gently pat my hand. I try my best not to flinch. "What do you love about band, Harper? Why are you here and why does the idea of not letting you march make you anxious?"

I swallow, entirely unprepared for this. Because now, I know the answer. I know it in my gut and in my heart, I just don't know how to convey it with words. Not in any way that makes sense. "Because I . . . I feel like I belong here?"

Mrs. Devereaux nods encouragingly. "Keep going."

I draw in a breath and try to dig deeper for the words. There's got to be something more meaningful rattling around somewhere inside of me. "I'm part of something, I guess, something bigger than me that makes other people happy. Like, did you know that Margot has a little sister named Issy?" Mrs. Devereaux smiles and nods again. "She's the cutest kid ever and loves to play with Margot's drumsticks and watching the band makes her happy. And—and Bellamy, right? They love conducting, and I love that I can be a part of that for them."

Her laugh is gentle. "Those are all good reasons to enjoy band," she says. "But they're reasons to enjoy band for the sake of people who aren't you. You like making them happy, sure. But why does band make you happy?"

I finally cave and sink against the back of the chair. "Because it's . . ." I close my eyes and pinch the bridge of my nose, racking my brain for something. "Because it's something I chose for myself. Because I'm good at it, sometimes, and because I love making other people happy. Seriously. Making them happy makes me happy, and it makes holding my saxophone feel like it's an extra limb, like a third arm or a third leg or some weird alien extension that's part of me. And—and I feel like—it feels—Jesus. It feels like I belong some-where. And feeling like I'm a part of something when I've never felt

153

part of anything is . . ."

"Freeing?" Mrs. Devereaux offers softly.

"Yeah, exactly." I reach up to scratch my face and brush away the hair that's tickling my cheek and chin, but my skin feels wet and my lips taste salty. Fuck, when did I start crying? Mrs. Devereaux pats my hand, accepting that she's pushed me to some breaking point I didn't realize I was standing on. I sniffle and draw in a breath. "It feels freeing, and if I can't march tomorrow or you kick me out of band, I lose that. I can't make people happy and I lose that extra limb and I won't have anything left; just a bunch of fucking articles about Dad taking me to get ice cream."

Mrs. Devereaux hands me a tissue box from the far side of her desk. "Those articles don't mean anything, Harper, and you can't control how everyone else responds to them. But you can control how you respond to their responses. Don't you think that, maybe, missing rehearsal and possibly not getting to march tomorrow is letting those shoddy journalists and people like Rebecca take advantage of how deeply you feel things?"

I wipe my nose with a tissue. "Maybe."

"Don't you think that, maybe, if you allow yourself this little bit of happiness here at school, doing what you love and being a part of something great, you could allow that for yourself once you graduate, too?" Mrs. Devereaux takes back the box of tissues. "People are always going to talk, Harper. They'll always want to stop and stare. But to hell with them, because you're better than that."

"What if I'm not, though?"

"You are," Mrs. Devereaux reiterates. She takes my hand and squeezes it firmly. "Because you are not the product of your environment, and you're certainly not the product of your parents. Dianna and Marcus didn't make you a musician, Harper. They didn't make you fall in love with marching. You did that because you wanted it. You wanted it, you went for it, and you're a musician I'll be sad to see go because no one else has ever been so dedicated. But just think, Harper, think of everything else you could do with your life if you take that same dedication and apply it to something in college. Sure, you can be a lawyer, but will you love it?"

I sniffle and shake my head. "No."

"Exactly," Mrs. Devereaux says, giving my hand a little shake. "Your parents are who they are, Harper. They dug their graves and someday, they're going to have to lie in them. I imagine they'll have regrets when they do, but you don't have to have those same regrets. You are more than capable of learning from their mistakes and knowing not to repeat them. So to hell with all those articles and just forward march because that's not who you are. Don't you ever let your parents hold you back."

There's something in Mrs. Devereaux's determined voice, something in the way that she knocked me down a peg and built me back up twenty more. In all of my years of performing for her, we've never shared so many words, but I guess that doesn't mean she's not been watching me. It's nice to have some encouragement, a nudge in a different direction that's not down the path my parents have always wanted me to take.

"Does this mean I get to march on Friday?"

Mrs. Devereaux shrugs. "Only if you tell me what you want," she says. "Where you want to go to college and what you want to study."

A weird, comforting little cry cracks out of me, starting in my stomach before bursting up and out without notice. It's a minefield of emotions I can't navigate, some bitter and some hopeful and some that are fiery and hot, burning with rage. Mrs. Devereaux is right.

"Ithaca," I say, rubbing my nose with the back of my hand to wipe away snot and tears. Mrs. Devereaux winces, plucks out a clean tissue from her tissue box, and hands it to me. "I've thought about Ithaca, in New York. Google says they have a good music program."

"Yes!" Mrs. Devereaux says, full of enthusiasm and pride. "Absolutely, yes. Oh, or somewhere like Berklee! I could help you prepare for an audition."

I giggle to indulge her and rub at my eyes with my palms, feeling the slightest bit lighter. "That'd be great," I say. "So can I march?"

Mrs. Deveraux bounces out of her chair and hugs me tightly around the shoulders. It's weird, something unfamiliar, but I guess, maybe, it feels nice. "Absolutely, you can march. You can play a damn solo if you want."

I don't want to, and Sarah shouts in outrage when I join my friends in the band room. "Dude, you totally should! I could film your solo and send it to a fancy-ass music school! Oh, and Margot could go with you! I bet you guys could duet."

Margot snorts as she slings her arm around my hips, hugging me to her side in a way that looks friendly and casual. Sort of. She hugs Sarah like this all the time. "I don't think a snare and a sax can duet," she says. "But I'll play with Harper any time."

I bite my lip and look down at her. "Really? Because if so, I have a proposition for you." Margot raises an eyebrow while Sarah makes a disgusting kissing sound. "I want my chair back, but I need help getting it. Do you think the three of you can rehearse with me, just us?"

Margot's face breaks into a grin that shows off her dimples. "Fuck yeah, we can! Some extra time with my snare and helping my lady win her seat back? Count me in."

Bellamy cups my face between the palms of their hands and

plants a kiss on my forehead. I try my best not to recoil. "Of course I can help," they say, just before wrapping Margot and me in their arms, squeezing us with me in the middle. Sarah nearly leaps onto their back to include herself. "Rebecca is a shit saxophonist."

"She doesn't know how to march on step, either."

I press my face into Margot's leather-covered shoulder, hiding the tears hanging from my lashes. But Margot must know that I'm about to cry because she rests a gentle hand on my hip. "We've got you, McKinley. Now and always."

CHAPTER TWENTY

A T THE END OF EVERY OCTOBER, OUR BAND PERFORMS AT THE Renaissance festival in Annapolis. It's a day off campus, mostly out of uniform, and after a quick trip around the village, we're unleashed onto the dusty dirt roads of a medieval town to eat giant turkey legs and shop.

Or throw axes at a wall, if you're Margot Blanchard.

"Ha!" She throws her fist into the air when her ax almost sticks. It knocks against the outer ring of a faded red bullseye, then drops into the grass with a thud. At least she hit it this time. "I'm gonna make it stick, Harp. I'm gonna do it. Are you watching?"

"I'm watching," I say dryly. Margot picks up the ax in front of her, testing its weight as if she's watched one too many episodes of *Vikings* and actually knows what she's doing. "Hit the wall again, and you might actually impress me."

Margot whirls around as quickly as if I'd grabbed her by a dainty shoulder and spun her. "Are you flirting with me, McKinley?" she asks, tucking a new dreadlock behind her pierced ear. Her mom had taken her to get her hair done last weekend, and now Margot spends most of her time tickling my cheek with a lock when I annoy her.

Margot and I aren't official yet. We're not holding hands or stealing awkward kisses when we think that no one's looking, though Sarah's been encouraging us to behind her back "if we want to." Margot won me a keychain from a medieval claw machine, and I'm the one who'd paid for the ax she's pointing at Sarah, but really, I swear we're not official. We've agreed to take things slow and navigate whatever this is with a tentative caution, so we are.

"I would never, Blanchard."

Sarah sighs dramatically. "Throw your ax, asshole. I'm hungry."

Margot turns back around and rolls her shoulders. She adjusts her grip on the ax, slides her fingers farther up the handle, and then down again, trying to find a comfortable fit. It's not a heavy piece of medieval weaponry, but Margot acts as if it weighs a thousand pounds. If I didn't know any better, I'd say she was really trying to impress me.

I hold my breath as Margot raises her arm, flexes her fingers around the handle of the ax, and flings it at the wall with all her strength.

It thuds into the grass just before reaching the wall.

Her shoulders slump with defeat. "Goddamn it."

I pat Margot's arm as she juts out her bottom lip in a pout. "You tried," I say encouragingly. She tries not to smile. "That always counts for something. Come on, let's get something to eat."

Margot loops her arm through my elbow, the only physical contact we've allowed ourselves to share on this trip. It feels different than when we've done this in the past, though, like it's a fill-in for hand-holding in a place where we can't show affection. "What are you hungry for, my lady? Lunch is on me."

Sarah skips to my other side and slings her arm around my waist. "I'm hungry for one of those giant turkey legs," she says. Margot snorts. Sarah isn't the kind of friend I've always wanted, or even someone I imagined myself ever spending time with. But she and Margot are a package deal, and she's really starting to grow on me. "I think your options might be limited though, Margot. I haven't seen anyone walking around with a salad."

We manage to track down a vendor selling deep-fried pickles on a stick. She doesn't like that they're fried or have been in grease, but Margot still devours them with a shocking ferocity while Sarah and I share a basket of dumpster fries.

We find a small picnic table with a striped umbrella near a stage of comedic sword jugglers. Margot sits on the table instead of the bench beside me to watch. "I want to juggle a sword."

I roll my eyes and point at her with a seasoned french fry. "Absolutely not."

Margot has the nerve to look affronted, and she points back at me with her empty pickle stick. "Why?"

"Because you'll skewer yourself," Sarah says, shoveling a fry into her mouth

"Hello, beautiful maidens." Bellamy appears, grinning, from somewhere deep within the heart of the festival's food court, huddled over a basket of fried zucchini. They nod to the empty seat at our picnic table. "Mind if I sit?"

I pat the bench beside me. "Of course, friendly patron."

"Wait," Margot says skeptically. She leans over the table and looks into Bellamy's basket, inhaling so deeply her nostrils flare. "You can sit down only if you share those. Christ, Bell, where'd you find zucchini in the middle of the fucking dark ages?"

Bellamy laughs and indulges her, sliding their basket into the middle of the table. Margot immediately plucks out a piece of seasoned zucchini and pops it into her mouth. "I found them at a vendor up the road," they supply. "He's got all kinds of food, even veggies for you weird vegetarians. Harp, I think he's even got deep-fried Oreos."

I shoot out of my seat. "I will be back," I announce, digging into the pocket of my black overalls for my change purse. "With deep-fried Oreos."

Margot steals another piece of Bellamy's zucchini and hops off the table with a smile. "I'll come with you."

I bounce on my heels as Margot takes her sweet time using her overalls as a napkin to wipe off her hands. "Come on," I complain. "You've had your lunch. It's my turn."

I take Margot's arm and drag her down the dirt path Bellamy indicated will lead to my salvation. "This is, like, the only place in Maryland that has them."

"I've never had one."

I stop us both in our tracks. Margot's eyebrows shoot up into her hairline. "You've never had a deep-fried Oreo?" I ask. "Like, ever?"

Margot looks like she might laugh, but doesn't. "I have not."

"And you judged me over a s'more!" I cry. Margot bursts into bubbling laughter; it's infectious. I love the sound. It's the prettiest thing I've ever heard, even if she snorts, and I'm smiling so hard my cheeks hurt. It's hard not to join in, so I do as I take her hand, pulling her down the path again. "You're trying one. Right now. It's a necessary American experience."

Margot gently shakes me loose and loops her arm through my elbow again, a reminder that our no-hand-holding rule was my idea, my requirement if we want to be together. "You know we probably have those in Canada, right? They're likely not specific to the United States."

"Yes, well, these ones are specific to Maryland, and you have to try one."

The line for the deep-fried Oreo vendor is long, stretching across the pebbled path and a grassy field where people dressed in pirate costumes are sword fighting. Margot waits patiently and watches them, her fingers twitching like she wants to pick up a sword and join in. She likes doing anything hands-on, anything where she'll learn something new or she gets to be creative and messy. It is, without a doubt, my favorite part of her.

We've spent nearly every day together since Nadia gave her our room key and Margot came to our dorm almost a month ago. We sit together at breakfast with Sarah and Bellamy, and we've started eating dinner together, too, the four of us occupying a table that's never too far from Nadia and Evelyn's sulking. It's been weeks since Bellamy and I have spoken to them, and when we do talk, it's never more than a few short words at a time.

When it's our turn at the vendor window, I order us each a basket of three Oreos. Margot swoops in to pay for them before I can hand the girl behind the register my mom's credit card, adding a basket of fried zucchini to our order. "You know Bellamy and Sarah didn't save us any," she says by way of excuse.

"To be fair," I say. "They were Bellamy's."

"Yeah, but like, sharing is caring, Harper."

We drift out of line once we have our food. I snatch Margot's basket of deep-fried zucchini slices before she can pop one into her mouth. "Try an Oreo first."

She pouts and picks up an Oreo, pinching the flaky outer layer of fried pancake batter between her fingers. I watch her carefully, anxiously, as she takes a bite. I really want Margot to like it, just like I'd liked her s'mores.

She blinks and takes another bite, then stuffs the rest of the Oreo into her mouth.

"Is it good?"

Margot licks powdered sugar off her fingers. "Shit, Harp, where have these been all my life? You can keep the zucchini. I think I'm gonna get another basket of these."

I grin and eat one of mine, tucking Margot's zucchini basket beneath my Oreos. It's warm and sickeningly sweet, the kind of sweet that'll give you a toothache if you eat too many in one sitting. But I don't give a damn. I'd eat a hundred Oreos if I could.

"Hey, Harp?" I blink out of my stupor to find Margot biting her lip with her phone clutched to her chest. "Can I take a picture? Just one? You look so frickin' happy right now."

I swallow my Oreo and shuffle nervously on my feet. "You can't post it anywhere."

Margot makes a show of drawing an X over her heart with her index finger, effectively crossing it. "My eyes only. I promise."

Margot quickly takes the picture, standing on her toes to get a better angle of both me and my basket of Oreos—Oreo. She flips her phone around to show me and get my approval before she saves it in a locked album in her gallery. "I want to make it my lock screen," she sighs. "But I know I can't. Not yet. I just like seeing you so happy."

"I'm sorry," I say quietly, and I hope she knows I mean it. "I just . . . I can't risk my parents finding out right now. Not with this election and while I still need a place to live."

It's crossed my mind one too many times what my parents might do if they find out that I like Margot, that we spend so much time together because we want to be together. Expelling me—or Margot, for that matter—from Golden Oaks, as Mom did to Christian, is a strong possibility, though I doubt they'd send me off to military school.

It's not a risk that Margot and I feel comfortable taking yet, so we haven't. We're still trying to work out the kinks in all of our possible contingency plans, ranging from staying with Margot's family until college next fall to moving with her back to Canada.

Margot busies herself with fixing the hood of my jacket. "I understand, Harp. I promise. Don't ever think that you have to put yourself in danger because of me. I can wait."

I fiddle with my Oreo basket, picking at the cardboard until it tears. "What if we took a selfie?"

Margot tilts her head as she tugs on the drawstrings of my jacket, pulling until each cord is an even length. "What for?" she asks. "I mean, we can, but are you sure?"

"I think so," I say, shuffling closer. "We've spent all day together and have nothing to look back on later. One picture won't hurt, and friends take pictures together all the time, right?"

"Right," Margot says tentatively. She turns on her phone's front-facing camera. "Promise me you're sure?"

"Promise me you won't post it anywhere?"

Margot draws another X over her heart. "You have my word."

I bend my knees until I'm Margot's height and drop my head onto her shoulder. She grins and leans her forehead against my temple, her thumb hovering over the capture button. "Let's do it. This'll make a cuter lock screen, anyway."

CHAPTER TWENTY-ONE

TONIGHT IS OUR LAST AWAY GAME OF THE PRE-PLAYOFF SEASON, AND it's raining so hard by halftime that, for our safety, Mrs. Devereaux decides that we'll perform on the track in our pregame block. On a good day, if I wasn't frozen to my bones, I'd be thrilled to play on the track. We don't have to move between songs or even do our dances, which Margot has helped me choreograph for my section, but with the added weight and width of our insulated raincoats, there's barely enough room for us to breathe. We're practically standing on top of each other, Aiden Callahan's elbow digging between my ribs because he has nowhere else to put it.

It's not our worst halftime show by any means, though it's certainly not our best, either. By the time we've finished performing and Mrs. Devereaux has released us for our third quarter break, I have to tip my saxophone upside down and empty out the rainwater that's gathered inside the bell. I'll need to take it back to my dorm tonight to let it sit out so the keypads and corks can dry and hopefully not split or fall off.

Margot has pulled her arms inside the sleeves of her raincoat when I find her huddled up next to Sarah in the bleachers, convinced she has the flu because she's been snotty and coughing all over everything since yesterday. I take the empty seat beside her anyway, far less cautious than I should be because of my asthma, and Margot flops into my side and buries her face into my shoulder. "I'm dying."

I roll my eyes and gently pat her on the back. "Is she always so dramatic when she's sick?"

"Always," Sarah snorts. She leans around Margot to hand me the cup of hot chocolate she's just poured from the water cooler sitting next to her. My numb fingers leech the warmth from the Styrofoam as steam billows off the rim. "Thank God for band moms."

Margot shivers and wriggles closer to me. "I am so ready for this season to be over."

"We still have two more home games before the playoffs," I remind her. "And God only knows how far we'll make it this year. Last year we were marching in the snow."

"We're undefeated," Sarah adds, blowing on her hot chocolate, precariously filled to the rim. "I bet you both a pair of My Chemical Romance tickets we go all the way to the championship."

Margot's whimper is barely audible against my raincoat. "I hate Mother Nature," she says. I'm surprised she's not jumping at the chance to steal Sarah's concert tickets. Margot tried to snag tickets for My Chemical Romance's reunion show in Baltimore with no luck, but Sarah's older brother won two off the radio. She must not be feeling well if she's passing on a potential opportunity to see her favorite band. "I just want to play my drum and live to tell the tale."

"Jesus, Margot." I set down my hot chocolate and press my gloved hand against her cheek. Margot practically melts into it. "Better?"

She turns her entire face into my palm. "Where did you get hand warmers?"

"My mom stocks up on them every year. If I'd known you didn't have any, I'd have brought extras." I hold Margot's face between both of my hands to warm her cheeks. "You look miserable."

"I feel miserable," she says. Margot places her hands over mine so that I'm squeezing the warmth into her skin. "I can't even go home this weekend. Mom doesn't want me getting Issy sick, so she's picking me up tomorrow morning to take me to urgent care."

"That's good," I tell her, tucking one of her dreadlocks back behind her ear. "They'll probably give you some antibiotics."

"Yeah, for a million dollars," Sarah chimes in. "American health-care sucks."

"Here." Margot and I look up to find Nadia standing in front of us, her feet shuffling nervously over the cracked cement that the bleachers are sunken down and bolted into. She's holding out the pack of hand warmers I'd left on her desk this morning. "I, um. I overheard you talking. I haven't opened these ones. You can have them if you want."

Margot eyes her skeptically and doesn't take them. "What's the catch?"

"There isn't one," Nadia says. She looks at me and bites her lip as if she's about to word vomit right into my lap and is trying her best to contain it. "Consider it a peace offering. I'm just so tired, Harp. I hate that we're not talking."

"Yeah, and whose fault is that?" Margot snaps, and I elbow her between the ribs. "Ow."

"Harper, please," Nadia sighs. She tightens her ponytail and adjusts the headband covering her ears. "I overreacted, okay? I've been over-reacting. We should've just sat down and talked everything out like we normally do. I never meant for it to go on this long, and I'm sorry."

I swirl my hot chocolate, watching as the bits of melted marsh-mallow lap over the sides of the cup. "It's been two months, Nadia.

Why now?"

I hear her sniffle, so I look up. Nadia's eyes are wide and full of tears, and her bottom lip is quivering. "Because we're not even talking and you still remembered to give me hand warmers. I mean, they're the same ones I'm trying to give Margot, but still. You didn't have to leave them out for me, and you did, even after I've been such a bitch to you."

Margot scoffs as she takes my hot chocolate and sips from the rim of the cup. "You're kissing her ass because of some hand warmers? Do you know how shitty you've made Harper feel about herself?" I can't tell if Margot's hands are shaking because she's cold or angry, but either way, I take the closest one and grip her fingers, wringing some warmth into them. "You made her feel worthless, like there's something wrong with her when there's not. You turned her friends against her because you're petty, then you cornered her after practice and she nearly had an asthma attack. She's supposed to just forgive you for all that because you're offering me the hand warmers she gave you?"

"Margot," I say softly, touching her shoulder. She whips her head around and blinks at me, and I know she has loads more ammunition to fire at Nadia. "I said some pretty crappy things to her, too. It wasn't all Nadia's fault." I reach up and take the hand warmers from her. "I'm not going to sit with you and Evelyn at mealtimes, and probably not at pregame, either. Margot and Sarah are my friends now, too, and I'm not abandoning them just because you and I are on speaking terms again."

Nadia rubs her nose and nods. "I get it," she says. "It was wrong of me to be jealous of Margot, and I'm sorry. To both of you. I've just . . . I've been trying to figure some things out, and I thought you were stealing my best friend."

Margot snorts. "You're welcome to take Sarah as retribution. I'm not petty enough to get angry over friend-swapping."

I flick Margot's cheek with a gloved finger and thumb. She yelps and swats me away with a drumstick. "Shut up and take the damn hand warmers before you get frostbite."

She snatches the unopened plastic bag from me and rips it open with her teeth in some weird display of dominance that Nadia flinches away from. "Fine," she concedes. "But only because I'm cold and can't feel my fingers. But *you*." Margot looks up at Nadia and glares at her with all the wrath of the rain still pelting us through our raincoats. "Harper might forgive you, but I don't. Not yet. I still remember the rock bottom we had to help pull her out of because you couldn't be bothered to do anything except throw a toothbrush at your depressed roommate."

I roll my eyes and force myself to smile up at Nadia, who looks as if Margot has just slapped her across the face. Her eyes well up with tears, but nothing Margot said was a lie, so I can't find it in me to scold her. Or defend Nadia. "Trust me when I say she means well."

Nadia sniffles and wipes at her eyes with the heel of her hand. "Are we okay now?"

It's been so long since Nadia and I were any kind of okay, and all I want is to walk into our dorm and not be smothered by tension so thick you can cut through it with a knife. Maybe Nadia wants that, too—she must if she's trying to make amends—and I'm not so heartless that I'm unwilling to forgive her. Margot doesn't have to like it, but I know that if she were in my shoes, if Sarah had done to her what Nadia has done to me, she'd probably forgive her, too.

"Yeah," I say. Nadia bursts into a fit of tears that Margot rolls her eyes at, but I see her mouth twitch with the threat of a smile. "We're good."

CHAPTER TWENTY-TWO

"I AM GOING TO THROW THIS GODDAMN THING AT THE WALL," I say to no one in particular, struggling to untangle my auburn hair from around the metal plate of a curling iron. "Who invented this ancient contraption, anyway?"

Nadia sets down the makeup brush she's using to apply highlighter to Evelyn's cheeks. "Probably someone with needle-straight hair who wanted curls." She strides over the few steps between her desk and mine and takes the curling iron away from me. "I told you I'd do this for you when I finished Evelyn's makeup. It's not my fault you're impatient."

"I'm not impatient," I say, slouching in my chair as Nadia unravels my hair for me. It falls over my shoulder in a perfect ringlet that she carefully pulls apart with her fingers, then scrunches near my scalp to give it some extra volume. "I just know Margot. She doesn't know the meaning of showing up somewhere on time, and I can almost guarantee you she'll be early."

"It's homecoming," Evelyn says dryly. She's sorting through Nadia's makeup bag and setting aside whatever she wants to use, building herself a mountain of precariously stacked eyeshadow pallets. "It's a five-minute walk across campus. Margot can wait for you in the common room. Besides, it's not like Nadia won't be dolling you up again next weekend."

I frown at myself in the mirror. "I don't need her to 'doll me up again' next weekend."

Evelyn snorts as she opens up a pallet and smudges a line of purple eyeshadow across the back of her hand. "That's right, I almost forgot. You'll need all the help you can get to look good for a state dinner with the president, so your mom's probably taking you to a professional." She glares at her hand like it's offended her, then chucks the pallet back into Nadia's makeup bag. "Must be nice to have that kind of money to waste."

I turn to face her, Nadia huffing because I've moved. "What's that supposed to mean?"

Evelyn studies a tube of lipstick without even bothering to acknowledge me as she says, "It means that the only reason you were invited is that everyone thinks you're fucking Harrison. It's not like anything else makes you exciting and worthy of an invite."

"Evelyn!" Nadia snaps at her. She must see the way that my face has fallen in the mirror, the way my shoulders are caved in around me. Evelyn isn't usually so cruel. "That's enough. Harper hasn't done a goddamn thing to you, Eve, so can you just leave her alone?" Nadia's lips press together in a thin line as she returns to sectioning off my hair. She twines a thin lock of red around the curling iron, working its ancient metal clamp open and shut. "If you want to borrow my makeup, fine, but stop being mean to Harper. It's not her fault you're pissy about a silly dinner." Evelyn snarls a remark beneath her breath, so Nadia adds, "Just let me do her hair really quick, then I'll come over there and help you find a shade that's not green."

Nadia gives my shoulder a gentle squeeze, a silent apology for

Evelyn's shitty behavior. It doesn't help the all-consuming embarrassment or the hurt that flares inside my chest, but at least Nadia stood up for me. For once. I reach up and touch her hand; a silent thank you for not letting Evelyn maul me.

I don't like dances, especially not now. They're boring and stuffy. I get my fancy party fill at fundraisers, and state dinners, apparently. But Margot had asked me to be her date during last week's game, between sips of hot chocolate and hiding her face in my raincoat, and I hadn't thought twice about saying yes. We've spent the last several days coordinating my dress to her outfit, which is a powder-blue pantsuit that I've only seen in dressing room selfies.

Homecoming isn't an official date because Margot and I aren't actually together, but we're letting ourselves revel in what it might feel like to someday go on a real one. Sarah is accompanying us tonight as an unofficial third-wheel, a faithful buffer between us so this whole thing doesn't blow up in our faces. My mom will be in attendance, probably with a yardstick to measure the appropriate distance between dancers, and the last thing we need is for her to think that Margot and I are there as a couple.

"I can do your makeup if you want." Nadia offers quietly. She looks hopeful as she meets my eye in the vanity mirror behind my desk. She's made quick work of curling my hair and has swept half of it up into a high, braided bun that looks too elegant for someone like me to pull off. "You don't need much," she adds, shooting Evelyn a glare in the mirror. She snorts. "Just some eyeshadow and mascara, maybe a little highlighter. I could help you."

Nadia has gone out of her way to, as Margot puts it, kiss my ass ever since we made amends at the game last week. She talks to me nonstop during study hours, convinced an openly resentful Evelyn to sit with me, Margot, Sarah, and Bellamy at mealtimes, and is sometimes a little too supportive of my and Margot's friendship. Nadia's repeatedly asked if Margot and I are something more, if I like her as more than a friend, but I'm not comfortable enough to share the extent of our relationship with her. We're not quite there yet, though she's suspicious.

"Sure," I say. I flash her a smile in the mirror. "Not too much, though."

Nadia grins back at me and manages to dance across the room, rifling through her makeup bag and the piles of sparkling product Evelyn set aside for herself. "You'll look so pretty with this new eyeshadow I just bought," she says. "It's this shimmery blue that'll make your eyes pop. Kind of like that color I wore when you came over for Lunar New Year, just not as clownish. Fuck, do you remember that? You and Mom spent all night trying not to laugh at me. Oh, and this." She twirls a stick of silver eyeliner between her fingers. "Eve, hand me my highlighter and the fan brush. You can't hoard it from Harper."

She's not-so-secretly wanted to do this for years, to give me a makeover that rivals Mia's from *The Princess Diaries*. I don't have a secret grandmother who's a queen, nor am I pining for my best friend's brother, but my dad is running for president, and tonight's photos will end up online. Mom will take them when I see her tonight, and Dad will post them on his social media to boost his supporters' morale and remind them that he's a family man.

Nadia is living for the opportunity.

It's more makeup than I anticipated wearing tonight, but Nadia takes her time dolling me up like I'm a charity project. She smears her eyeshadow across my eyelids with her index finger, curls my lashes and coats them with heavy mascara, then fills in my waterline with her silver stick of eyeliner. We're afraid I'll smudge her masterpiece and ruin my dad's promotional photos, so she and a simmering Evelyn help me into my dress, tugging it carefully over my hair.

It's a flowery gray-blue tulle with sheer quarter-length sleeves. The neckline is a cute little collar that buttons around my throat, removing any need for a necklace, and a thin belt wraps around my waist with tiny, pale blue gemstones. It's a modest dress, one that shows far less skin than most of the dresses I'll see tonight, but I like it. My only fear is that Margot won't. She hasn't seen it yet.

Nadia steps back to admire her handiwork. "You look beautiful," she says with a wide, thoughtful smile. "Seriously, that color looks great on you."

I laugh and wave her away. "Go do Evelyn's makeup before she kills me in my sleep."

I'm slipping into my shimmery blue flats when there's a knock on our bedroom door. Nadia races to answer it, blocking the threshold with her lanky body so that whoever's in the hallway can't see inside. "Hi, Margot. Wow, don't you look . . . am I supposed to call you pretty, or handsome? I, uh, don't know what vibe you're going for. But you look nice."

Margot snorts, and I can see her trying to peek around Nadia. "Is Harper ready?"

I bump Nadia aside with my hip as I sling a small silver purse over my shoulder. I smile nervously at Margot. "Ready."

Margot blinks at me with dark eyes perfectly rimmed in smoky black eyeliner. She's leaning against our threshold, her hands stuffed into the deep pockets of her faintly striped blazer. It's not the exact same shade of blue as my dress, but no one will notice in the dim cafeteria that Bellamy says is lit by twinkling fairy lights. Margot's dreadlocks are down around her shoulders, some of them twined with thin silver thread that matches her outfit and my makeup. She looks gorgeous, or handsome, or whatever she prefers I call her tonight.

I might settle for stunning if she'll let me.

She blows out a breath that ends in a soft whistle. "You look beautiful."

"I, um, thanks." I tuck a curl behind my ear and hate myself for sounding bashful. Maybe it's a good thing Nadia caked so much makeup onto my face tonight; maybe Margot can't see me blushing at her compliment. "You look lovely."

Margot grins and rocks up onto her toes, trying to match my height in the three-inch heels she's wearing. "Lovely, huh? I'll take it. Sarah's waiting for us in the common room, though. We should get going."

"Have her home by midnight!" Nadia trills. She's fiddling with my curling iron and has plopped herself down at my desk. Her reflection is smiling at me in the mirror, but it doesn't quite meet her eyes.

I slip into the hall and offer Margot my arm. "See you later, guys."

Sarah is still waiting for us in the common room, outfitted in a navy dress that complements our powder-blue formal wear. She's taking selfies on her phone, holding up peace signs, and making silly faces at her camera. Margot sneaks up behind her and covers her eyes, but Sarah only laughs and snaps a photo of herself trying to lick Margot's hand.

"It took you guys long enough," she says, taking another picture. Margot rests her chin on Sarah's shoulder and grins infectiously at the camera, then presses a quick kiss to her cheek. I'll likely see both pictures on Instagram later, captioned with some song lyric from an indie band they listen to. "Wow, Harper. You clean up nice. Do a twirl for me."

I raise an eyebrow and fiddle with my tulle skirt, fluffing it out a bit. "Do what?"

Sarah wriggles her phone, showing me that she's not on Snapchat or Instagram or anywhere else where she can record a live video. "Twirl for the camera," she amends. "It's for my eyes only, promise. And Margot's. Actually, probably just Margot's. I'll send it to her and then delete it."

"Oh, um . . ." Sometimes I forget that Sarah is a budding social media guru and wants to be a YouTuber and that she's all about documenting her favorite memories and sharing them with her few-hundred followers. She's never posted anything I'm in without permission, but I'm always afraid she will by accident while trying to upload something else. "I don't know, Sarah."

Margot takes my hand, her fingers warm against my palm, and spins me around. I giggle as my dress swishes against Margot's blazer and the tulle flares in a pale blue bubble between us. "There. She twirled. If you didn't record it, that's your fault." Margot grins and slings her arm around my waist. Sarah pouts and puts her phone away. "Shall we?"

"Bellamy's probably bored out of their mind," Sarah says. She loops her arm through Margot's elbow, effectively putting her in the middle of us. It's impossible to know who is who's date without asking, and that's exactly what we want—what I need if I want to have fun tonight. "They texted me a half hour ago and said, and I quote, 'Hurry your dramatic asses up. It's homecoming, not the Met Gala.' How rude."

Margot snorts. "Because they didn't spend three hours getting ready tonight."

I'm not sad that this is our last homecoming, only that Margot and I won't truly get to spend it together. We can't dance or stand too close. We can't hold hands or even get each other a glass of punch. Sarah and Bellamy are great, and I know that the four of us will have fun together, but my mother will be somewhere in the cafeteria tonight. We can't risk her finding out about Margot and me, so I won't get any time alone with her.

Or, maybe I will. It seems Margot has another idea.

"We'll be right in," she says, slipping her arm out of Sarah's embrace when we reach the cafeteria's double doors. A second black runner has been rolled out down the hallway and is duct taped to the tiled floor, which Sarah has made a game of prodding at with the toe of her heel. "You'll have to rescue Bellamy from whatever poor, unfortunate fate Mrs. Devereaux has bestowed upon them without us."

Sarah rolls her eyes, squinting against the glowing little lanterns that are strung up down the center of the ceiling. "I can take a hint," she says, waggling her eyebrows suggestively. My face flashes hot beneath my makeup, and I don't even know what she's implying. Not really. Or maybe I do and I just don't want to think about it. "Behave, you crazy kids. If you're gone all night, I will send Bellamy out to look for you."

Margot laughs and waves her hand in dismissal, shooing Sarah away. "Piss off, Lewis. Go dance."

Sarah winks at me as she yanks open one of the doors, a shower of gold glitter raining down behind her from the paper stars taped to the navy wood. School-appropriate music floods into the hallway, a promising indicator that Bellamy has worked out the kinks with the sound system, and a heavy bass swallows Sarah whole as she saunters into the dark cafeteria.

"I hope you don't mind," Margot says. She takes my hand as soon as the door swings shut, her calloused fingers wrapping around mine because I'm nervously shuffling in my flats. I have no idea what's so important that Margot couldn't have told me in a text, and felt it necessary to send her best friend away. "I just want to talk, I promise. Sarah is . . . just ignore her, please. Bell won't need to come looking for us."

"Talk where?" I ask tightly. "About what?"

Margot nods to the nearest classroom door and sheepishly smiles. "About us."

Every inch of me goes numb with an icy cold that settles into my bones, from my fingers to my toes. There's plenty for us to talk about where our relationship is concerned, but I didn't think she would pick tonight to do it. It's no wonder she sent Sarah away. "Oh."

I must make some kind of face, or maybe she hears the way my voice shakes, and Margot squeezes my hand. "It's nothing bad, Harp. I promise. Do you trust me?" She gives my arm a gentle tug, beckoning me to follow her into our calculus classroom.

My feet shuffle over the polished tile. I trust her and I want her to know that I trust her, even if it makes me nervous. Margot and I slip inside, sliding through a crack in the door so that no one will notice us swing it open. It's dark without the overhead lights and the flickering old smartboard that never works, so Margot turns on the flashlight on her phone.

"So," she says, leaning against a beige cabinet full of unassigned textbooks and graphing calculators. "Hi."

I sit on the edge of Mrs. Whitmore's desk, pushing aside the tray where we turn in our homework. "Hi."

Margot rocks onto her toes, worrying at her bottom lip and biting at the place where her lip ring used to be. If I didn't know any better, I'd think Margot is nervous, too. "So, um." She picks at her fingernails, chipping the black and silver polish she's painted them with. "There's something that I, uh, wanted to talk to you about. I'd do it later, or somewhere else, but this was my only chance to get you alone tonight. Sarah and Bellamy are hard to shake."

I try to remind myself that Margot has promised this isn't anything bad. "Okay."

She takes a breath and sets her phone on the nearby desk, flipping it screen-down so that the flashlight glows ominously between us. In this lighting, at this angle, I notice that Margot has a subtle gold highlight along her cheekbones, a soft shine that complements her beautifully. "I, uh, I know you're not out, or whatever, and that's totally fine. I'm not asking you to put yourself in danger for me. Until we graduate and you're somewhere safe, I don't think I want you coming out, though it's your choice, obviously."

I blink at her. I don't know where she's going with this. "All right."

Margot twirls a lock around her finger. "I just, um, I still . . . . Christ, what am I doing? Spit it out, Margot." She takes another shaky breath that makes my heart hurt. It's unlike her to be flustered and stumble over her words and not know how to talk to me. "Harper, I want you to be my girlfriend. Like, my actual girlfriend."

Of all the things I expect Margot to say—we can't be together, she's sick of waiting for me, this isn't worth it, it's too complicated—it's certainly not that. "What?"

Margot rocks back down onto her heels. "I know we couldn't tell anyone, but I don't need to tell anyone. You'd know, and I'd know, and that's good enough for me." Margot swallows when I don't immediately respond. What can I say? There are things Margot doesn't know yet, things that might make her change her mind.

Things I don't know how to tell her. "Unless you don't want to, of course. Shit, I shouldn't have assumed. I'm sorry, Harper. I—"

"There's something I need to tell you first," I say. There's no time like the present. The words tumble out before I can think them through or know what I'm saying. But they're important, and I need to say them as much as Margot needs to hear them. "I like you, Margot. A lot. And I want to be your girlfriend, but . . ." I wrap my arms around my middle. I don't know if Margot will understand, but her eyes are soft and inviting. "I, um, I'm ace. Like, asexual? I don't know if you know what that means, but—but I love spending time with you, and I like holding hands when no one's watching, and—and I want to be with you, as your girlfriend, just not—not with you. Physically."

Margot tilts her head at me. "Okay."

"I've been talking to Bellamy about it, and I've Googled what being asexual means, like, a thousand times. I thought about telling Sarah because she knows you best and I thought she might know how you would take it, if you'd be okay with it, but I didn't." The room is suddenly too hot, too small, and I pop open one of the buttons on my collar. "I—I don't know all the details about your past relationships, or your Tinder hook-ups, but asexual for me means that I, that I don't want a physical relationship, and I don't know if I ever will."

Margot raises an eyebrow and repeats, "Okay."

I think I might vomit on her shoes, shiny silver heels she bedazzled with rhinestones. "I understand that—that maybe this changes things because if you're wanting, um, a physical relationship, I don't think I can give that to you." I find a loose coil of tulle on my skirt and twist it around my finger. "I just thought you should know, and I, um, understand if you don't want to date me now."

Margot takes three slow, tentative steps to cross the space between us, her heels clicking in sharp staccatos over the tile. She takes my hand and gently grips my fingers, her thumb lightly tracing across my knuckles. "Harp, that's okay," she says. "I mean, it's fun, and I enjoy it, but it's not everything. I don't need it. Were you . . . were you that afraid that being ace was gonna be a deal-breaker for me? Is that why you've never mentioned it?"

All I can do is shrug and stare at the floor, stare at a speck on the tile that might be dirt or might be a rogue piece of glitter. It's hard to tell in the dark.

"Well, it's not," Margot says. She reaches up with steady hands to fix the collar of my dress, lifting the folds where I've tugged them flat while unbuttoning it. "I don't have any deal-breakers, Harp. Except for maybe a murder charge."

I chuckle weakly. "I thought you said you'd help me hide a body?"

Margot doesn't miss a beat. "I did, didn't I? I guess I don't have any deal-breakers at all, then." Her hand moves faster than I can register; Margot tucks a springy curl behind my ear, mindful of my small hoop earring. "I don't care if you're ace, Harper. I mean, I care, obviously, because it's a part of who you are, but it doesn't bother me. I like you because you're you, you know? This tall, gorgeous, complex little redhead who keeps me on my toes and feels everything so fucking deeply." Her thumb brushes across my cheek. "It also doesn't change my mind about wanting to be your girlfriend. Like I said, sex is fun and all, but I'm here for this. I like this." Margot pokes me in the chest to indicate the heart beneath.

"Really?" I ask, my eyes watering. I hope I don't seem as pitiful as I sound.

Margot's fingers are gentle as she takes my chin and tips my head up, forcing me to look at her. Her smile is soft, her eyes bright, and her skin is glowing in the dim iPhone lighting. "Really, really. So now that we've established that I don't have any deal-breakers . . . Harper, will you be my girlfriend?"

"Your secret girlfriend?"

She snorts and tugs on a curl, then tucks it behind my ear. "Until you're ready to let me blast it from a rooftop, yes."

I pick at my fingernails and consider what this means, how slapping a label on our relationship might change it. We already tell each other everything. We hold hands in private and spend whatever free time we have together. Margot teaches me French and we watch *Doctor Who* and argue about who's the better Doctor. She paints these beautiful galaxies that she rips from her sketchbook and gives to me, and I sit and read to her about faraway places that she and I can never visit.

Maybe there's nothing to change, even if you slap a label on it.

"We definitely can't tell Sarah."

Margot's mouth starts to lift at the corners. "We probably shouldn't tell Bellamy, either."

"As long as we're both in agreement."

Margot's grin is wider than I've ever seen it, showing all her teeth. "Are you saying yes?"

"I'm saying absolutely."

She flings her arms around my neck, squeezing me until I feel like I might burst. I wrap my arms around her middle, hugging her and marveling at the way she just fits. This isn't the first time I've hugged her, nor is it the first time I've tucked her head beneath my chin and gathered her up into my arms. But it's the first time I've noticed how perfectly we fit together, maybe in more ways than one.

Margot's dreadlocks tickle my cheek as she bounces on the tips of her toes, as she sways us both from side to side and holds me with a hidden strength. "You're my girlfriend," she says reverently.

I laugh and hold her tighter. "Your secret girlfriend. For now."

Margot wriggles out of my arms, though she keeps herself pressed against my knees. She fiddles with my collar again, smoothing out the fabric and buttoning the button I've popped open. In a book, I know what comes next, what happens after couples become official. Margot's eyes dip a bit lower, and she bites her lip as she stares at mine like she knows what she wants but won't ask for it.

I think I want to try it. Maybe I'll hate it or maybe I won't, but it's Margot. I would only ever try this with Margot.

"Margot?"

She's arranging my curls over my shoulders, twirling little sections around her index finger. "Hmm?"

I slide to the edge of Mrs. Whitmore's desk. "Can I, um . . ."

She quirks her head, her hands stilling in my hair, and I think she knows what I'm asking, that I'm doing it because I know that she won't. "We don't have to do anything," she stresses, but I see her glance at my mouth again. "Unless you want to."

I pluck at the tulle of my skirt. "Maybe just once."

"Are you sure?" Margot shifts her feet and leans into me; I can smell her minty breath and subtle hints of a cinnamon spray or lotion. She uses both, sometimes, usually vanilla or cinnamon. "You can say no."

"I asked," I point out, swallowing. "Kind of. I started to, then didn't, and I should have."

Margot's laugh is a whisper between us. "Stop rambling."

"Rambling. Right. Sorry. Can you, um, can I—"

Margot rises up and kisses me, her lips featherlight against mine. She touches her hand to my cheek, her thumb brushing over the highlighter Nadia painted me with, smearing it back into my hairline. But I don't care. Margot Blanchard is kissing me, and I don't hate it.

My heart is hammering in my chest, beating so hard that everything aches. There's no bolt of lightning or sparks of tingling electricity where we touch, but it's nice. I'd probably do this again, maybe, if she let me.

It's over as quick as it started. Margot sinks onto her heels and looks up at me, searching my face for any flicker of emotion. I try not to give any away. "How was that?"

My hands are shaking as I bunch up fistfuls of tulle. She takes them and smooths out my fingers and holds them. "It was nice," I tell her. Margot looks doubtful. "I'd do it again, but maybe not make a habit of it."

She nods and clutches my hands, the silver from her polished rings a biting cold against my knuckles. "That is fine. No habits." Margot smiles and carefully pulls me off the desk, her heels clicking sharply over the tiled floor as I drop onto my feet in front of her. She slings an arm around my waist, then stands onto her toes and presses a kiss to my cheek. Just a peck, nothing that lingers. "What about that?"

I throw an arm around her shoulders, drawing her in where she fits perfectly against me. "I think that's okay."

Margot's grin is wicked as we head into the school's cafeteria, standing close enough that people will know we're here together, but far enough apart that no one will think we're together-together. Sarah and Bellamy flag us down from near the refreshments table, Sarah already having stacked a plate full of frosted cookies and cupcakes. I'm surprised no one's told her to not be greedy and save some for the rest of us. Margot swipes a cookie from the top of her pile in case she doesn't, biting off a big enough chunk that there's frosting all over her lips.

Bellamy nudges me with their elbow. "Hey, Harp, you should help her take care of that."

I cough into the cup of fruit punch that Sarah's just handed me. "Christ, Bellamy."

They snort and give a little twirl, showing off the rainbow tulle of their handmade dress and the blazer worn over-top of it. "I'm just looking out for you!" they say, giving me a wink. "I know Margot didn't drag you into an empty classroom just to say hello or ask you to fix her tie."

I feel the heat as it creeps back into my cheeks. "Keep your voice down!" I say, slapping my hand against their shoulder. Bellamy bounces on their heels, giddy excitement drawn clear as day across their face. Five minutes in, and I've never once seen them this happy at homecoming. Probably because they usually go with Evelyn, who doesn't let Bellamy design their own outfits or do anything fun with their hair. Tonight, it's curled with a curling iron and pinned half-up on their head. "You can't tell anyone about us, Bell. Not a soul."

Bellamy's grin stretches so wide that it brings out the dimples in their cheeks. "Not a soul," they repeat, drawing an X across their chest with a finger. "I promise."

I lean in to give them a hug and thank them for keeping our secret when Mom's voice cuts through me. "Harper!" she gasps. I nearly collapse into Bellamy, a groan slipping out of me that's muffled by Bellamy's blazer. "Harper, baby, turn around. Let me have a look at you! Oh, Marcus, doesn't she look beautiful?"

Dad's attendance tonight is news to me as I spin on my heels to find Mom hanging off his arm. She's dressed in a dark blue gown that's too elegant for homecoming, but at least Dad's casual in black pants and a matching navy button-up. He holds a hand to his heart. "Jesus, Josie, look at you. You look—you're so grown up. Shit. When did this happen?" Dad reaches up to brush a finger beneath his eye, wiping away what look to be tears. "I remember when you were little and used to run around the house with just a diaper on and—"

"Okay!" I shout, clapping my hands together before something more horrifying slips out of his mouth to embarrass me in front of my friends. Margot is snickering behind her plate of sweets. "What are you doing here, Dad? Mom didn't tell me you were coming."

Dad beams at me as if I'm meant to be proud of him. "I signed up to chaperone last week," he tells me, opening up his arms for a hug. "I made some calls, canceled a meeting, and here I am. Now show your old man some love, will you? Pretend I'm one of your friends."

I offer him a smile as the tension drains from my shoulders; I don't remember tensing them in the first place. "It's good to see you, Dad." He scoops me into his arms as I wrap mine around his middle, trying not to smudge Nadia's makeup against his dress shirt. "I wish you'd have told me you were coming. I'd have made you bring me ice cream from Rizzo's."

Dad chuckles as he kisses the top of my head. "I'll shut down the shop," he says. "You and I can make a day of it. We can eat all the ice cream we can stomach, how's that sound?"

"Like a promise."

Having him here almost feels right, a normal dad and his normal daughter hugging each other as normal families do. Normal parents chaperone school events, hug their kids because they love them, not for personal gain, and because they support their daughters and want to be there and tell them how pretty they look at homecoming.

And then a camera snaps and flashes, and I'm reminded that we aren't normal, that Dad has never chaperoned a school event, or even hugged me in public for anything except a publicity stunt.

"Just ignore her, Jos," Dad murmurs. "Your mom wants pictures to share with family."

And the tabloids.

And President Shannon.

And Vice President Bentley.

And Republican senators that Dad needs endorsements from.

And his on-the-fence supporters who aren't sure if they're going to vote for him.

I wriggle out of Dad's arms, breath caught in my throat, and turn to look for Margot. She sets a half-eaten cookie on Sarah's quickly diminishing cookie plate, her dark eyes wide and searching my face for any signs of discomfort. Maybe it's in the way my cheeks have flushed and my bottom lip is starting to tremble, or maybe it's in the way that my hands are shaking and my spine has stiffened and my knees are starting to wobble, but she finds it.

"Mrs. McKinley," Margot says, sliding around Bellamy to sling a friendly arm around my shoulders. Sarah and Bellamy follow her, Bell's hand wrapping around my waist while Sarah hangs from Margot's arm. And at this moment, I appreciate them so much I could kiss them, especially Margot. "Do you think you could get some pictures of the four of us? My parents will want to see us all together."

Mom purses her lips as if the question has physically pained her. "Of course," she says tightly, turning her cellphone sideways. Dad grimaces next to her, staring at my friends and me through the screen. "Scooch in just—just a little bit closer. Not much. Miss Lewis, you cannot make an obscene gesture. Put your hand down."

Margot leans into my ear, taking advantage of Sarah's likely staged obscenity, and says, "I've got you. You're okay. Just breathe, yeah?"

"They're using me for Dad's campaign again."

"I know, Harp." Margot's fingers give my shoulder a gentle, promising squeeze. She would turn around and hug me if she could. "Fuck them both, okay? This is your night, not theirs. Don't let them take it away from you."

I let out a wheezy breath through my nose. She's right. Sort of.

It's not my night that this damn election is trying its best to steal, it's our night, mine and Margot's, and I will be damned if my parents take it away from us. So I smile wide as Mom holds up her phone, telling us all to say cheese in a voice that says she'd rather be anywhere else, photographing anything else, just not her kid with her openly queer friends.

"They're a colorful bunch," Dad comments, rubbing the back of his neck, and in a hushed whisper, he adds, "Only send that one to Harper. No one else."

Sarah reaches up and flips off the camera right as Mom snaps another photo. "Fuck the patriarchy!" she cries. Mom gives her detention for a week.

CHAPTER TWENTY-THREE

R OUND ONE OF THE PLAYOFFS IS TONIGHT, AND WE'RE GOING INTO THE game undefeated, 10–0.

Of course, that doesn't mean anything; you lose one game during the playoff season and you're done, finished, crying on the bus ride home because the season is over too soon.

And, of course, in typical Maryland-weather fashion, the sky is spitting out ice and snow, rendering the practice field hazardous. Nadia had slipped and nearly broken her ankle when she'd dashed to our room to fetch a pair of black socks, so we're rehearsing our set inside. We'll likely perform on the track again tonight because the stadium we're playing in has AstroTurf—a tuba and bass drum's worst nightmare.

While Bellamy leads us through halftime, Mrs. Devereaux is pacing alongside the chalkboard, beating on her dented cowbell with a spare mallet. The drumline is off their game tonight. They're a full measure behind the rest of the band because Margot, of course, is not feeling well. She doesn't have the energy to get them together because she's been guzzling cough syrup. Apparently, this is normal for her, head cold after chest cold until the weather warms up in the spring. It does wonders for my anxiety.

Margot looks miserable, but I know she'll never stay home tonight, even if Mrs. Devereaux has insisted she skip tonight's game to rest; being this sick is a reasonable excuse.

Our set is going to be a train wreck. We don't have the time to repeatedly play through each song or for Nadia to get her part right and stop screwing up her trumpet solo, but my hand shoots into the air before Mrs. Devereaux can tell us to put our instruments away and start changing into our uniforms. She looks at me with a raised eyebrow, though I know she and the entire band know what I'm about to do. "Yes, Harper?"

"I want to challenge for my chair."

"What? No!" Rebecca leaps to her feet and nearly knocks over her music stand, the neck of her saxophone crashing into the raised lip and sending her flip-folder flying, thudding to the floor beneath a freshman clarinet player. "You can't challenge for a chair on a Friday! That's not a thing."

"Actually," Bellamy pipes up, a grin lighting their smug face as they bounce on their heels behind the podium. "There's nothing in the rulebook that says she can't. Right, Mrs. Devereaux?"

She dips her chin and sets down her cowbell. "Bellamy's right," she says. A strangled cry of furious protest emits from Rebecca's throat, but I don't care. She's had my chair for too long, and it's time to take it back. "Harper, what song would you like to play?"

I turn the pages in my flip-folder. "Truth Hurts."

Mrs. Devereaux blinks at me, her mouth tightening with what I know is concern. "We haven't rehearsed that song yet," she says. "Are you sure—"

"I'm sure."

Bellamy, Margot, Sarah, and I have stayed after practice nearly every day for weeks. We've spent hours sitting in this room, Bellamy conducting while Margot beats on her drum. She's been tapping out eighth notes for me to play to and help me keep tempo lest Bellamy and I fall out of sync. I think there's a metronome burned into my brain now. Sarah had tried to help too, first by crashing her cymbals until Bellamy begged her to stop, then offering encouragement whenever I started to get frustrated. She's like my own little book of compliments.

I know every note, every rest, and every rhythm. I know where Bellamy's hands should be for every upbeat, downbeat, and everything that comes in between. I've never heard Rebecca play this before, and we've never rehearsed it as a band, but if Rebecca could pose a shady challenge to take my chair, then I'm within my rights to pose a shady challenge to win it back.

"This isn't fair," Rebecca spits, sinking back down into her seat. *My* seat. "We don't know that song!"

Mrs. Devereaux rubs her temple. "Once a song has been passed out, it can be challenged on. You know the rules, Rebecca. Harper, whenever you're ready."

I sit up straight in my seat. Bellamy is bouncing behind the podium, their hair flopping in a messy bun. They wait for me to settle against Rebecca's second chair, for me to take a breath and calm my thoughts. I am going to win this challenge.

"Ready, Harp?"

I bring my mouthpiece to my lips and nod.

Bellamy's hands rise up, come down, swing in and out before lifting back up to cue the first downbeat of the song. "Truth Hurts" starts with the trumpets, and after several beats of rest, I come in at exactly the right time, hitting every note with clean precision as my fingers stab at my saxophone keys, slide through every slur, and rise with every crescendo.

Nothing else exists in this moment, not Rebecca, not the game, not Mom or Dad, or the unanswered texts that they've sent to me. I hear myself, I feel the music, and I see Bellamy's arms flapping behind the podium until they cut me off, ending the song on a note that blasts through the band room.

"Hell yeah!" Margot's voice is the first sound that breaks through my saxophone-induced cloud nine. A moment later, I feel her at my back, her arms snaking around both me and my saxophone as she hugs me from behind. Her chest rattles against my shoulders. "That's how you do it! That's how you frickin' win!"

I laugh and turn my head away, grateful for Margot's support but unwilling to catch whatever it is she has. "Sit down and stop breathing on me," I say. "Rebecca still has to play."

"Yes," Rebecca snaps in agreement. "Getting up to congratulate your girlfriend before I've even played is so unprofessional."

Margot leans around me and snarls at her, "Bitch, it's high school. Talk to me about professionalism when you actually beat Harper in a challenge. And she's not my girlfriend."

"That's enough, Margot. Harper, well done." Mrs. Devereaux says, smiling at me as if she's been waiting for me to take back my chair and put Rebecca in her place. "Rebecca, whenever you're ready."

Rebecca is angry enough for steam to pour out of her ears when Mrs. Devereaux declares me the winner. It's a formality, but for Rebecca's sake, our director asks if she'd like to try playing the song again. She doesn't, and first chair is mine. When Rebecca gets up to look for her uniform in the storage closet, I pick her saxophone case and place it on the chair I've been keeping warm for her.

CHAPTER TWENTY-FOUR

I'VE PROBABLY BEEN TO A HUNDRED BLACK-TIE EVENTS SINCE DAD'S first plunge into politics. They haven't been fun since my parents stopped bringing Christian, who'd always found a way to cause trouble, be it crawling beneath tables or the time he'd zapped Gideon Bentley with one of those electrified prank pens. Fortunately, he'd laughed it off, but not before his Secret Service nearly put my brother in a chokehold.

Fundraisers, galas, private parties anywhere on Capitol Hill; they're all excuses for the obnoxiously rich to get dressed up and blow through money. Get my parents drunk enough, Dad's putting in bids on old, ugly paintings he'll toss into the trash the next morning or donate to Golden Oaks' art gallery.

I've never been to a state dinner before.

My parents and I are waiting in a mile-long receiving line to meet the Canadian prime minister and snap a quick picture for the press before being sequestered to our dinner table.

Mom's more reserved than usual tonight, a dull accessory hanging off Dad's arm in a dress costing more than my tuition. She's all soft smiles and kind, warm-welcome eyes, a make-nice trophy wife whose sole purpose is to make my dad look good to anyone with money who could endorse him. It's the reason I'm here, too. I'm only here to fake pretty smiles and talk about how wonderful my father is, who pulled strings to have me added to the guest list.

If Mom is his dull accessory, then Dad is the polished gem she's to complement, shining bright in the golden chandelier lighting. He's smiling a megawatt smile, showing off all his teeth, and slaps his hand into anyone's who is willing to shake it. Here, in some renowned hallway of the White House, Dad is in his element, a charming politician who can pin you with his eyes and coax you into spilling your darkest secrets. Maybe he'll blackmail you, maybe he won't, but you'll tell him anyway because talking to my dad is almost as easy as breathing.

At least it used to be. I don't tell him much anymore.

My only consolation is that Margot is somewhere in the White House tonight, either in this line or already seated at her family's table in the State Dining Room. Canada's prime minister is a close family friend, and he'd insisted that the Blanchards be invited.

"How much longer?" I ask, grabbing Dad's arm to steady myself. My feet are aching. "These shoes are going to kill me."

Mom cuts me a sharp look from around Dad's broad shoulders. "Don't whine, Harper, it's embarrassing. You're in the White House."

"Oh, leave her alone, Dianna. My feet would hurt too if I had to wear those damn death traps all night." Dad winks and kisses my temple, then gently nudges me with his elbow. I can't tell if it's a warning not to complain, or if it's a silent reassurance that he has my back. Maybe it's both. Or maybe he wants the approaching reporter to film him acting fatherly. "It won't be too long, now. I can see Pete's ugly mug."

The sight of the president makes my skin crawl.

"There he is!" Pete Shannon grins at my dad with yellowing teeth and a fever-blister hidden beneath makeup. He slaps his hand into Dad's palm and turns to Canada's prime minister. "This here is a real son-of-a-bitch, I'll tell ya. Good man, good family."

Dad turns up the wattage of his smile and claps Pete on the arm. "I think you're getting senile with age, old man." He turns to the prime minister as Pete laughs heartily, spitting little droplets that spray between me and Mom. "Senator Marcus McKinley. Pleasure to meet you."

I don't remember his name, even if Margot has told me a thousand times, but the prime minister smiles and shakes my father's hand. "Anthony Gallagher, and the pleasure is all mine. This is my wife, Davina."

Dad loops his arm around Mom's waist, suddenly remembering we exist. She tilts her head and smiles up at him. "My wonderful wife, Dianna." He reaches around her and carefully ruffles my hair. "And my beautiful daughter, Harper."

Anthony and Davina Gallagher embrace both Mom and me warmly, a hint of recognition in Davina's eyes as she gently takes my hand. They're friends with the Blanchards—something about Anthony and Leon being roommates in college.

"Lookin' gorgeous as always, Diane." Pete slings an arm around Mom's waist as we turn and pose for photos. Her mouth tightens at the corners, but she doesn't correct him. "Good Lord, Harper, you get prettier every time I see you! Harrison is one lucky bastard, I'll tell ya."

I stiffen between Dad and the First Lady. "I'm sorry?"

Pete winks at me, and Dad steps warningly on my foot.

A camera flashes, then a dozen more snap in rapid succession. "I'll tell you what," Pete begins, patting Dad on the back. "Mark my words, this lot will make a fine First Family come Inauguration Day."

The air whooshes out of my lungs. I angle myself toward Dad and cough into my sleeved elbow. He thumps me hard on the back, half warning, half concern, then takes my arm and spins me back toward the cameras. They flash in quick bursts of finger-clicking permanency, their accompanying journalists speaking softly into small, hand-held recording gear.

Pete thinks Dad will win the election.

I think I might vomit on his shoes.

We're shuffled down the Cross Hall by someone from the president's security team, and our arrival is announced as we enter the White House's State Dining Room.

Our table is near the front of the ballroom, closest to the podium where President Shannon and Prime Minister Gallagher will give speeches tonight. It's set with polished white dinnerware and more plates and forks and fancy napkins than anyone in this room even needs. A towering, three-post candelabra has been placed in the center of the table, its flames flickering ominously between vases of lilies and what I think might be artificial maple leaves.

"Yes!" Margot's raspy voice cuts between the cluttered floral arrangements. I lean around Mom to find our table already occupied by the Blanchards, our apparent companions for dinner tonight. Mom purses her lips as the realization strikes her, too, but she knows better than to object to the president's seating chart. "Maybe tonight won't suck after all."

"Margot," her mother sighs, reaching around Issy to fuss with one of Margot's dreadlocks. Most of them are swept into an elegant bun to keep them out of her face, but she's left a few down to fiddle with. "Harper, do teach my girl some manners, please."

I smile warmly at Elizabeth. "I'll try," I say, sliding into the empty seat next to Margot. She immediately brushes her hand against mine, her pinky finger curling around my thumb beneath the table. She gives it a gentle pinch before letting me go to get situated. "It's nice to see you again, Mrs. Blanchard. You too, Leon." Margot's dad and I are on a first-name basis now. He buys me pretzels at playoff games, and I keep his kid out of trouble; it's a fair trade. "Hello, Issy. You look beautiful tonight."

Margot's little sister offers me the faintest of smiles. She's foregone her usual cat-eared headband in favor of glittery hair clips holding back her curls, and like Margot, Issy is dressed in a burgundy dress that complements her complexion.

"What about me?" Margot pouts quietly. She waits until our parents are exchanging stiff pleasantries to ask, "Don't I look pretty, too?"

I pat her knee beneath the table. "You look gorgeous. That color suits you."

It does. Margot's dress is the darkest shade of burgundy, the color of the wine that Mom's already sipping from her wine glass. It's a full satin skirt with a lace bodice and a neckline that skims beneath her collarbones, teetering the line of what is and isn't appropriate. I'm surprised to see her in a dress and that she's chosen not to wear one of the dozen pantsuits I've seen in her closet back at school.

"You look stunning," Margot murmurs, eyeing me in a way that makes me feel as if I've laid all my secrets out in front of her. I shift nervously in my seat but don't back down from her—never Margot, even if I disagree with her assessment. "That dress is . . . I want it."

"It's itchy," I tell her, scratching at my arm. "And I think Mom forgot about my asthma when she laced me into it. I can barely breathe."

Margot pats the small purse sitting dutifully in her lap. "I have your inhaler if you need it. I snagged it from Nadia after the game last night." She looks nervous. "I knew you'd probably forget yours. I hope you don't mind."

I blink at her, at Margot's never-ending thoughtfulness, and feel a tightening in my chest. I don't know what I've done to deserve her. "Thank you. I did forget mine."

We spend the few minutes before dinner chatting, Issy our attentive listener. Her dark eyes dart between us, studying our faces in the washed-out lighting of the banquet hall. I lean around Margot and talk to Issy, too, cherishing her little smiles and the way she nods her head. Issy and I are pals ever since their parents started bringing her to the playoff games. We always share the mini-pretzels that Leon buys me during break; Issy likes them plain and leaves the cups of cheddar cheese for me.

Servers in white button-up shirts come by with bowls of broccoli cheddar soup. Margot surveys the spread of silverware in front of her, skeptical of her option of three different spoons. Issy hesitates, too, waiting to see what Margot will do. "It's been a while since the last time Dad dragged us to a fancy dinner," she says. "Remind me again which one we're supposed to eat with?"

I snort and tap on her soup spoon, the one that sits between her dinner plate and an empty porcelain teacup. "This one," I say. "And put your napkin in your lap. I know you, and that dress is too pretty to ruin."

Margot huffs and takes the gold napkin from her dinner plate. I spend the next few hours reminding Margot and teaching Issy the proper etiquette for dining at black-tie affairs. Issy listens intently, but Margot says to Hell with it when the main course arrives and rummages through her vegetables with her cake fork.

We're shuffled into the East Room for entertainment and dancing after dinner. The room is smaller than I remember, the ugly floral rugs rolled away to reveal an even uglier wooden floor. Margot, Issy, and I huddle together near a small orchestra, listening to the myriad of violins and cellos that fill the ballroom while our parents mingle. Mom and Dad are busy chatting up whichever politicians they think will endorse Dad, and the Blanchards are catching up with the prime minister.

"Please tell me the night's almost over," Margot begs. She's threatened to kick off her heels and walk around the White House barefoot. Twice. Even Leon, with horrifying ease, had paused mid-conversation with my parents to tell her she'd better keep her shoes on. "How much more mingling can these rich asshats even do without one of them dropping dead of old age?"

"Margot!" I hiss, clocking the security guard standing near the window behind us. I imagine him picking up Margot and tossing her little body over his shoulder, acutely aware she's not actually a threat to security, but needing to detain her anyway. "You can't say things like that! Jesus, do you want to be tackled or removed by the Secret Service?"

She jabs me in the ribs with her elbow and a sly grin. "Maybe."

"Evening, ladies." Harrison's voice makes my skin crawl as he materializes from behind the orchestra. His father is standing behind the cellist with his arms crossed, his pinched, splotchy face angled in our direction. Sweat has gathered in the creases of Gideon's forehead, the same frown lines Mom has had filled in with Botox. "Are you enjoying yourselves?"

"Cut the pleasantries," Margot snaps at him. Harrison winces, sipping from his gold-rimmed wine glass as if it's a necessity for dealing with Margot. The sloshing, lip-staining liquid is a dark red, and I wonder if he's sweet-talked a server into giving him wine. Or maybe you don't deny the vice president's son, even if he's underage. "What could you possibly want?"

Harrison sighs and swipes a hand through his perfectly styled hair. "My father demanded I come over and make nice with Harper," he admits, loosening his navy tie that both does and doesn't match his slate-gray suit. "And I need to show her something."

Margot's spine stiffens as she tugs Issy closer and drapes an arm around her shoulders. "The last time you offered to show a pretty girl something, it was a certain body part in a very unflattering mirror selfie." Harrison's face flushes a bright scarlet, and even Issy looks a little uncomfortable. Maybe it's because Margot's voice has risen a full octave. "Yeah, Sarah showed me. Next time, maybe don't Snapchat my roommate during study hours."

Harrison sighs and slips his phone into his hand. Gideon must not have given him the same lecture that my parents had given me about no electronics tonight. "I need you to brush off the chip on your shoulder and shut up for, like, a solid three minutes, Blanchard. I'm trying to give Harper a heads-up." Harrison taps and scrolls with a slightly trembling thumb. I don't know if it's the wine or his father's staring that's making Harrison shake. "A friend of mine sent this to me a few minutes ago."

"Is it your *friend's* certain body part?" Margot quips. Harrison grinds his teeth, his temple pulsing with what I assume is frustration. "You should know, Harper won't appreciate it."

"Margot," I murmur, touching the inside of her palm. "Stop it."

She purses her lips and falls quiet, her arm still slung around Issy's delicate shoulders.

Harrison hands me his phone, and I blink disbelievingly at the CNN article on the screen.

BREAKING: *President Shannon Endorses Senator McKinley of*

Maryland

Margot peeks at the screen from over my shoulder and spits out a string of French curse words. "When did that happen?" she asks in English. "I've never heard that half-wit say anything about endorsing Marcus, not even on Twitter."

"In the receiving line," I tell her numbly. "Pete said it right in front of the reporters, that we'd make a good First Family. I—I didn't think . . ." I look up at Harrison and start to pick at my fingernails. He looks as nervous as I feel, and I wonder what he thinks this might mean for him. "Is that even a real endorsement?"

Harrison rubs the back of his neck. "It is to the press," he says. "And Pete does nothing without some self-serving purpose. He's probably hoping that Marcus will recruit him as some secretary so he can keep his foot in D.C. The bastard likes a good power play, and he just made your dad look damn good to his supporters."

"I wouldn't be so sure," I say softly. "He's talked about asking Gideon to be his VP." Harrison pales to an alarming shade of white, looking as if he might run from the White House screaming. "Sorry, Second Son. You might be America's most desirable bachelor a bit longer."

"Fuck." He drags a hand down his squared jaw and dimpled chin that's starting to fill in with dark stubble. "My dad hasn't said anything about this. Maybe Marcus hasn't pitched him the proposition yet. What about Reinhart? Or Ayers? Christ, literally anyone else. I can't handle this crap for another term."

"Yes," Margot croons. "Such a sad life, little VP. All those parties and galas you get to go to. How awful it must be."

Harrison glares at her, his hands shaking. "Shut up, Blanchard. We all have our shit, okay? I'm glad you don't have the stakes that Harper and I do."

Margot opens her mouth to snap back at him, so I angle myself in between them, my back to Margot as I look up at Harrison and smile thinly. "Thank you for the heads-up. My dad will have a field day when he sees the article."

"Articles," Harrison corrects. "There are more. But you're welcome. And, uh, thanks for the heads-up, too, about Marcus considering my dad. Party's almost over, in case you guys were wondering. It's past Pete's bedtime." Harrison fiddles with his tie to loosen it. "Enjoy the rest of your night. The next time there's a dinner, I'll try and mark you off the guest list."

Margot snorts and takes Issy's hand. "Privilege of the Second Son?"

Harrison shrugs and chugs the last of his wine. "A perk of being Pete's favorite godson. Good night, Harper. And good luck with the media shit-storm. You might want to stay offline."

In the car, on our way back to campus, I delete Twitter and Instagram from my phone.

CHAPTER TWENTY-FIVE

MARGOT AND SARAH'S DORM IS EVEN MESSIER THAN MY HALF OF mine. The floor is covered with dirty clothes and bits and pieces of their uniforms; a cardigan is tossed over Margot's desk and a rogue skirt hangs from the windowsill. There are thin little brushes speckled with paint scattered across the stained beige carpet, and rolled-up tubes of empty acrylics lay stomped on, stepped over, and forgotten.

Even I can't thrive in this chaos.

Margot and I are curled up against her headboard while Sarah watches television from the lumpy beanbag chair beneath the window. She's reading a battered copy of *They Both Die at the End* by Adam Silvera out loud to me in French, skimming over the words so I can follow along with her index finger. My head is resting on her shoulder, and Margot's arms are wrapped around my waist as she holds the book in my lap.

It's hard to follow along and focus on the story when all I want is to listen to the sound of her voice. Her gentle rasp is still heavy with sleep, rounding out her tone between the lulls of plot and dialogue.

Margot had slept on the floor last night, having built herself a nest of pillows and blankets so that I could sleep in her bed.

We'd gotten back to campus after midnight, and since Nadia hadn't responded to the half-dozen messages I'd sent her on the car ride home, I'd slept here to avoid the risk of waking her.

"Look!" Sarah cries, launching a pillow at Margot's head that knocks an oversized pair of reading glasses off her face. "Harper, you're on TV!"

My eyes flick up from the book in my lap to the coverage of last night's state dinner. Sarah's been watching CNN all morning, trying to find Margot and me in the crowd. The news anchor is analyzing Dad's newest endorsement, his lead in the polls, and the footage on the screen is of our meeting with the president and prime minister.

In this particular video clip, Pete is announcing that my parents and I will make a fine First Family after Dad wins next year's election. My eyes visibly widen, and a moment later I'm stifling a cough into Dad's massive shoulder. "Great. Of course they filmed that."

Margot pats me on the back as I sigh and slump against her chest. "Everyone knows you have asthma," she reminds me. "Besides, who cares if you coughed? You looked so good in that dress I doubt anyone noticed."

Margot kisses my cheek and adjusts the book in my lap, finding our place somewhere halfway down the page. She starts to murmur in French again, starts to trace over the words as she drops her chin against my shoulder. Her hair tickles my skin, a loose dread sliding over my cheek and curling against the curve of my neck. I absently twirl it around my finger, and I feel Margot smile against my ear as she continues to read her favorite book to me, her voice hardly above a whisper.

"Uh, guys?" Sarah's voice snaps me back into the dorm room, back into a place where Margot and I aren't the sole inhabitants. Sarah's sitting up on her knees, her arm stretched forward as her thumb repeatedly stabs at the TV remote. It takes me a moment to realize she's turning up the volume. "Shit, you guys. Shit. You have to see this."

I know I shouldn't look up, not when Sarah's mood has audibly shifted from giddy excitement to absolute mortification. I can imagine the look on her face, the wide eyes and slack jaw that accompanies a tone of shock, and I know that I shouldn't look up. I should keep staring at *They Both Die at the End*, should pretend that I don't hear Margot suck in a breath behind me; she's looking, and I can feel her heart pounding inside her chest between my shoulder blades.

"Fuck," she whispers. "Fuck. How did they get those messages?"

BREAKING: *Daughter of Presidential Hopeful Has Found an Endorsement of Her Own*

Onscreen are pictures of Margot and me: a selfie of Margot with her drumsticks and the photo Mom took of me in California, the one where I'm standing on the pier in Oceanside. But they quickly fade and are replaced by screenshots of what looks like our Messenger history, except I didn't send those messages—would never have sent them.

I declined Margot's offer to show me the Tinder messages before she deleted the app. I was too embarrassed to see them; too shy and scandalized and everything in between. But now I'm seeing them on television—everyone is seeing them on television—and I should have let Margot prepare me for this.

They're graphic. They're disgusting and obscene and I cannot believe that someone took the time to do all of this. The messages look bad for Margot, all the winking emojis and desperate pleas to meet up somewhere, but they're world-ending for me. I've offered to send her nudes I've never taken. I've told her what I'm wearing beneath my clothes, how I'll take Margot's off if she ever gives me the chance. I don't know what any of it means, but Margot sounds thrilled about what I've offered to do to her.

My phone vibrates on the nightstand. Margot reaches for it, thinking it's hers, and then hands it to me.

Incoming Call: *Mom's Cell*

I don't answer it. Can't answer it. Can't breathe.

New voicemail.

Incoming Call: *Mom's Cell*

New voicemail.

My hands are shaking and Margot throws aside her book.

Incoming Call: *Dad's Office*

New voicemail.

Margot is touching my face, smoothing back my hair, and brushing her thumb across my cheek.

Mom's Cell: *Harper Josephine you had better answer your phone.*

Mom's Cell: *WHAT DID YOU DO?*

Dad's Cell: *Josie, honey call me.*

Margot tells Sarah to find her purse, and Sarah scrambles, throwing aside pillows and digging through the fabric of our dresses.

Bellamy Parker: *Fuck, Harp, where are you?*

Bellamy Parker: *Are you okay?*

Incoming Call: *Bellamy Parker*

New voicemail.

Margot, I think, is talking to me. I can't hear her. Can't see her. Can't breathe.

Incoming Call: *Mom's Cell*

New voicemail.

Incoming Call: *Dad's Cell*

New voicemail.

Harrison Bentley: *Oh my God, is it true? You and Margot?*

Harrison Bentley: *Can you call me when you get a minute? I think we should talk.*

Dad's Cell: *I'm on my way, Josie.*

Mom's Cell: *You'd better be in your goddamn room.*

Margot takes my phone and tosses it away. It thuds somewhere on the floor. "Harper," she says, holding my face between her hands. Her palms are cold and sweaty, a stark contrast to their usually comforting warmth. "Harp, you need to calm down. We can fix this. The profile wasn't yours. It's fine. You'll be fine. But I really, really need you to fucking breathe right now, okay? Sarah can't find your inhaler."

"She can use mine. Here." Sarah thrusts an inhaler into Margot's shaking hand. It's her rescue inhaler, the one she'd given me during halftime all those weeks ago. Margot shoves it between my lips without asking and presses down. I cough and turn my head away. "Christ, Harper. Just use it, okay?"

My phone is vibrating on the floor; Mom or Dad or Bellamy or Harrison—everyone who has my number. Margot's phone is blowing up, too, a high-pitched trill that blatantly announces her dad is calling. Sarah answers it and scurries to the corner of the room to whisper into it.

"Harper, please," Margot begs, fiddling with Sarah's inhaler. She forces it between my teeth again. "Just take a deep breath, okay? Just one. Please. For me, Harper. Just do it for me."

I can't. I don't want to. I don't deserve to. "They know."

Margot cups my face, leans forward, and plants a kiss on my forehead. "I know," she says. "I'm sorry. I'm so, so sorry. But we'll fix it. I'll fix it. This is not your fault."

"They know, they know, they know—"

Margot shoves Sarah's inhaler into my mouth and presses down. She grips the back of my neck, tangles her fingers in my hair. She does not let me move, turn my head away, pull back from her. Albuterol blasts down my throat; it's bitter on the back of my tongue. I cough, and Margot holds me.

"I don't think it's her asthma," Sarah says, pacing the length of the room, Margot's phone still pressed to her ear. "That's a panic attack."

"Yeah, well, whatever it is, she can't breathe. Her fucking lips are turning blue." Margot cups my face again. Her eyes are wide. She gives me a little shake. "Calm down, calm down, calm down. Please, Harper. Please. Sarah, tell them I'll call them back later. Call an ambulance."

Sarah's dials. I can hear her speaking to a dispatcher. Margot holds me in her lap, pulls her fingers through my hair, and whispers in my ear. I don't hear her—can't hear her. Blood is rushing in my ears and my pulse is too loud and I'm gasping against Margot's shoulder. She hugs me and presses a kiss to my temple. She's shaking all over, and I think she might be crying.

My parents know about the profile. The school and the band and Harrison know. Everyone watching CNN read messages I didn't write and that Margot had written in confidence. I don't know what will happen to either of us, if Dad's campaign has been derailed or if Margot will be expelled from Golden Oaks.

She can't be; I won't let her be. This isn't Margot's fault, either.

Footsteps storm up the hall. Sarah swings open the door. Margot is giving someone my name, my age, and what she thinks might be wrong with me. She doesn't let me go, even as she turns me and sits me on the edge of her bed. Gentle fingers poke and prod at my neck, beneath my chin, around my wrist. A paramedic straps a mask to my face, a nebulizer with medicine that mists down the back of my throat.

I must be crying, too, because Margot is wiping away tears. My tears. Her thumbs brush beneath my eyes and across the top of my cheekbones. "It's okay," she says, her voice cracking. The sound of it pierces through me, jars me into curling against Margot's chest and burying my face into her shoulder. She cradles the back of my head. "It's okay. Just let them help you."

Only now do I feel the ache growing in my chest, the way that my lungs have twisted into knots. Their fancy mask isn't helping me. It's not forcing my airways to open back up like it's supposed to. Maybe this is what it feels like to die, to sit here and gasp as if someone's wrapped a fist around my throat, like a full breath of air's not enough.

"Harper," the paramedic says. My eyes burn. They flash to his face. He's young, maybe Christian's age. There's two of him. "Do you think you can try and stand for me?"

"No." I barely hear myself say it. I don't feel my mouth move at all.

I don't feel him lift me or lay me down on the stretcher they've rolled into Margot's room. He straps my legs to a stiff and uncomfortable board and clips a belt around my waist that's meant to keep me from falling. Margot clutches my hand, screaming down the hallway, and ordering people back into their rooms.

I don't remember being wheeled down the stairs or down the sidewalk or through the garden that opens into a parking lot. An ambulance sits where the grass bleeds into the blacktop. Margot is speaking with the medics, begging, screaming for them to let her go with me. Sarah grabs her arm and pulls her back, snapping at her to calm down and call my parents. Margot pales. She won't do that.

But she doesn't need to call anyone.

"What the—hey!" I know that voice. I dread that voice. It sounds like he's speaking underwater. "That's my daughter! Where are you taking her? Josie!"

Dad shoves past Margot, claws at the medic who's Christian's age, and scrambles into the back of the ambulance. I don't remember being lifted into it. He steps over wires and tubing. Picks up my hand and studies the IV I didn't feel slide beneath my skin. "What is this?" he demands. Authoritative. Dad is the one in charge here. "What have you done to her?"

The paramedic is annoyed. His nostrils flare. "I'm trying to calm her down. Her friends say she has asthma, but is there anything else I should know? Any allergies to any medication?"

"No, not that we're aware of. Her asthma is triggered by stress." Dad has moved to sit behind me. I can't see him, but he's petting my hair. My heart twists in my chest. I don't deserve his understanding. Not now. Not when I've ruined everything he's worked so hard for. "Josie, baby, what happened?"

"It's not mine," I say. The words squeeze through my airway, are muffled by the mask and the medicine. "Not mine, not mine, not mine. It's not mine. I didn't do it. Daddy, I swear I didn't do it."

He presses a kiss to my temple. I haven't called him Daddy in years. "We'll talk about it later, okay? I don't care about what you did or didn't do. Not now. You've got to relax, Josie."

"Harper!" Margot has crawled halfway inside the ambulance. Her foot is perched on the step, and she's hoisting herself up despite Sarah pulling her back. "Harp, I'll meet you at the hospital. I'll meet you there, okay? Bellamy's going to drive us. I'll see you soon, I promise."

Margot's face is blurry. There are two of her, too. Sarah yanks her down, locking an arm around her waist and spitting out some kind of warning. Margot bursts into tears.

"Close that door," Dad snaps. The medic huffs his irritation. He's busy poking a syringe into my IV's injection port. Maybe steroids to open up my lungs. "I don't know if one of them worked her up like this. Close that goddamn door. Now. Or I'll file a complaint."

The medic obliges if only to shut him up. I doubt he cares about a complaint that Dad will never file. He steps over a tank of oxygen and dances around the tubing that attaches my IV to a saline drip. He grabs the handle and slams the back door shut, closing it in Margot's face as she clings to Sarah and cries.

I've never seen Margot cry before. Not like this.

Dad keeps petting the top of my head as the ambulance surges into motion. As we hurdle toward the hospital with Margot in the car behind us, I can hear Bellamy blaring their horn.

My eyelids are heavy.

They shut.

Dad smooths back my hair. "Sleep, Josie. We'll fix this."

I'm too tired to tell him that he can't.

CHAPTER TWENTY-SIX

I WAKE UP ALONE IN A ROOM I DON'T REMEMBER FALLING ASLEEP IN. The lights are dimmed to a soft, fluorescent glow, bright enough for visitors to navigate the room but dark enough still for me to sleep. It's uncomfortably silent, smells too clean and too sterile, and I'm reminded of how much I hate the hospital. I've hated it since I was six years old and first diagnosed with asthma. I've spent too many nights in a room like this, with an oxygen cannula poking up my nose and a thing clamped to my index finger.

I flick it off and an alarm dings somewhere in the hallway.

I worry, for a moment, why I'm alone. Is leaving me here without any company Mom and Dad's way of punishing me? I vaguely remember Margot saying she would meet me here, that Bellamy was driving her and Sarah to the hospital. I have no idea where they are, but maybe I've been here for too long. Maybe a night has passed and they're back at Golden Oaks in class, or in bed. I don't know what time it is, either.

Dad's blazer is tossed over the recliner pulled to the edge of my bed. A cup of still-steaming coffee sits on the windowsill, and the floral curtains are drawn shut and pinned in place by Mom's heavy purse. The television is on, though it's muted, and an episode of

Criminal Minds is playing. My parents are somewhere in the hospital, probably doing damage control because I don't know how to not ruin things.

There's a soft knock on the door, and I know it can't be my parents. Neither of them would've knocked, they would've simply barged in without a care if their kid was still sleeping or awake. They're just not good at being quiet, though maybe they would've tried under the circumstances. The television is muted, after all, and they've left to talk outside the room.

A younger woman with colorful hair slips inside through a small crack in the door. She smiles at me, gives me a little wave, and rolls over the computer that's been pushed into the corner of the room. "Hi, Miss McKinley. I'm glad to see you're finally awake. I'm Brielle, your—"

"Margot," I say, clearing my throat because it's tight and full of mucus. Brielle's expression softens into something subtler, less blinding than her bedside-manner smile. "Is—is she here? She's short, and she's got hair like yours but without all the color, and—and she's probably worried sick. Fuck. Is she here? Can I see her?"

"Such a sweetheart," Brielle says, and I know she must mean Margot. My heart swells inside my chest. "She was here when they first brought you in, but your parents weren't allowing any visitors. Poor little thing sat in the lobby and cried for over an hour."

My heart thumps into overdrive, confirmed by the monitor above my head. "Is she okay? Has anyone talked to her? Does she know I'm okay and she's got no reason to worry? Can I—"

"Slow down, Miss McKinley." Brielle types something into the computer as she talks. I try and slow my breathing before I launch myself into another asthma attack. "I think what's best for everyone is that we get you taken care of, okay? Can you tell me how you're feeling?"

It's a loaded question: Am I anxious? Can I breathe? Does my chest hurt? Brielle waits patiently for my answer, watching me intently as she clicks her mouse and navigates through the hospital's charting system. I wonder how long she's been doing this, because she's maneuvering through it all without looking.

I'm not anxious, not really, except I wish I wasn't alone and knew if Margot was okay. Breathing hurts and it feels like I've been punched in the chest, but it's not caving in and my lungs don't feel like they're in knots. But those are messy answers, the complicated ones, and they'll only pose more questions: On a scale of one to ten, do I think I can rate my pain for her? Should she get a breathing treatment ready for me? Am I at risk of having another asthma attack?

I settle for telling her, "I'm fine."

Brielle clicks on something in my chart, still not looking at the screen. She glances at the monitors hanging near my bed instead, the ones I'm connected to by wires, and studies their numbers before frowning. "You took off your finger clip, didn't you?"

"It's annoying."

"It's important," Brielle chides, her bedside-manner smile returning. "Your dad warned me you'd be a difficult patient. Think you could help a girl out and put it on for me? It'll tell me if I need to increase your oxygen."

I sigh through my nose and clip it back on. I know from experience that if I don't, they'll tape it on and I won't be able to get it off. "Do you, um, do you know where my parents are?"

"I do!" Brielle clicks her mouse. "Your mom's down the hall, in the lobby. I think she's on the phone. Your dad went down to the food court." Brielle stands and fiddles with the oxygen behind my bed. "They should be back any minute, but I can page them and tell them you're awake?"

"No," I say quickly. Brielle finally frowns. "Don't rush them. Do you, uh, know what kind of mood they're in? I . . . they're probably not happy."

"Oh, honey, they're worried about you." She places a comforting hand on my shoulder. I wonder if she's seen the news, if she knows who I am or who my parents are. Who my dad is. "Your mom hasn't sat down since she got here, and your dad's eating his way through the hospital's food supply. Did you know he's a stress eater? Dear Lord, I don't know where he puts it all!"

"He runs it off in D.C."

Brielle laughs. "Is there anything I can get for you, Harper? Some water, anything to eat?"

I shake my head as the door creaks open behind her, praying that somehow it's Margot. But I know better. "No, thank you."

Dad comes in with enough food to feed a small army. He's carrying a brown paper bag that's nearly bursting at the seams, and I can see the outlines of at least four different carryout containers. He is stress eating.

"Josie," he says, blinking warily from the doorway. "You're awake. Why weren't her mother and I notified?" He glares at Brielle from over the bag before setting it on the counter by the sink. "I told the nurse's station to page us—"

"I told her not to," I say quickly, hoping to spare Brielle from Dad's wrath. His features soften, his tired eyes crinkling at the corners. "I've only been awake for a few minutes, and I didn't want you to rush back. But there better be something for me in that bag. I'm starving."

Dad strides to the edge of my bed and plants a kiss on my forehead. It's a lingering kiss, the kind that tells me how worried he's been. I think his lips might be quivering. "How are you feeling?" he asks, waving Brielle away when she announces her departure. "I thought you'd never wake up."

"I feel fine," I tell him. "Just tired. How long was I asleep?"

He looks at the watch around his wrist. "Six, seven hours? They, ah, sedated you in the ambulance. Said it was the worst panic attack they'd seen in months, and it was only making your asthma worse." Dad sits in the recliner next to me and takes my hand, his wedding band cool against my skin. I don't know when he started wearing it again; his fingers swell and he's had to have it cut off twice. "I was so scared, Josie. You wouldn't understand, but as a father, you just— you never want to be in a position where you can't help your child, and I couldn't help you. Your face was turning blue."

It's been so long since Dad's been candid with anyone, least of all me. Seeing him like this, his hand trembling over mine and tears lining his eyes, I've never felt guiltier, and not even just for a profile I didn't make. "I'm sorry," I say, and I hope he knows I mean it. "I didn't—I didn't mean to get so worked up, or to ruin everything, or—"

"Stop," Dad says gently. He smooths his thumb across my knuckles. "We're not discussing what happened. Not here. There'll be plenty of time for that later. Right now, your job is to rest, not damage control."

"But the profile isn't mine," I tell him anyway. Dad heaves a sigh that might be relieved, maybe exasperated. Either way, he lets me finish. "I didn't send those messages. I swear. You can check my phone if you want. Or—or have your friend from the CIA hack it and look at my history. I never downloaded that app."

"I should certainly hope not." Mom sweeps into the room in a blaze of fiery frustration that straddles the line of shame and blatant disappointment. "Do you know how hard it is to wrestle with freedom of the press? There are dozens of media outlets talking about those messages, Harper, and I can't shut a single one of them up. I've been on the phone for hours trying to convince them that you weren't involved in this."

Dad raises his hand and pins Mom with a glare I know well to steer clear of. It can burn right through you if you let it. "Harper doesn't need the added stress of you bitching about doing your job as her mother to protect her. Take it back into the hallway. I won't have you getting her all worked up again."

"I am protecting her!" Mom snaps. "While also trying to save your campaign. The press is having a field day with this, Marcus. It's a goddamn free-for-all on CNN and Fox, in case you haven't been paying attention."

Dad glances at the television, and I realize that maybe *Criminal Minds* isn't on for my sake. "For crying out loud, Dianna, Harper is a child. The election won't hinge on a high school prank gone wrong. If Josie says she didn't send those messages, then I believe her. But if this Blanchard girl has had anything to do with any of this—"

"No!" I yank back my hand like he's burned it. Mom crosses her arms, prepared to inform me of exactly how she plans to punish Margot. Expulsion is on the tip of her tongue. "Leave Margot out of this. She's just as much of a victim here as I am. Someone tricked her into sending those messages, into thinking she was talking to me. It's not her fault."

Dad's frown is deep enough to wrinkle his forehead. "Did you know about this?"

I feel myself balk at the question. "I—"

"You knew," Mom says, her eyes narrowing. She storms to the edge of my bed and points her finger in my face. It feels as belittling as it does concerning, but it's not concern for me. "You knew, and you let this happen?"

Dad's voice is pained as he begins, "Dianna, let her explain—"

"We could've prepared for this!" Mom cries. "We could've shut this down before it began! Of all the reckless, immature, selfish things you could've done to this family, Harper—"

"Dianna!" Dad stands up so fast his recliner flies out from under him. It's enough to make Mom stop talking, to stop yelling at me, but she doesn't back down. Not from him. She crosses her arms and glares at Dad with me lying between them. "Let. Harper. Explain." Each word is clipped, edged with a sharp warning.

Mom blows out a breath through her nose, unfurls her lip from where it's drawn back over her teeth. I've never seen her snarl before, but I'm surprised she's not salivating. "Fine," she snaps. "But it'd better be a damn good explanation."

Dad settles at this as if he's won some challenge. He sits back down and touches the top of my head, smoothing back my hair before offering me a wary smile. "Go ahead, Josie. Tell us what happened. The truth."

I don't realize I'm crying until Dad wipes a tear from my cheek. "The profile isn't mine," I repeat. My voice cracks. Dad nods encouragingly. "Margot told me about it the weekend before school started. She didn't know she hadn't been talking to me. But she said that the account went quiet, that she'd tried messaging it to find out who was behind it, but they never replied. I—I wanted to tell you, but Nadia said if the account was quiet and wasn't causing any trouble, I should just leave it alone and forget about it."

"Ah, yes." Mom drags a hand through her hair. It's down around her shoulders, unbrushed and wild from last night's updo. "Because listening to your friends is always the smart thing to do.

God, Harper, do you even understand the position you've put us in? No one's going to believe that you weren't a part of this."

"But I wasn't," I stress. Dad places a hand on my shoulder. "I told you, check my phone. And—and Margot, this isn't her fault. They tricked her. She thought it was me."

Mom scoffs and puts her hands on her hips. I hate it whenever she stands like that, asserting her dominance at a time when it doesn't need asserting. I know exactly where I fall on the food chain. "I warned you that that Blanchard girl was trouble. The things she wrote, even if not to you, were disgusting. Do you even know what any of it meant? Was it explained to you? It was—it was—Lord, what do you kids call it these days? Smoot? Smut? Pornographic. Those messages were nearly pornographic. They painted a very clear picture."

My face heats with a blush that creeps up my neck, warms the tips of my ears. Dad coughs into a fist. "I think what your mom's trying to say, Josie, is that you probably shouldn't spend any more time with her. The Blanchard girl."

"Margot," I say stiffly. "Her name is Margot. And she's my friend."

"I don't care if she's your friend," Mom snaps. "I have half a mind to expel her. Those messages were sent on school grounds and discussed hooking up in the dormitories. I could lose my job over this, Harper. Do you understand that?"

"You can't expel her," I insist. I sit up straighter in my bed, my spine cracking and chest aching with protest. I've been laying still for too long. "It's our senior year, and Margot doesn't deserve that. Don't you think she probably feels awful that this happened? Christ, Mom, those messages getting leaked affects Margot, too. Find whoever did this, and punish them instead."

"Oh, I intend to. But in the meantime, I do not want you around her, especially if you don't want me expelling her." Mom's tone is final, the equivalent of her pointing at a door. It rattles every bone in my body. "Friends come and go, Harper Josephine, and Margot is one who needs to go."

I shake my head. My stomach gives a little flip, and I think I might vomit all over the crisp white bedding. There's no way that I can just let Margot go, forget about everything we've been through, and act as if none of it happened. We share too many memories, too many experiences that are bad and good and everything in between. Margot isn't just my friend or someone I speak to in high school but will never see again once we graduate. "No."

Mom raises an eyebrow, her forehead wrinkling despite the Botox. "Excuse me?"

"I said no," I repeat through my teeth. My heart pounds out a warning, and my lungs twist to remind me why I'm in this bed, but I don't care. "I'm not staying away from Margot. You don't get to dictate who my friends are like you dictate everything else."

Mom squares her shoulders. She puffs up her chest and sticks out her jaw to remind me that I am the child here. She doesn't care if stress triggers my asthma or if half the hospital has likely heard her yelling at me. I'm the child and she's the adult, and whatever she says goes. "Harper Josephine, don't you dare—"

"Margot Blanchard is my girlfriend," I announce to the room, to my parents, to the nurses in the hall, and to the group of residents making their rounds on this floor. Everything about Mom deflates; her shoulders, her chest, her face. She opens and to closes her mouth, and I use her silence to surge ahead while I'm still in control of the conversation. I know I won't be for long. "With or without that profile, and with or without your approval, Margot is my goddamn girlfriend, and you are not going to ruin that."

I think she's gone into shock; I think I've gone into shock. This isn't how I planned on coming out to them, not in a fit of rage over being told I'm not allowed to see Margot. It was always meant to be through an email, or a text I sent Dad from my dorm room in a college across the country. My hands are shaking in my lap, and my tongue feels heavy behind my teeth as if it knows what I said is damning.

It's Dad's voice that eventually breaks the silence. "Josie," he says tightly. "Honey, what are you saying?"

I've already come this far, have already told them what Margot is to me. There's no sense in not going all the way. "Margot's my girlfriend," I tell them again, though my eyes are fixated on Dad's emotionless face. I can't read him. I can't tell how he might be feeling. It's the face of Dad the politician, the one he's practiced in the mirror so people don't know when they've rattled him. "In the grand scheme of things, I think I identify as a lesbian."

"Think?" Mom's voice sounds as if it'll snap into splinters. "*Think*? You're not even sure? You're putting everything we've worked for at risk because you *think* you might be a lesbian?"

Dad pinches the bridge of his nose. "Christ, Dianna, stop talking. I'm—I'm trying to wrap my mind around this."

"Wrap your mind around it? Wrap your mind around *what*, Marcus? She doesn't even know what she's saying!" Mom drags a hand through her hair, flips it back and tosses it over her shoulder. Her eye is twitching, her eyebrow jumping every time she breathes. "You're just—you're confused, Harper. That's all. Margot's made you confused."

"Mom—"

"Dianna—"

"Jesus fucking Christ."

The voice in the doorway is tired and worried and sober and familiar.

Dad's body becomes rigid, his breath catching in the back of his throat. I wonder if he might need my oxygen.

A strangled cry escapes from Mom as she slaps a hand across her mouth. Her other hand falls to rest above her heart as if she's trying to contain it in her chest. "Christian?"

My brother crosses his arms. "I see not a damn thing's changed."

CHAPTER TWENTY-SEVEN

E VERYTHING ABOUT HIM IS DIFFERENT.

The last time I saw my older brother, he was sickly thin and looked like a skeleton, one that even I could have taken down despite his years of combat training. Christian had stumbled drunk into the Christmas tree, reeking of booze as if he'd just come over from the bar, and Mom had thrown him out, telling him not to come back until he got his shit together.

Apparently, it hasn't been together until now.

Christian is taller than I remember. It's like someone has stretched him all out, then filled him with muscle until his skin threatened to burst at the seams. His hair has grown out, and his eyes are clearer than ever. He bolts to my side to keep me from leaping out of bed.

I sit up on my knees and crash into Christian's chest, nearly knocking him off balance. My arms barely fit around his torso as I hug him, but he envelops me in a hug that's a little too tight.

"Harper, be careful!" Dad cries. "You'll rip out your IVs!" He grabs my hospital gown to pull me away from Christian, but Christian holds me tight. He folds me in close and tucks my head beneath his chin, cradling me and rocking back and forth as I let out a sob that makes him wince.

Dad's still fluttering around us, patting and tapping at my wrists and arms to ensure I haven't ripped out my IVs. I'm almost positive I haven't, but I couldn't care less if I bleed all over him or my brother. Christian might deserve it if I weren't so happy to see him.

I don't know where my oxygen has gone, though, and that's a problem.

"You—you—ugh!" I cry, slamming my palm against the center of Christian's chest. He doesn't flinch. It's like he's prepared for this. "You big ass behemoth! I've sent you so many messages! I called your old number and left you a dozen different voicemails!"

Christian flinches and has the nerve to look like I've slapped him. "I know," he says, and the break in his voice has tears springing to my eyes. "God, Josie, I know." Only he and Dad ever call me that. "I am so, so sorry. I can't even tell you how sorry I am."

I bury my face into his shoulder, gripping his shirt between my trembling fingers. I'm afraid to let him go. I never got to hug him goodbye or tell him I loved him before Mom kicked him out on Christmas. There's a chance she'll do it again now, even if Christian seems sober, but I won't let him go before I'm ready.

But Mom is hugging him, too. She's kissing his temple and crying into his cropped brown hair. "My baby," she says, holding his head against her chest. Christian's gone rigid. I can tell he doesn't want her to touch him. "I'm sorry. I'm so sorry. I can't believe you're here."

"Of course you can't," Christian remarks. His body vibrates against mine, his words booming up and out, and I wonder how long he's been storing up whatever it is he's come here to say. He and Mom have never seen eye to eye, and I doubt, for him, that's changed. "You weren't even going to try and get a hold of me, were you?"

Mom presses her palm against his cheek, but Christian swats her away. "Chris, baby, I would have. God, I would have tried if I knew how! But she's only been here a few hours, and we've been trying to get a handle on the press—"

"Josie could have died," he says dryly. "And all you care about is the media. Typical. I didn't come here to see you. Either of you." Christian glances pointedly at Dad, who's sitting silently in his recliner, watching Christian and I cling to each other. "I'm here because I knew Josie needed me."

"How?" I ask, rubbing my nose on his shirt. He doesn't seem to mind that there's snot and tears and day-old make-up staining it. "If they didn't call you, who did?"

Christian pets my hair. He takes the rogue oxygen cannula hanging from Dad's index finger and tucks it behind my ears. "You have a very bossy friend," he tells me. My brow furrows as I frown at him, but I have a gut feeling I know who he's talking about. "Some girl named Margot called the base in Arlington. I'm not stationed there anymore, but she badgered the civilian running HR into telling her where I work. She tried calling there, too, then messaged me on Facebook and ripped me a new asshole. I like her."

"Shit," I breathe. Christian chuckles. "She called you? Did you get in trouble?"

"A friend of mine answered the call, so no. But remind me to show you the message. She was brutal. Efficient, but brutal. I met her in the lobby." Christian hugs me a little tighter. "She told me to tell you she'll see you as soon as she's allowed. Apparently, they won't let her in." He looks directly at Mom, but I know that he means Dad, too.

I twist away from my brother. "Wait, she's still here? She'll worry herself to death if someone doesn't tell her I'm okay!"

Mom is wiping her eyes, smearing her mascara. "I told you I don't want you seeing her anymore. She's trouble and has gotten you confused."

"She got ahold of Christian," I snap at her. "You weren't even going to try. I'd say that warrants a thank you, and maybe an apology depending on how you've treated her. Actually, you should probably just apologize. I know you."

Dad sighs heavily from his recliner. "Josie," he says. He sounds exhausted, as if he hasn't slept in days. Maybe, with everything going on, he hasn't. "This—this queer thing. It's new for us, okay? We need time to—to figure out what it means. To wrap our heads around it. The entire country found out at the same time we did."

"Marcus," Mom retorts. "Don't indulge her."

"I'm not indulging her, Dianna. She's our child, and this is— it's—don't be so goddamn thickheaded." Dad drags a hand down his face, rubbing his jaw and the dark stubble that's growing there. "We didn't make a single effort to understand Christian and his . . . problem." He winces as the words come out. So does Christian. "We booted him off to military school and hoped that it would fix him. We have to go about this differently. I won't lose Josie, too."

Because that's the deal with Christian; they've lost him. He's gone a year without returning their calls, answering my messages, or showing up at holiday dinners. And he didn't come here for our parents. He probably would've preferred to not see them at all. Dad knows this, understands this, and in a weird, regretful way, he accepts it. I can see it on his face as he stares at my brother with tears in his eyes.

It wasn't his decision to send him away, after all.

It's why Christian's being harder on Mom, why he can't even look at her without a snarl curling his upper lip. Maybe someday he'll make amends with Dad, but he will never forgive Mom for not helping him, sending him away when he needed her the most.

"I had a problem," Christian says. He doesn't shy away from admitting it, but he can barely tolerate looking at Dad. He doesn't elaborate on his health or if he's truly sober or how he might have gotten that way. It's none of their business. "Harper doesn't. You can't just fix her like you thought you could me. She's not broken."

Dad raises his hands to fend him off. "I know. I didn't mean that, I just—"

"Oh, for Christ's sake." Mom snatches her purse off the windowsill. She shuffles across the room, pointy heels clicking over the polished white tile, each staccato note driving through my skull like a knife. "We need to talk, Marcus. Now." She throws open the door and points her finger into the hallway. "In the lobby. Alone. Christian . . ." Her voice cracks over his name, a piece of her heart audibly breaking when he doesn't bother looking up at her. She sniffles. "Stay with your sister."

"I planned on it."

Dad stands with a pained groan and holds a hand to his back. I hear it snap as he twists his hips and stretches. I think he might be stalling. "I swear to God, Dianna, if you make one more scene . . ." He plants a kiss on the top of my head, then hesitates. Christian's not looking at him, either, so Dad's hand flutters unsurely at his shoulder. He settles for giving him a quick pat. "Keep an eye on her. Don't let her take off the oxygen again."

"Will do."

His sigh is suffering as he follows Mom from the room, closing the door behind them. I can hear them bickering in the hall, and Christian's shoulders cave in around him the moment we're sealed in here alone. "I can't believe I ever missed them."

"What about me?" I ask. I sit on the bed across from him, so I can see his face and commit each detail to memory. It's likely he'll end up disappearing again. A scar slashes through his eyebrow, a pale pink line that cuts down into his eyelid. It's new. So is the crookedness of his nose. "Did you miss me?"

Christian frowns. "Of course I did," he says. He reaches between us and takes my hand in his. His fingers are rough and calloused, and I try not to think about the things he's done to make them that way. Even before he cut us off, Christian wouldn't talk about his deployments or what the army has made him do. "Shit, Josie. You're the only thing I've missed about this place. I just—I wasn't ready to see you, you know? Or talk to you. I was fucked up, and I . . . I needed to get better. And I couldn't do that here, or anywhere near Mom and Dad. They're smothering, and you know how they can be when they're disappointed. I couldn't handle it."

I pick at a loose thread on the blanket, twisting it around my finger until my skin turns purple. Christian watches me intently. "You could have messaged me," I say quietly. "Just once. Just to tell me you were okay."

My brother nods solemnly. "I could have," he agrees. "But I wasn't okay, Josie. Not for a long time. It's—it's hard. Being back here. Being so close to that shit-storm they call a school." Christian rubs his brow, the scar there, and I wonder if maybe it still hurts him. "I couldn't be the brother you needed, and you did not need me the way I was. But—but maybe now, I can be. I don't drink anymore, or do anything that even classifies as trouble. I haven't in almost a year."

I figured he was sober just by looking at him, but it's a breath of fresh air to hear him say it. "How, um. How'd you . . ." I don't know how to ask, but Christian seems to understand.

He smiles fondly. "I, uh. I met someone. About two years ago. They were helping me get my shit together, but I screwed up on Christmas when I knew I had to see Mom and Dad. I got drunk just before coming over." Christian leans on the raised guardrail meant to keep me in bed. "I'm—I'm really sorry if I ruined Christmas. I don't even remember what happened."

"Best not to talk about it," I say. "The Christmas tree hasn't recovered."

Christian winces. "I'm sorry."

I pull my fingers through my hair, grumbling at the tangles twisted through my curly auburn locks. Margot will beg to brush it out, ask if she can braid it. She loves to play with my hair. I'll let her as long as she hasn't been expelled by the time I return to campus.

"So, uh." Christian clears his throat. "Are we going to talk about those messages? I, um, heard about you and Margot on the news this morning. I was going to message you after work, but I ended up coming here instead."

Everything inside of me does a flip, shrivels up and dies from embarrassment. Of course he watches the news. It's probably his way of keeping tabs on us. "I never sent Margot those messages," I say. I tell him all about the profile, how Margot and I met, and how I realized I'm queer. Christian listens intently, nodding when appropriate and squeezing my hand when I start to get choked up. He knows all about our parents, their constant disapproval, and how bad they can make a person feel, especially Mom.

He blows out a breath when I'm finished. "Shit, Josie."

I give him a wobbly smile. "So that's everything! Now I have to worry about Mom sending me away. She's probably outside research-ing electroshock therapy or conversion camps."

Christian's eyes widen to the size of a quarter, and I'd laugh if I didn't feel like crying. "What? Hey, no, listen. I'm not gonna let that happen, okay? I promise." Christian pulls me into his arms, hugging me close so I can bury my face into his shoulder. His shirt is still wet with the tears I've already cried, but he still doesn't seem to mind. "You can come live with me if she tries anything. I have a condo in D.C. with a guest room. You can have it."

I sniffle against Christian's chest. "You're twenty-three and bought a condo?"

"Well, I mean, we're renting it, but—"

"Wait, we?" I scramble out of his embrace, wriggle in his arms until he lets me go. Christian bites his lip. "Oh my God. You really met someone if you're living together! Is it serious? Are you going to marry her? Are you already married? Wait, let me see your hand." I pick it up and inspect his finger for a ring. There isn't one. "Good, okay. I didn't miss anything. Christian! I can't believe you found someone!"

"Yeah, Josie, about that—"

There's a soft knock on the door, a startling sound that bursts through my excitement and has Christian sucking in his breath. But we both know it can't be our parents; neither one of them would give us the courtesy of knocking. Christian tentatively says, "Come in."

A younger man dressed in a lab coat slips through a crack in the door. He smiles and fiddles with his tie. "Hello, Harper. I'm Dr. Benjamin—"

"Go away," I cry, flopping against Christian's chest.

He grunts and sighs into my hair, but every bit of him has relaxed. He's glad it's not our parents. "You'll have to forgive her, doctor. My sister's an awful patient."

Dr. Benjamin raises a perfectly manicured eyebrow. "Yes, so I've been told."

"Hey, I was nice to the nurse!"

Christian pushes me back. "Come on, Josie. You have to be nice to him, too. He's only here to check up on you. Sorry, but she really hates doctors."

"I get it," Dr. Benjamin says kindly, offering me a friendly half-shrug. "I used to hate them, too." He studies the monitors that hang from the pole behind Christian, who looks up to watch him. "Your dad told the nurse's station to check your IVs in case you'd accidentally ripped them out. Has anyone else been by yet? You took off your finger clip, too, I see. And your heart monitor."

"None of that's important," I say quickly. Dr. Benjamin's mouth quirks with a knowing little smirk. "Don't trouble yourself trying to hook it all back up."

"Those things are important, actually." He pushes a button on the monitor. "The heart monitor tells me you're alive, though so does your sass, and the finger clip measures the oxygen in your blood. For someone who came in for their asthma, that's something we need to know." Dr. Benjamin crosses his arms. "The IV, of course, is how we give you medicine if you need it. It'll only take me a minute to stick you if I need to."

Christian snorts and leans back on my bed, flopping into the pillows that are still flat from where I slept on them. I'm surprised to see him so relaxed, so calm, when Christian doesn't like doctors either. "Do you need the IV to sedate her?" he asks. "Because that's the only way you're gonna poke her with a needle. See, Josie? I remember. We used to have to hold her in a bear hug just for blood work."

Dr. Benjamin chuckles. "Reminds me of someone else I know. They fainted trying to get a tattoo. I had to pick them up off the floor."

I'd ask to hear the full story, but Christian bolts back upright, his jaw falling slack as he glares at Dr. Benjamin. "I did not faint, you asshole. I told you, I tripped over the chair."

I blink; clearly I've missed something. "Wait a minute," I say. "You know him?"

Dr. Benjamin smirks again, still fiddling with the monitor. I think he's searching through the history, checking my stats before I ripped everything off. "Yes, sir, do you know me?"

Christian drags a hand down his face, his cheeks scarlet with a blush. I've never seen my brother blush before. "For Christ's sake, Ben. Harper, this is . . ."

"Ben," Dr. Benjamin says. He holds out his hand in offering. "Your second-year resident, and this handsome guy's boyfriend. Sorry, love, but you were taking too long. I could hear her squealing about marriage in the hallway."

CHAPTER TWENTY-EIGHT

HAVING A DOCTOR FOR A FUTURE BROTHER-IN-LAW HAS ITS PERKS. I got to have ice cream for dinner last night, and he's arranged to sneak Margot into my room while my parents are away from the hospital today. Her dad's picking her up early from school, and Ben agreed to be our lookout. "No one told me she can't come in, and letting you know I saw your parents on the elevator is a courtesy."

I like Ben, even without his perks. I like the way he makes Christian smile. The way he calls him "love" and rubs his back when he's stressed. He's confident, if not a little cocky, and I especially like the way he'd looked our parents in the eyes and said, "Hello, my name is Ben, and someday, I'm going to be your son-in-law."

Mom nearly had a breakdown.

Dad shook his hand. Bravery transcends homophobia, apparently.

Seeing them together warms my heart, too, and it gives me hope for Margot and me.

Ben also has the patience of a God, and every time I ask, "Is she here yet?" he calmly tells me, "No." He's been texting with Margot all morning since he first started his shift and my phone is wherever Margot threw it. He's been busy making his rounds, but I think he likes having me as a patient; he slips into my room whenever he needs to take a breather.

"So," I say. "What exactly does Christian do now? Is he discharged?"

Ben pretends to listen to my heartbeat with his stethoscope. "Honorably, as of six months ago. Now he works security at the Smithsonian. Boring, but safe. Nothing in the museum can kill him, and I swear to God if that's a *Night at the Museum* reference about to come out of your mouth, I will strangle you with your oxygen."

I snort and draw in a breath, then turn and cough into my elbow. My chest still aches from yesterday's asthma attack, and Ben's been insisting I do a breathing treatment ever since he looked at my medical history. "That was an accident."

Ben rolls his eyes and wraps his stethoscope around his neck. "You sound fine, just a little wheezy. Someone warned you about getting all excited to see your girlfriend." He reaches behind me and increases my oxygen. I groan. "Hey, I don't want to hear it. The sooner I'm convinced you can breathe, the sooner I can bust you out of here."

"How'd you two meet, anyway?" I sink back down into my pillows, watching him click through the computer he's rolled over to my bed. "He doesn't seem like your type."

A small smile tugs at the corner of his mouth. "I'm sure it won't come as any surprise to you, but we met at a gay bar in Baltimore two years ago. He was in town with some friends from the base, and I was in my last year of med school." Ben is quiet as he types something into my chart, hopefully an estimated discharge date. "He got into a fight with some asshole over a game of pool. That scar above his eye? He got hit upside the head with a beer bottle."

I lean in closer, gripping the guardrail. "Were you there? Did you see it?"

Ben nods. "I was sitting at the bar with my boyfriend. We were already on the rocks, but there was blood everywhere and I left him to go patch up Christian. He was pissed. So he stole my car keys and stranded me there, even though I lived on the other side of town. I ended up calling an Uber and taking your brother back to my place. Bastard couldn't remember the name of the hotel he was staying at, and I couldn't exactly leave him at the bar, so . . ."

"You're right," I sigh. "I'm not surprised. What happened the next morning when he was sober?"

Ben winces, and I wonder if Christian was ever really sober those first several months. "I lived across the street from a Starbucks, so I went out and got us some coffee. When I came back, Christian snapped awake and immediately put his fists up. He punched me right in the jaw before I even knew he was coming at me. The bastard is quick on his feet." Ben chuckles grimly and absently rubs his jaw. "I don't know how he didn't break it, but Christian likes to joke that it's because of my 'beautifully sharp jawline,' and it hurt him more than it did me. But he didn't know where he was or who I was, and he was scared, and I think a little paranoid. He'd forgotten he was even stateside." Ben slips his phone out of his pocket. "It took me an hour to calm him down. I was convinced the entire time he was going to hit me again or put me in a chokehold, whatever he could do to get away. You know, fight or flight, or whatever, and he woke up on a stranger's couch. Coming from the army, his instinct was to fight and get the hell out of dodge. But he settled down when he realized I wasn't going to hurt him and collapsed onto my couch and cried. We've been nearly inseparable ever since."

I tug my knees into my chest. "Are you the one who helped him get sober?"

He hesitates, probably wondering if it's his place to tell me this part of their story. Ben sighs and sweeps a hand over his cropped hair, a careful zigzag buzzed around his ears. I hadn't noticed it yesterday. "I got him into some rehabs, called in some favors to a few psych friends from undergrad who specialized in substance abuse. But ultimately, Christian had to want to get better, and for a long time, he didn't. So I gave him an ultimatum, and he took it."

"What ultimatum?"

"That I loved him, but I couldn't want his sobriety more than he did. He had to get better if he wanted me to stay, because I couldn't keep watching him kill himself." Ben clears his throat, probably wondering if maybe he's taken this too far, then continues, "It's where he was headed, eventually, but he took my offer and let me help him. He had slip-ups, obviously, like on Christmas, but he hasn't touched anything since."

I stare at Ben for a long, long while. He stares right back at me, doesn't even blink his warm, dark brown eyes. It's unnerving. "Could you, um, come here, please?"

If he finds the question to be unusual, Ben doesn't let on. He strides to the edge of my bed, and I push myself up onto my knees. Ben stands perfectly still as I throw my arms around his torso, as I hug him and bury my face into his lab coat. "Thank you."

He wraps his arms around my middle, and I think he kisses my hair. "You never have to thank me, Harper. Not for helping him. I love your brother, too. And you by association, by the way. He's told me so much about you, I feel like I already know you."

"I wish he'd told me about you, but I understand why he didn't."

There's a loud thud in the doorway, a strangled cry from a raspy voice I recognize. "Sorry, sorry. I don't want to intrude on a moment, but like, the last time I saw you, you couldn't breathe, and it's been twenty-four hours, and if I don't get to hug you within the next three seconds, I am going to lose my mind."

I fly out of Ben's embrace, and the only thing that keeps me confined to my bed is his hand planting firmly on my shoulder. "Margot!"

She sprints across the room, her hair splaying out behind her, and skids to a stop in front of me, her hands fluttering as she bounces on her toes and whines in the back of her throat. "I—I want to— can I—will I hurt you?" She looks up at Ben with tears in her eyes. "Can I hug her?"

Ben smiles reassuringly. "Be gentle, but Harper is fine. Safe and sound, as promised."

Margot wriggles between us and loops her arms around my waist, careful not to hug me too hard. "Are you okay? I tried to come see you, but your mom threatened to have me arrested. Arrested, Harper. Do you know how badly it could've gone for me had your mom called the fucking cops?"

I squeeze her against my chest, ignoring Ben's sigh as he pinches the bridge of his nose, murmuring something about non-compliance. "I'm sorry. I'm so, so sorry. I can only imagine how awful that would have been. Had I known, I would have—I would have done something. I would have come down there. The nurse told me you were here, but then Christian—Christian! Margot, you got a hold of Christian! You—he came here—I saw him." I bury my face into her shoulder. She's shaking like a tiny little leaf. "He was here, and I saw him, and he's better now. And I never would have known if you hadn't done what you did."

A soft whimper slips out of her. "I didn't know if you'd be mad, but you missed him. I thought that having him here might help you. I didn't know he'd show up, or that he'd even respond to my message, but I had to try."

I pull back enough to look at her. Margot's cheeks are ashen, stained with tears both fresh and old. She's not even wearing any eyeliner. I cup her face between my palms. "You're the best, most wonderful creature on the face of the earth, and I'm not mad at you. For anything. I can't—I can't even thank you. I could say it a thousand times, but it would never be enough."

Margot sniffles, and I brush my thumb beneath her eyes to wipe away a few stray tears. "They just—they slammed the ambulance door shut. In my face. And all I knew was that they hadn't, like, fixed you before taking you away. And Sarah, she said she's only had one asthma attack as bad as the one you had, and that it was the worst feeling in the world." Margot gives my waist a little squeeze. "Are you—are you better now?"

"Good as new," I tell her. She doesn't need to know that my chest hurts, or that Ben says I'm wheezy because I got too excited about seeing her. "Ben's taking really good care of me."

Ben smiles as Margot looks up at him, tears still hanging from her lashes. "Harper's a popular patient," he says. "All of my colleagues keep stopping by to check on her. They know she's family." Ben lightly pats my shoulder. "I need to get going, though, because I do have other patients. Christian's only working a half day today, so he'll swing by when he gets off. I'll pop in when I can, but I think you're probably in good hands."

Margot rubs her eyes with the sleeve of her cardigan. "Is there—should I do anything? Does she need to, I don't know, avoid lying flat or something? Sarah said it's easier for her to breathe if she's sitting up during an asthma attack."

My heart swells in my chest. It's endearing to see her so concerned, though I'm not sure I deserve it. It's my fault we're here in the first place.

Ben doesn't miss a beat as he shows her how to look at my monitors, read the numbers, and know when she might need to send for him. He doesn't anticipate her needing to, but teaching her what to look for seems to make Margot feel better. "Try to keep her in bed if you can," he adds on his way out the door. "She's been up pacing since this morning. If she absolutely has to get up, make sure you stay close by. And don't let her take off her oxygen. Every time I come in, she's flung the damn thing behind her bed."

Margot is visibly making a mental checklist, ticking things off on her fingers as she repeats it all back to him. "Stay in bed, stay close by, and don't let her pull the plug on herself. Got it, McDreamy."

Ben nearly slams into the threshold. "Jesus Christ. Don't even."

Margot beams and sits on the edge of my bed. "Too late. I watch *Grey's Anatomy*."

"McDreamy" looks up at the ceiling, and I wonder if he might be praying. "I'll be back in an hour to check on you. Hit the call button if you're dying." Ben slips through the door before another reference can pop out of either of our mouths.

I flop back into my pillows when he's gone. "He said he'd come by if anyone sees my parents so he can smuggle you out through the staff elevator. Do you know when your dad's coming back for you? Maybe Christian can give you a ride back to campus."

"He said he'd stay in Bethesda until I call him to pick me up." Margot crawls over my legs, mindful of my IV and oxygen. She curls up and snuggles into me, resting her head in the curve between my neck and shoulder. She absently fiddles with my hospital gown, smoothing out the papery blue fabric. "Your phone is in my bag; remind me to give it to you before I leave. I can't—I can't go another twenty-four hours without hearing from you. Not while you're here."

I turn onto my side to face her so I can study her and hold her hand between us. Margot laces her fingers through mine. "I am so sorry, Margot. This is all my fault. Christian and I spent half the night talking about why someone would do this, and I don't think it had anything to do with me and you, not really. Someone's always planned on leaking those messages."

Margot nods. She traces her thumb across my knuckles. "They did this to hurt your dad, probably. That's why it came after the endorsement."

"Maybe not him specifically, but his campaign," I say. Margot nods again, like they're synonymous. I guess, in a way, they are. "I am so sorry you were collateral in all this. None of it is fair for either of us, but especially not you. It's not what you signed up for."

"Harper," Margot says fiercely. Her eyes blaze with a kind of grim resolution. "I sent those messages. No one made me match with that Tinder account, and no one made me say the things I said. I knew what I was doing, I knew who you were, and I knew who your father was. I sent them anyway. I have a responsibility in all this, too."

"But they tricked you," I say. "You thought it was me."

"Yes," she agrees. "And whoever did this is a bitch I want to punch in the face. But I played my part, too, and it's not your place to apologize. You didn't do anything wrong. Besides, I'm not even upset that this happened. The being tricked part, that is. I hope whoever leaked the messages burns in hell."

I feel my brow furrow as I frown at her. "You don't care that someone tricked you?"

"No," Margot confides. She reaches up with a steady hand and tucks my hair behind my ear. "We never would've met if they hadn't. Not really. You'd have asked to borrow another pencil, then forget to give it back to me after class."

"That happened once—"

"Once was enough," she says. "I don't ever want to be some useless memory for you."

I don't like the look on her face. I don't like the way she's not looking at me, or the way she's stopped tracing her thumb across my knuckles. I don't like the way my heart breaks, and I wonder if she feels this way about Emily, if she's afraid a memory is all she'll ever be to anyone.

But she'll never be just that for me.

"Hey," I whisper. Margot grunts an acknowledgement, so I take my fingers and place them beneath her chin. Her eyes snap up to meet mine. "You will never just be some memory for me, okay? Never. And I'm sorry I was so oblivious before all of this. I should have paid better attention. I should have given you back your pencil when I borrowed it."

Margot lets out a little chuckle, a soft brush of air that's warm against my cheek. "Every time I tried to make small talk," she muses. "I always hoped it'd become more than that. You were so serious about band, about whatever book you brought to class that day. I liked it. I liked you. And I knew you were more than the girl whose mom was the dean. That's why I swiped right on your profile. I wanted to prove myself right."

I wriggle just a little bit closer, until nothing but my oxygen tube separates us. "What about now?" I ask. Margot tilts her head. "Do you think you might still like me?"

She lifts my hand and kisses the back of my fingers. "I think," Margot says quietly, offering me a timid smile. "I think I might be in love with you."

CHAPTER TWENTY-NINE

"I WANT YOU TO USE THIS EVERY SINGLE DAY—TWICE, EVEN, IF you have to—once before bed and once when you wake up in the morning." Ben places a brand-new nebulizer on the hood of Christian's car. It's the fancy kind, a mask that covers your mouth and nose so you don't have to suck on a tube. "New inhaler, stronger dose, use as needed." He tucks the inhaler into the pocket of my cardigan, and I feel like a child being sent off to their first day of school.

Ben and Christian offered to bring me back to campus, even though my parents were at the hospital when Ben discharged me. I didn't want to be trapped alone in a car with them, so Christian and I waited in the food court for the end of Ben's shift so they could bring me back instead.

Christian was quiet the entire drive back to Golden Oaks, drumming his fingers against the wheel while Ben and I chatted to fill the silence, a nervous thread strung between us. I know being back here is hard for him, he'd rather be anywhere else, so I'd told him he could wait in the car. Christian's still sitting in the driver's seat, his eyes closed and head thrown back against the headrest, though he's opened his door so I can lean in and hug him before I go.

"Ben," I whine, bouncing on my heels as a cold wind whips at my cheeks. "I'll be fine, I promise. You need to get going while it's still daylight. I don't want you driving home in the dark."

Ben rolls his eyes before holding open his arms. "Come here, little McKinley. Let's get you inside before you catch pneumonia."

I hug Ben and press a kiss to his cheek. I've known him a total of three and a half long days, but I feel like I've known him all my life. We bonded in the hospital, and he's as much of a brother to me as Christian. "Take care of him, okay?" I whisper it softly enough so Christian can't hear. "I don't want any of this to set him back. And—and if talking to me is too much, tell him that he doesn't have to. But maybe you can text me every once in a while to let me know how he's doing."

Ben presses me closer, and I bury my face into his shoulder. "I don't think you understand how much he needed this—needed *you*. Christian has missed you, Harper. More than you're ever going to realize." He kisses the top of my head. "I'm off work on Saturday. If you want, I can pick you up, maybe take you to the Smithsonian. We can bug Christian at work."

"Absolutely not," he says, popping open one eye. "The two of you together would get me fired, and I happen to like this job. I get to see mummies and dead things."

"Harper, McDreamy, Soldier Boy!" Ben groans as Margot's voice pierces the stillness of the parking lot. He lets me go before Margot crashes into me. He likes to pretend she annoys him, but I see him smiling over her shoulder. "Harper, you're back! Oh my God, I've missed you. You got here so fast."

I laugh and breathe her in, hugging her around her middle. "I missed you, too. We're going to the Smithsonian on Saturday. Want to go?"

Margot nods against my shoulder. "I'll call dad and tell him I'm not coming home this weekend. Speaking of which, there's a playoff game two days away, and it's the second to last of the season. Can Harper march at halftime?"

Ben hesitates. "I'd prefer she not push it."

I sigh into the curve of Margot's neck. "He's a tyrant."

"All right," Ben says, clapping his hands to mark the end of this discussion. "Margot, get Harper inside before she catches a cold. I guess we'll see you both on Saturday. I'll text you with a pickup time once Christian stops looking so mopey."

"I am going to get fired."

I twist out of Margot's embrace. "Cheer up, big brother. We'll be on our best behavior." I slip around the car door and lean into the front seat to hug him. "Love you. I'll see you soon."

He kisses my forehead and gives me a pat on the back. "Love you too, Josie."

"Text me as soon as you're home," I say, kissing his cheek. "Let me know you got there okay."

Christian rolls his eyes. "Get inside. The temperature's dropping."

Margot hugs them goodbye, too, and we stand on the sidewalk as Ben climbs back into the car. Christian honks his horn after backing out of his parking space, then speeds away with a quick wave as if he can't get away from this place fast enough.

Margot loops her arm through my elbow. "Just so you know, everyone on campus is still talking about those messages." She guides me across the practice field to my dormitory. My chest aches from the thought of someone confronting us, prying into our relationship like it's anyone's business but ours. "People have been staring at me all week, and I just wanted to warn you in case they stare at you too. I know you like flying under the radar."

"Has anyone been mean to you?" I ask. I wonder how hard I can hit someone over the head with my nebulizer, which Margot has tucked beneath her arm. Ben's probably told her to make sure I use it before bed tonight. "My mom hasn't cornered you, has she?"

She shakes her head and kicks at a rock in our path. "She called my parents and told them she doesn't appreciate their daughter's 'deviant behavior' on campus, but my mom pretty much told her to go screw herself. She said I'm not Dianna's child to parent, and that they're capable of navigating all of this on their own. I have detention every day for a month, though. Mom and Dad both agreed to that."

I blow out a breath through my nose, wincing at the frost lingering in the air in front of me. "Are they upset?"

Margot shrugs her shoulders. "They're more disappointed than anything, but it's not like they didn't know I'm a lesbian. They're worried, too, obviously. Dad's afraid this might affect my college applications."

I pull open the door of my building, groaning at the blast of warm air heating my skin. Margot seems to melt a little, too. "I am so sorry that you got caught in the middle of all this." I shake off the mud clinging to the bottom of my shoes, the same way I've been shaking away my guilt. "But we're going to get through this, okay? Together." I try and offer her a smile, but it's hard to do. I know there's going to be backlash—for both of us. Margot takes my hand. "But a part of me is glad that everything is out in the open, you know? I was so worried that something would happen with that profile, and now that it has, it feels like a weight is off my chest. I know it sounds weird, but I'm relieved. The worst is over."

Margot unwinds the scarf wrapped around her neck, then drapes it across my shoulders and uses it to pull me close. She presses a kiss to my nose. "I'm just glad I don't have to hide that you're my girl-friend anymore."

"We haven't confirmed anything, you know." I smile. Margot blinks like it hasn't dawned on her that neither of us has spoken publicly about our relationship. "But my parents already know, so I don't care who else does."

Margot heads for the stairs and waits for me to follow her up, eyeing me as I try not to wince. Climbing them makes me winded. "Have they mentioned anything about, you know, doing to you what they did to Christian?" She doesn't want to say 'do they want to send you away,' but I know it's what she's asking.

"No," I say, gripping the railing to haul myself up the stairs. "But Christian said that if they try, I can stay with him and Ben. He drove me by their condo in D.C. It's nice. They have a golden retriever named Buster."

Margot presses a steadying hand to the small of my back as we turn into the corridor on my floor. "Are you surprised?" she asks. "That he's gay and has a boyfriend you never knew about?"

"A little," I admit, grabbing Margot's hand and lacing my fingers through her gloved ones. She smiles so wide it brings out the dimples in her cheeks. "I'm just glad he found someone, you know? Ben seems like he's good for him."

"Yeah," she agrees. "I like him. They're cute together."

"Harper!"

We're halfway through the empty common room, and I barely have enough time to let go of Margot before Bellamy knocks us both over. Their arms come around my shoulders, and Bellamy heaves a visceral sob that wracks my entire body. It shakes the wind right out of me.

"Harper, oh my—oh my God." Bellamy hugs me until my chest

hurts and Margot wedges herself between us, pushing them back to give me enough space to breathe. But Bellamy doesn't let me go. They grip my wrists and are crying so hard their every inch is trembling. "Are you—are you okay? Margot said she saw you and you were fine, but you weren't replying to my messages, and I thought maybe something had happened, and——"

"Bellamy," I say sternly, tugging myself free to place my hands on their shoulders. I should've asked Margot not to tell anyone I was on my way back, to give myself the chance to settle in first. Bellamy hiccups and I give them a gentle shake. "Bell, I'm fine. Calm down. I didn't have my phone for the first day and a half, then it died when Margot brought it to me, and I had to bum a charger from my nurse. Margot said she kept you updated, though."

Bellamy nods, their bottom lip quivering and scabbed as if they've been picking at it. "She did, but—shit, Harper. Everyone saw the ambulance leave, and Sarah and I brought Margot to the hospital, but your mom wouldn't let us see you, and—and you're my best friend, Harp, and I love you so much, and——"

I wrap my arms around their middle, hugging them tightly and letting Bellamy cry on my shoulder. Margot pats them on the back to help me comfort them, but I know from experience they'll cry for hours if I let them. This isn't the first time I've found Bellamy waiting for me after a hospital stay, though Nadia is usually here, too.

"Hey, come on," I say, taking a step forward so that Bellamy will take one back. I nudge them in the general direction of the worn-down couch that sits adjacent to the television. "Sit down and we can talk, okay? I'll tell you everything."

Bellamy sinks onto the couch and drags a hand through their hair. "What happened?" they ask, sniffing back snot before rubbing their nose with the sleeve of their dirty cardigan. "Margot said you had an asthma attack, but Sarah said it was a panic attack, and I know that sometimes your asthma gets worse when you're stressed, but I didn't think . . ." Bellamy tugs on the collar of their polo, their knees bouncing and heels slapping noisily on the wood. "Was it because those messages got leaked?"

I sit on the floor at Bellamy's feet while Margot perches on the armrest. "Something like that, yeah." I pick at my fingernails and pull at a hangnail until it bleeds. Margot taps me with her foot. "Those messages were really bad, Bell. My mom can barely look at me because she still thinks I had something to do with it, and she threatened to expel Margot for writing them on school grounds."

They draw in a breath, demolishing the dam on their tears. "Harper, I am so sorry," they begin. A sob is building in their chest, one that's shuddery and guttural and makes me flinch when Bellamy finally unleashes it. I don't understand why they're apologizing. "I didn't know, and—fuck. Please, just listen to me, okay? I didn't know she would do this."

Margot grabs the collar of Bellamy's cardigan, yanking them back. The blood in my body runs cold. I suck in a breath and hold it. "You didn't think who would do what, Bellamy?" Margot's fingers curl into fists, but I see in her eyes what I'm trying to shove down deep: betrayal. "I swear to God, Bell, if you had anything to do with this—"

"I'm sorry!" Bellamy cries, twisting out of their cardigan because Margot won't let them go. They slide off the couch and sink onto their knees in front of me, clawing for my hands. "Harper—Harp, please. Just listen to me, okay? Let me explain."

"You did this?" I ask, something inside of me splitting open wide as the accusation rolls off my tongue. I've missed something, some misunderstanding. Bellamy would never do this.

Their face twists with something akin to heartbreak. "Harper, please. It was supposed to be harmless!"

"Harmless?" Margot snarls. "You put Harper in the hospital!"

"No!" Bellamy cries, their voice breaking over a sob that pierces through me. "No, no, it wasn't—we never meant for this to happen! Please, Harp, you have to believe me. It was Evelyn's idea to make the profile, but—but I thought—you never put yourself out there, you know? And I thought that if we could just find someone for you, you wouldn't hate us for doing it." Bellamy grips my hands, their own shaking like little leaves in mine.

It takes everything in me not to shove them away because the sight of their face is making me want to shatter things.

"Evelyn was so fucking insistent," they continue, barely taking a breath. There's no room for me to get a word in. "We wanted to stop when you were close to finding out. But we didn't want to make her mad, and—and you know what she's like when she's mad, how cruel she can be, especially when she's mad at me. It was Evelyn who sent Margot all those messages, I swear. I think she wanted to, you know, dirty up your record, or something? To make everyone at school think you were finally on the dating scene. But we didn't—I never thought she would take it this far—she's just so fucking jealous of you, you know? Of your family and your dad and the fact that people just like you." Bellamy sucks in a wet, shuddery breath as if they're on the verge of sobbing if I don't say I forgive them. "We didn't know she'd do this, Harp. I promise. We never meant for you to get hurt—you or Margot. Nadia and I just did the swiping, and—"

Everything inside of me cracks open, a floodgate that releases every emotion my body is capable of feeling. It hurts—I hurt. I don't think I can handle this.

"Nadia was a part of this?"

Bellamy snaps their mouth shut, and it's all the confirmation I need, the driving force that has me scrambling to my feet because anger and pain are smothering my desire to be understanding.

Bellamy jumps up, too, grabbing my elbow and whirling me around before I can storm down the hallway. "Harper, wait. Please. I'm not making excuses for either of us, okay? I swear. But Nadia, she's—she had her reasons for doing this, but she feels awful." I scoff and bat them away, slapping my hand against their forearm. Bellamy lets me go, rubbing their eyes with the sleeve of their cardigan. "Look, be mad at me, if you want. But go easy on Nadia. Please, that's all I'm asking. There are things you don't understand. She hasn't been to class or rehearsal all week. Mrs. Devereaux is talking about not letting her play on Friday."

"I don't give a shit if she plays or not," I snap. Bellamy flinches. "Especially since neither of you gave a shit about what might have happened if anyone found out about that profile. Fuck, Bell, you could have at least told me!"

"We thought you'd rat us out to your mom!" Bellamy cries. "She has this way of just—making you fuckin' talk to her, you know? You tell her everything, even if you don't want to. She's just that good. And we knew that if Dean McKinley found out about this, she'd expel us!"

"Oh," I say, spitting out a harsh laugh. "So it was okay for my mom to consider expelling Margot, who's just as much of a victim as I am, but God forbid she consider expelling all of you, the people responsible in the first place!"

Bellamy's face drains to a splotchy, ashen pale, perhaps realizing that expulsion is not off the table. "You're not going to tell her, are you? Fuck, Harp, please. You can't. My parents will kill me, and I have a scholarship—it'll ruin everything!"

I don't know if I care how expelling them might ruin their life. They contributed to ruining mine and Margot's. They're the reason my mother can't look at me. They're why Dad is still walking on eggshells, why he constantly asks if I'm sure or if maybe this is a phase I'm going through. If Margot doesn't get accepted into any colleges, she's talked about going back to Canada, and then all of my friends will have contributed to her leaving.

They're exaggerating. Bellamy's parents would never kill them. Ground them for life or take away their absurd allowance, but never so much as lay a finger on them. At least they came out on their own.

"Harper," Margot says sternly. She vaults off the armrest of the couch and wedges herself between Bellamy and me. Only then do I realize that I'm crying. My chest is tight and Margot is holding my nebulizer. "Calm down. They're not worth it, and your face is getting flushed."

"I don't care—"

"I care," Margot snaps at me. She places her hand on my shoulder, a steadying weight dragging me back down to earth. Margot draws in a breath, holds it, then slowly exhales through her nose. "Breathe. Please. Like Ben taught you. I cannot handle calling another ambulance."

Bellamy shuffles behind her. "I'm sorry. I didn't mean to—"

"Shut up," Margot spits at them. Bellamy lets out a whine and takes a step back. "Harper, breathe. Now. Or I'll call Ben and Christian and tell them to come back."

I don't want that, not when they're likely almost home, so I draw in a breath and watch the rise and fall of Margot's chest. In for five, out for seven, repeat. In for five, out for seven, repeat. Margot breathes with me, studies my face as if I'm a puzzle in need of solving. After a moment, she sighs and lightly pats my cheek, smoothing her thumb over my freckles. "Good," she deems. "Now, what are we going to do about this?"

"I'm going to talk to Nadia," I say, ignoring Bellamy's nervous fluttering behind Margot. "And then I'm gonna take a damn nap, steal some of the snacks I know you have hidden in your room, and then decide whether or not I call my mom to tell her that they were all involved."

I finally look up at Bellamy. Tears are rolling down their cheeks, and I force myself to remember all the times they've been there for me, how they've offered me comfort, and how they eventually chose me over Evelyn. Maybe this was personal for her, some convoluted scheme to sway an election in her dad's barely existent favor. But I don't know what to believe where Bellamy's concerned. "You're supposed to be my friend," I say. My voice breaks in the middle, an ugly waver that makes all three of us cringe. Bellamy recoils. "I don't know what I'm going to do, but if I only rat out Evelyn—and that's a big *if*—I'm not going to stop her from running you over if she throws you and Nadia under the bus."

Bellamy's expression is pained, but they nod with grim resignation. "I get it."

Margot tucks my hair behind my ear, her fingers skimming over my cheek. "Do you want me to come with you?"

"No," I say. Something like pride flashes in Margot's eyes. Her mouth twitches with the threat of a hidden smile, one that would show her dimples if we hadn't just learned that our friends betrayed us. "I have to do this on my own. She's—she was my friend, and I want answers that Bellamy won't give me. She might not talk to me if you're there."

Margot nods and presses a kiss to my forehead. "I'll wait here."

I try not to storm down the hall, to jingle my keys as I tug them out of my pocket. She doesn't deserve to know that I'm coming so she can prepare any excuses she might have. But Nadia is curled up in bed when I slip into the room through a crack in the door, a trembling ball of teenage betrayal hiding beneath her floral duvet.

I let the door slam shut. "Sit up."

Nadia sniffles as she pulls back the covers, and I don't show my surprise when she looks at me through bloodshot eyes. Her nose is red. It's as if she's spent the last few days rubbing it with the sleeve of her cardigan, which is wrinkled and clearly slept in. "Harper," Nadia croaks, dragging a hand through her oily, messy hair. "You're back."

"Bellamy told me it was you," I say. I don't have it in me for small talk. Nadia lets out a little cry. "I know you had something to do with this, and that you and Bellamy made that profile with Evelyn. But they didn't tell me why—why my best fucking friend stabbed me in the back and made a profile that got leaked to the media."

Nadia's face crumples, all of her soft, delicate angles pinching sharp and tight. "Harper, I—I never meant for you to get hurt. You have to know that." Her voice cracks. She swallows what I think might be a sob. "You were in D.C. at that youth conference when Evelyn downloaded Tinder. I didn't want to do it, but Evelyn and Bellamy insisted, and—"

"And what?" I snap, slamming my hands against the footboard of Nadia's bed. She jumps. "I'm glad that outing me to the entire country constitutes not hurting me, Nadia. I'm so glad we've settled that."

"We didn't make the profile to out you," Nadia says. She fiddles with a tissue she's pulled from somewhere beneath her pillow. "We didn't even know you were queer. We tried swiping for guys at first, but we weren't matching with anyone."

I snort, but I believe her. "Is that supposed to make me feel better?"

Nadia shakes her head. "No, but . . ." She blows her nose and sniffles tearfully into her tissue. "Margot's the only person we matched with, and—and I'm not telling you to make you feel bad about yourself, but there aren't any other messages to be leaked. Just whatever Evelyn sent to Margot. The app was on her phone, not ours."

I cross my arms and stare at her, piecing together every breadcrumb my friends have left in their wake. They did this.

Nadia had insisted I forget about the profile, that I not tell my parents when it wasn't causing anyone any trouble. The messages stopped coming after Margot confronted me in front of her, and she must have told Evelyn to lay off and let the profile go dormant.

On the first day of school, Evelyn and Bellamy had been laughing at something on her phone, an inside joke they hadn't let me in on; Bellamy always let me in.

All three of them had shut me out, chased me from our circle because of my friendship with Margot, the one they made happen. Evelyn never apologized for it, even when Bellamy and Nadia did, and she never came around to accepting me back into the group.

I dig my fingernails into the footboard. "Why?" I ask, pretending not to hear the way my voice cracks. Nadia flinches. "Why did you do this? Why me? You could have been anyone else, used anyone else's pictures to make that profile."

"It was Evelyn's idea," Nadia says. "She thought people would match with it because, well, it was you. She said they'd be curious to see what the dean's daughter was about. But I never thought Evelyn would leak those messages." Nadia blows her nose again. "If I had, I never would've let it happen. I swear. I'd have—I'd have said no, said I didn't want to be a part of it."

"You could have told me!" I say, trying not to think about all the opportunities where Nadia could've come clean. "Apart from not having done it, you could've told me it was happening. Instead, you acted like a jealous bitch when Margot and I actually became friends."

"That's why I didn't tell you!" Nadia argues fervently. She sits herself up on her knees, tossing aside her tissue. "You got Margot out of it, and—Christ, Harper, you'd have told your mom, and Bell and I would get expelled. It wasn't that serious!"

"Nadia," I say slowly, and I can feel the hair starting to raise on the back of my neck. I'm going to yell at her, scream at her, have campus security beating down the door. I don't care. "My mother could lose her job, Dad could have to drop out of the election, and my very homophobic parents had to find out that their daughter is a lesbian on CNN because of that fucking profile. What about any of that isn't serious, Nadia? And what about Margot? She could be expelled, or not get into college, or have to move back to Canada! None of us knew her, and the three of you dragged her into the middle of a bullshit political scandal! Or does what happened to us not matter so long as you and Bell stay in school? Because that seems to be all you two care about."

Her eyes well up with tears. "Of course, all of that matters, Harper. You matter, and so does Margot, okay? But you're treating me like I leaked those messages, and it's not my fault that you chose to be queer for Margot, of all people."

"Are you serious?"

The ice in my blood has thawed. I'm burning. My chest aches, torn open wide and raw. I know I need to walk away, to put as much distance between us as I can. She's upset, I'm simmering, and we'll never work anything out like this. I don't even know if I want to work things out with her, if it's worth it, if I can ever come back from this hurt.

"I didn't *choose* to be queer, Nadia. I *am* queer. And Margot was there for me when you weren't." She flinches at that. "But you chose to make that profile, and like it or not, part of this is your fault. It's not all on Evelyn's shoulders. At least I know why she did it. But you still won't tell me why, and damn it, I deserve to know! The three of you put me in the hospital!"

Nadia sucks in a breath, her bottom lip quivering as she tries to steady it between her teeth. "Because I fucking love you, Harper. Okay? Is that what you wanted to hear?" My heart stops dead in my chest, sinks like a stone in an endless pond. "I love you, and you're untouchable, and your father is running for president. You have money, and I don't, and—I will never be what you want."

Tears are rolling down her cheeks, dripping from her chin and pooling in the circles beneath her eyes. Nadia is gripping her blanket, her body trembling as she stares and waits for my response, her chest heaving as she slowly rocks herself back and forth.

I don't know what to say—what I can or am supposed to offer. I don't know how to make any sense of this thing—this chasm of chaos and emotion and thoughts I don't know how to process. I don't understand why she would love me, how those feelings could exist for her, or why I never realized it before now.

"I don't understand."

Nadia snorts and rubs at her eyes. "Of course, you don't," she says. "You have Margot, and that's all you care about. I wasn't an option for you before, and I'll never be one now." Her nostrils flare as she sniffles. "And you don't know what that's like, wanting someone so much it hurts, but you know you can never have them. At first,

I thought you were straight, but now, you have Margot, and you'll always choose her over me. I will never, ever be good enough."

"Nadia, I—" I drag a hand through my hair, and Nadia looks up at me expectantly. I take a breath and try to find my anger again, that rage Nadia snuffed out with her unbelievable love. Or maybe it's not so unbelievable. Maybe it's always been there, poking and prodding and begging for me to acknowledge it. That would explain her jealousy; explain why she shut me out and made such a big deal about texting Margot during study hours.

But it doesn't explain the profile, and I let that betrayal fill me up again.

"You still haven't told me why," I say. "If you loved me, you wouldn't have done this."

Nadia's eyes flutter as she tucks her duvet beneath her chin. "I knew you'd never love me back, and that I couldn't be with you because of your parents. But Bellamy kept on teasing me after I told them, kept insisting that I shoot my shot and just tell you. But I—I couldn't. I didn't want to ruin our friendship. Bell and Evelyn thought it was hilarious; they thought I was a joke. So when they talked about making the profile, I agreed to help because—because I thought it would prove I was over you. I thought they'd stop teasing me."

A new rage ignites in the center of my chest, one that'll burn right through me if I let it. "You had nothing to prove to them, Nadia. You didn't have to do this because Bellamy and Evelyn were being assholes. For Christ's sake, you haven't even apologized!" My voice rises to a shout that echoes off the exposed brick along the window wall. "You told me why you did it, like loving me is a good excuse to wreck my life, but it's not an apology. Not once have you said that you're sorry to me or to Margot, who has just as much at stake as I do!"

Nadia's mouth opens and closes, something on the tip of her tongue she can't quite get out. "I'm—"

"No." I fling out a hand in dismissal. I've never felt more like my mother than in this moment. But Nadia deserves to be dismissed. This is not how you prove that you love someone, nor how you prove that you're over them. "Don't say you're sorry just because I'm asking for an apology. Try again later when you think you might actually mean it." I throw open the door with more force than necessary, barely catching it before it can slam into the wall. "I'm staying with Margot tonight. And tomorrow. I'll send Sarah over for my clothes."

Nadia nods with a sullen sort of acceptance. "Okay."

"And don't forget to feed Mickey and Martha," I say, glancing at the tank that's full of murky tap water. The filter needs changing. "I can tell by the dust on the bottle that the fish food hasn't moved." Maybe it's a low blow, but it's better than throwing a toothbrush at her and telling her to brush her teeth.

They're meant to be my parting words as I step back out into the hallway, but Nadia scrambles to the edge of her bed and catches me by the wrist. "Wait," she says, her brow furrowed and bottom lip caught between her teeth. There's a question on the tip of her tongue, I can see it in the way her eyes are searching my face. But then her shoulders slump and she sighs. "Are you going to tell your mom?"

"I don't know yet," I say, pulling myself free, and swing the door shut behind me.

CHAPTER THIRTY

O F ALL THE TIMES I'VE BEEN TO D.C. WITH MY PARENTS, I'VE NEVER been to the Smithsonian. Neither has Margot, but she doesn't have the same appreciation for history that I do, which is why she's more concerned with hauling me into the cafe than she is exploring the museum. "Come on, McKinley! I'm starving, and you made us miss breakfast."

"But the elevators are right there!" I whine, twisting against the arm Margot has slung around my waist. "All we have to do is go upstairs, see the mummies, and then we can come back down. I promise. The map shows that they're right down the hall from the—"

Margot groans and gives me a half-hearted tug. "But food, Harper."

"But mummies, Margot."

"Ladies," Ben chides, tapping on his phone from his seat at the table he's snagged beneath the life-size megalodon hanging from the ceiling. He doesn't look up, as he's likely texting Christian, but I know his raised eyebrow is meant for Margot and me. "You're causing a scene. Come sit down."

"But Ben—"

"This isn't my first rodeo trying to wrangle a McKinley," Ben says. He sets his phone screen-down on the table. "Sit, or we'll leave after lunch and no one sees the mummies."

"Come on, Harp!" Margot says cheerfully as she sits and pulls out the seat next to her, giving it an inviting little pat. "The mummies aren't going anywhere. They're dead. Sit down and eat, and that's the first thing we'll see when we're finished. I promise."

I sigh and slink to the table, sliding into the seat she's pulled out for me. "Buzzkills."

"Christian's clocking out now," Ben informs us. "He gets an hour for lunch and is off again at five, so if you think you can wait around for a few hours, he and I can both drive you back to campus."

Margot snorts and steals a fry from the tray in the middle of the table, waiting for Christian be damned. "If you think Harper can't spend the next five hours staring at a couple of corpses, well . . . you've got a lot to learn, McDreamy. She lives for this stuff."

Ben pinches the bridge of his nose. "You're never gonna let that go, are you?"

"Nope!" Margot pops a fry into her mouth, grinning.

"All right, you little shits. Why does Ben look like he's ready to have a stroke?" Christian appears from behind us, his mouth quirked with an easy smile as he unbuttons the collar of his shirt. "I told you two to go easy on him." Christian plants a kiss to the top of my head before plopping into the seat next to Ben.

"They haven't been that bad," Ben tells him earnestly, leaning in to kiss my brother. Christian's eyes light up as he indulges him, not a care in the world that someone might be watching them. Margot and I aren't quite there yet, but my brother and Ben give us hope. "We spent nearly an hour looking at dinosaur fossils, then another two in human origins."

"Have you seen the mummies yet?"

I groan and flop back into my chair. Margot pats my shoulder. "*No.*"

Christian snorts and digs into the tray where Ben has stacked our lunch. He bites off a hunk of pizza crust with vigor while Ben frets about Christian getting sauce on his uniform. "So," he says, ignoring Ben. "Let's talk about you two. I want to know what happened to the assholes who made that profile."

Margot, who has lettuce hanging out of her mouth, chews a little slower. She glances at me from around her veggie burger and frowns. "Do you want to talk about it?" she asks softly, nudging my foot beneath the table. "You don't have to." Margot looks up at Christian and smiles with a tinge of sadness. "It's still an open wound, Soldier Boy. They're assholes, one of whom she still lives with."

I sigh and pick at my food, pushing a glob of ketchup around my plate with a french fry. "Mom expelled Evelyn," I say, shifting in my seat. Knowing she's gone, even after what she did, doesn't give me any satisfaction. It doesn't make me hurt any less. She was, at one point, tolerable. "She's the one who sent those messages to Margot, then leaked them. Her dad's running for office, too—or he was; I think he dropped out—and she was trying to create some fucked-up sex scandal to derail Dad's campaign. She moved out of her dorm this morning."

Evelyn's parents had argued with my mother for hours, insisting that Evelyn didn't deserve to be expelled for a teenage prank gone wrong. But Mom had held her ground, demanded she be moved out by noon, and pointed them out the door.

"What about the other two?" Christian asks, licking pizza sauce from his fingers. Ben huffs and gives him a napkin.

I glance sidelong at Margot, who busies herself by opening the cap on her water bottle. "I didn't tell Mom they were involved."

Christian blinks as he settles back into his chair. He leans over the curved black metal until his spine cracks. "Why not?"

It's a good question, but I don't really have a good answer. Not one that Christian would understand. "They were my friends," I tell him. "And ruining their lives over swiping on a dating app didn't feel right. They didn't send those messages, and they didn't leak them to the press. Evelyn got what she deserved, but punishing Bell and Nadia felt wrong."

Ben takes a drink of coffee. "I think you did the right thing," he says. Christian whips his head around to gawk at him, but Ben presses forward before my brother can argue. "I won't make excuses for Evelyn; she knew what she was doing when she sent those messages and leaked them all to the press. But your friends? I think they were just being kids."

Margot scoffs and takes a bite of her veggie burger. "Being kids isn't an excuse. Bellamy said they were trying to find someone for Harper, but that's bullshit." She pulls a tomato from beneath her bun and flicks it into her basket. "Whatever Evelyn wants, Bellamy gives. Period. And Nadia, well . . . I guess I kind of feel sorry for her."

Christian coughs around his straw and sets his drink down. "Why the hell would you feel sorry for her? She's not the one who got outed."

"No," I say quietly, twiddling a fry between my fingers. "But she did come out to me, and all I did was yell at her. Apparently, Nadia's in love with me, and she helped with the account because she thought it would prove she was over me."

Christian slaps his palms against the table, a cackle rising up and out of him. "I knew it," he says. "I fuckin' called it years ago.

Don't you remember how she held your hand everywhere the two of you went?"

I swallow and rub at my temple. "Yes, but I thought nothing of it."

"What does it matter, anyway?" Margot spits. "It's still bullshit."

Ben winces. "Maybe so," he concedes. He takes a sip of his coffee. "But I think we're all missing the point here. What Bellamy and Nadia did was shitty, yes, and coming from a guy who just finished his psych rotation, their reasons don't make any sense to me."

They don't make any sense to me, either. I don't understand how Nadia and Bell can justify the part that they played. Bellamy, at least, apologized on Instagram, through text messages, and in emails. They even seek me out after rehearsal, but Sarah fends them off and swats Bell away with Margot's drumsticks.

But Nadia just sits and stares at the peeling paint on our walls, at the stars we've stuck to the ceiling. Once, I think I caught her counting them. She's not yet told me how many there are.

"But it doesn't sound like either of them intended to hurt you," Ben says, and I know, deep down, he's right. Probably. Somehow. I'm still on the proverbial fence. "Not from the things you've told me. Evelyn, however . . . I'm glad your mom expelled her. I don't know what made her think that a seventeen-year-old child could run your dad's campaign into the ground, but it backfired. It did the exact opposite of what she wanted. He's rallied some of the moderates in the queer community to his side of the ballot for the way he's handled you being outed."

Marcus McKinley the people pleaser, a newly minted ally to queer voters in America. His statement to the press had been brief. A quick, "I love and support my children. Always. No matter who they choose to love." It wasn't perfect, and it didn't necessarily confirm anything, but Christian and I are now the new poster children for queer kids in politics.

Mom still hasn't come around yet. She and Dad can't stand to be in the same room, nor can she look me in the eye whenever I run into her on campus. Dad says it's her loss, both shutting me out and having sent Christian away, and he's done his best to try and make amends with my brother. But Christian's not ready to forgive him yet, even if Dad did invite both him and Ben out to dinner last night.

"Look," Ben continues, reaching across the table to gently pat my hand. I snap out of a daze and look up at him. "No offense, but teenagers are irresponsible. I don't think that, consciously, your friends meant to hurt either one of you. Not truly. I know they did, but I don't think it was on purpose. I don't peg either of them as schemers."

Margot nibbles on the fry she's stolen from my plate. "How would you know, McDreamy?"

Ben tries not to roll his eyes. "I was a teenager once, too, and I did my fair share of careless shit. I hurt people I never meant to hurt. You guys have dating apps and Instagram, and we had three-way phone calls and AIM."

I tilt my head. "What's AIM?"

Ben heaves a sigh and looks at Christian with a pout. "Kids these days. They're so uncultured."

Christian laughs and presses a kiss to his temple. "AIM," he says. "Was an instant messaging system back in Ben's day. Kind of like Instagram, but more fun."

"Back in *my* day?" Ben slaps his hand against Christian's chest. "I'm hardly any older than you, ass. I skipped fourth grade and graduated high school a year early."

"Yeah, yeah, you cougar." Christian points at him with his uneaten pizza crust. "We know you're a certifiable genius. Sit down."

Ben purses his lips and fondly glares at Christian. "As I was saying, teenagers are irresponsible. You have a right to be upset with your friends, but I think you did the right thing by not turning them in over swiping on some dating app. Evelyn? She made her bed and now she has to lie in it. She got what she deserved by sending those messages and leaking them."

Margot's expression is blank. "That's a pretty detailed analysis, McDreamy, getting all up in the teenage mind like that. Maybe you're not as old as the fossils we saw upstairs."

Ben throws his hands into the air. "I give up."

"Did she ever delete the profile?" Christian asks.

"I downloaded Tinder again last night," Margot says. Ben and Christian both raise an eyebrow in unison. It's creepy. "Just to see if the account had been taken down. I couldn't find it, and all our messages were gone. Harper watched me delete the app when I was done."

"Good," Ben says, taking a drink of his coffee. "That's really good. Harper, you're being quiet. How do you feel about all of this?"

I blink and meet Ben's gaze, his kind eyes and warm smile the epitome of a doctor's bedside manner. "I feel . . ." Margot traces her thumb across the top of my hand beneath the table. "Relieved, I think. I'm glad the profile is gone, and I'm glad I don't have to lie to my parents anymore. But I think I'm still hurt, too? Nadia has been my roommate since we were seven, and she and Bellamy were my best friends. I still can't believe they played a part in all this. And, like, I got outed to the entire country on CNN before I was ready to come out."

Ben nods solemnly. "I'm sorry that this is how it happened for you."

"It doesn't have to be, you know." Margot is staring at the tomatoes she'd picked off her burger. "In your dad's statement, he never really confirmed that you're queer. You can still come out on your terms. Sort of. If you want to."

I angle myself toward her, twisting in my chair until my knees knock against Margot's. "What do you mean?"

She shrugs and smiles a bit. "You have social media, and you're not under a gag order. You don't have to do anything, but you can still come out on your own when you're ready. Fuck CNN and that profile. People don't know shit about shit."

"A punk with a point. I like it." Christian dodges Margot's kick beneath the table, grinning. "I think it's a good idea, but only when you're ready. Don't rely on Dad to speak for you. Or Mom—especially not Mom. This is your life, Josie, and you deserve to live it however you want. Just know that Ben and I aren't going anywhere. We'll back you the entire way."

"Me too," Margot adds, leaning over to plant a kiss on my cheek.

My eyes fill with droplets of salty emotion that start to roll down my cheeks. They're sad tears, full of anger and betrayal and everything in between. But some of them are happy, too. The worst of this is over, and I have my brother and Ben to navigate this screwed-up road with me. I have Margot at my side, a beautiful light in what sometimes feels like a never-ending dark.

She wipes them all away with her thumb. "What do you want to do?" she asks quietly.

I don't want to hide Margot's light or Ben's or Christian's or even mine. Not when we all deserve to shine. I slip my phone out of my pocket. "Which of you has longer arms?" I ask, sliding it across the table after turning on my front-facing camera. "Ben, you look pretty lanky."

He rolls his eyes and snatches my phone off the table. "Come over here, you little queers."

Margot and I move to stand behind them. She drapes her arms around Ben's neck and sticks out her tongue at the camera. Christian snorts and holds up his fingers to give her bunny ears. Ben sighs dramatically as I lean between him and my brother, smiling to show all of my teeth. "On three," Ben says, hovering his thumb over the capture button.

"Three!" Margot supplies without a countdown. Ben snaps a picture anyway.

"Ew, no, delete that." Christian crinkles his nose. "I don't like the way I look in it."

Ben hands me my phone. "You look handsome, love. As always."

I plop back down into my chair, and Margot leans over the back of it, resting her chin on my shoulder. I open up Instagram and upload the photo to be edited, staring at the faces of three of my favorite people. Margot helps me pick out a filter that casts the four of us in a rainbow gradient of greens and yellows and oranges.

"Are you sure?" she murmurs, watching my fingers hover over the keys to type a caption. "Once it's out there, you can't take it back. Don't hit 'share' unless you're sure."

I tag the three of them in the photo, link it to post to my Twitter account, and tap on 'share' before I can change my mind.

Harrison Bentley is the first person to like it.

Sarah retweets it to her hundreds of followers on Twitter.

I read over the caption and turn off my phone to enjoy the day with my family.

Love wins.

EPILOGUE

"WHAT ARE YOU DOING?!" MARGOT WAVES HER DRUMSTICKS IN the air, hopping up and down until I grab her by the collar of her uniform. I drag her back before she can jump into the end-zone. "Reinhart, take him down! Tackle him! Do something!"

Christian raises an eyebrow as he digs through his walking taco, a small bag of Fritos that a band mom from the concession stand has filled with melted cheese and beef. "I didn't think Canadians were into football. Is that even what you call it up there?"

"Shut it, Soldier Boy. I'm trying to get our team together before we lose the championship." Margot crouches down and monitors the field like a hawk, her brow furrowed in concentration. "Reinhart, goddamn it! Tackle the bastard before I come and do it for you!"

"What she means to say," Leon sighs, shaking his head at his Margot, not Issy, who's standing quietly at his side watching the game through a pair of sparkly blue sunglasses. "Is that yes, Canadians like football, and yes, that's what we call it. But Margot only likes it because she thinks it makes her sound impressive."

"Not true," Margot says, still crouched down beside me. "I won over Harper without my knowledge for the game."

"I think your sister's finally losing it, Issy. She thinks she's won me over."

Issy offers me the smallest of smiles before handing me our shared basket of pretzels. There's only one left, so I break it in half and give her the bigger piece. She smiles just a little wider.

Margot lets loose a guttural groan as she stands and stomps her feet. "Montgomery just grabbed their linebacker's face mask, so now there's a flag on the play and the refs are pushing us back. We're gonna lose. They're playing terribly tonight."

"We're winning," Ben points out, wincing as our receiver is tackled face-first into the mud. "I never understood this sport. I was finishing up my ER rotation at the beginning of this season, and do you have any idea how many football players were brought in for broken bones and concussions?"

"What about broken bones and concussions?" Sarah sidles up behind me, a thin slice of pizza half wrapped in foil in her hand. "Also, have you seen how pathetic they look? I'm starting to feel sorry for them. Halftime was a train wreck."

I don't need to ask who she's talking about.

Nadia and Bellamy have been sitting in the bleachers all night. Bellamy only stands to conduct, and I haven't seen Nadia dance or sway since the game started. It's so unlike them to not be jumping around or standing and screaming when our team scores a touchdown. They're sitting shoulder to shoulder in the bottom row, staring at the field as if we've already lost the game, their expressions pinched and grief-stricken.

Margot follows my gaze the second I bite my lip. "I know that look," she says, reaching around Sarah to take my hand and press her fingers into my palm. "You want to invite them over, don't you?"

"No," I say. Margot raises an eyebrow. "Maybe. I don't know, okay? It's been over a week, and all Nadia does is sit in our room and cry. I feel guilty. I know I'm not the one who did this, but I feel like we're giving Evelyn what she wants if we decide not to forgive each other."

Ben smiles as he leans into Christian's side. "Evelyn really does win if the lot of you don't learn to forgive."

I look at Margot. She's studying my face, and I make a note of her pursed mouth and the way her nose is crinkled. "If you want to invite them to dinner," she says. "I support you. But I'll also have Sarah kick their asses the second they make you upset."

Sarah raises her a half-eaten pizza crust, an improvised toast to the idea. "True that."

I might laugh if I didn't think they were serious.

With Margot squeezing my hand, I take a breath and turn to face the bleachers. "Nadia! Bell!"

Bellamy nearly falls out of their seat, and Nadia turns around with subdued skepticism. She blinks at me from behind the fence, nudges Bellamy in my direction, and whispers something in their ear. Bellamy's head snaps up and they look at me, their face twisting with what I know is regret. It's enough to knock the wind out of me.

I lift my hand and wave the two of them over.

She sets down her trumpet and wraps her arms around her middle, trailing behind Bellamy, who speed-walks across the track to greet us.

"Hi, Harp. Hey, Margot." They smile tentatively at the three of us, nodding an acknowledgment at Sarah. She grunts one back and rips off a chunk of her pizza crust with her teeth. I think it's meant to be threatening.

I look Bellamy over with apprehension. Their skin is pallid and circles hang beneath their eyes like they haven't slept since the last time Margot and I spoke to them. Maybe they've been crying as much as I do at night when the lights are out and I can hide my face under the blanket.

Nadia clears her throat, shifting uncomfortably behind Bellamy. She looks like she'd rather be anywhere else, and I don't blame her. We've not spoken since I stormed out of our dorm room a week ago.

We stand, staring at each other, for a long while before speaking, Bellamy forgotten between us.

"Harper, I—"

"Nadia—"

"All marching badgers, to your instruments! One minute till the final quarter of the season!" Mrs. Devereaux is pacing over the track, screaming into her megaphone with unhinged excitement. We're winning. Barely. The score is 37–33, and it's still anyone's game.

Nadia sighs and hangs her head in resignation. "Never mind."

She spins to retreat to the bleachers, but I grab her by the wrist and stop her. "Later," I tell her. "After the game. We'll talk. We're, uh, we're going out to dinner when it's over. You and Bell should come if you want."

Nadia rubs her nose. "Yeah," she says. I hear the wobble in her voice. "Yeah, all right."

"Marching badgers, let's go! Stop dawdling and get back to your seats!"

We part ways with my brother and Ben and Margot's dad and Issy. Margot is still harnessing her drum when I climb to the top of the bleachers, my saxophone waiting to be clipped to my neck strap and played. I tap my fingers along the keys, twist my mouthpiece, and adjust my reed so that a smooth, rich sound will spill from the horn for my last ever performance in marching band. Of course, concert band comes next, but we don't wear our uniforms for that. We don't get to stand beneath stadium lights and march over a torn-up football field.

The fourth quarter is a nail biter. Everyone is sitting on the edge of their seats. They score, then we score, and somehow we're tied when the timer on the scoreboard hits zero. The clock resets for an additional ten minutes of overtime, and I can hear Margot screaming from the bottom row of the bleachers. I can hear Nadia and Bellamy, too, and Sarah is yelling over the sound of her crashing cymbals. Normally, Mrs. Devereaux would scold her, but she spins around and lifts her megaphone to give us our final command.

"Seniors, down to the track! Show our boys some support!"

I know I'm not meant to take my saxophone. We're not going down there to play, but the bleachers are packed and everyone is stomping their feet, and I'm afraid my instrument will slip between the stands and crash into the rocks below. I saw it happen last year with Carmen Mendoza's clarinet. It was ugly.

"I'll watch it," Rebecca says, holding out her hand in offering. I don't give it to her, clutching my saxophone against my chest like I'm worried she'll take it by force. "Jesus, Harper. I'm not going to toss it over the bleachers. Just give me your sax and go down to the track before Devereaux calls you out over the megaphone."

"It's okay, Harper." Cassidy smiles and slides between Rebecca and me. "I'll keep an eye on it. Don't worry. Go have fun."

"Listen to the freshman, McKinley." Rebecca's smile is forced. "I want your chair, not your instrument in pieces. Plus, your life kind of sucks right now. I'm not going to make it worse."

I unclip my saxophone. "Thanks."

Margot is stomping back and forth over the track, wearing a path in the asphalt. She spins around and takes me by the shoulders, giving me a solid shake. "We're gonna lose. We came all this way just to lose."

"You're going to jinx it!" Nadia cries, bouncing on her heels as she holds Bellamy's hand and nearly rips their arm from the socket. "Happy thoughts, happy thoughts, happy—Warrick! What are you—"

"Steal the fucking ball back, you jackass!" Margot has moved into the grass, about to stand on the team's empty bench when I grab her arm and haul her back. "This is it. They're going to score and we're going to lose and this is the last time I'll ever wear this uniform."

"Mar—"

"They got it back!" Sarah screams, barreling past me to stand on the bench I've just yanked Margot away from. "Go! Run, run, run! Reinhart, run!"

Margot leaps onto my back, scrambling for purchase as she claws at my shoulders and wraps her legs around my waist. I stumble for balance, almost drop her into the mud, then brace my feet and give her the boost she needs to see the field. Her fingers are tangled in my hair, heels digging into my hips, and she's yelling a stream of French and English curse words into my ear.

"Run!" she cries, beating her palm against my shoulder. "Run, run, run! Go! You're almost—fuck! Flag? What flag? There was no flag on that play! Ugh!"

"The clock is still counting down!" Sarah screams.

There are ten seconds left on the clock.

Margot jumps off my back to join Sarah on the bench.

Five.

Bellamy takes my hand and drags me into their embrace, their arms slung around my and Nadia's shoulders.

Three.

Nadia covers her eyes. "I can't look. Oh my God. Let me know when it's over."

One.

Warrick bolts into the endzone, flipping into the grass where he lays sprawled with the football clutched to his chest. I can see him panting from here.

The stadium goes silent. A heartbeat passes, two, three, before the referee throws up their hands to indicate the play was complete. The game is over and Golden Oaks has won. Someone somewhere starts singing "We Are the Champions." I think it might be Sarah.

Spectators pour from the stands, flooding the field with blue and gold as they gather around our football team. I'm lost somewhere in the shuffle, bobbing along in the sea of cheering Badgers fans. The gleam of the championship trophy rises above the crowd, passed around from player to player until Warrick is lifted, too, holding it high for everyone in the stadium to see.

"Harper!"

I'd recognize Margot's voice anywhere; pick her out of any crowd and always find my way back to her. She's weaving between parents and football players, shoving aside coaches and barreling past the seniors in her way. "Harp!" she cries, flinging her arms around my neck when she reaches me. "Harper, we won!"

I wrap my arms around her middle, holding her close and burying my face into her shoulder. "Yeah," I say, breathing her in as we sway and move with the crowd. "We won."

Margot pulls back to look at me. Her dimpled cheeks are wet with glistening tears, but her mouth is curved with a smile so wide it's infectious. I beam right back and cup her face between my palms. "Fuck, Margot. We *won*."

Margot stands on the tips of her toes and crashes her lips against mine. It's quick, messy, but I don't care who might see me kiss her, and I don't mind that she's kissing me at all. Not now. Not here. Not when Margot and I have won and we can finally live as free as Ben and Christian. Sort of. We'll have to get through graduation first.

Margot drops back onto her heels, her dark eyes searching mine, and I think I know what Margot's been waiting to hear from me. It's only taken me four months to figure it out.

I bend my knees and press a kiss to her cheek. "I think I'm in love with you, too."

THE END

ACKNOWLEDGMENTS

A S A QUEER MUSICIAN WHO SPENT YEARS BENEATH STADIUM LIGHTS, a love for music was instilled in me from a very young age. I will never forget picking out my instrument in the fourth grade and deciding on the clarinet because I wanted to be like Squidward. Never in my wildest dreams did I think that love would transpire into this, but I'm forever grateful it did.

But I didn't make it here alone, and this is the part where I get sappy.

To Jen: This book would not exist without you. Period. I never would have written it had I not had you and your unwavering encouragement. Thank you for retrieving *Forward March* from a virtual trashcan while standing in line at Taco Bell. I owe you nachos and love you more than you'll ever know.

To Mariah: Thank you for being the best little human and my best little friend. Your heart and creativity inspire me more than you will ever know. Everything I do is for you. An author I might be, but being your aunt will always be my favorite, proudest title.

To Moe Ferrara: Thank you. Thank you for giving me a chance and coming to my rescue when I was lost, hysterical, and hyperventilating. Your support has been unwavering and I am so happy that our author-agent paths crossed when they did, even under unusual circumstances. Everything happens for a reason, and I'm ready to take publishing by storm with you!

To Tamara Grasty: You believed in my girls from day one and I cannot thank you enough. You've been one of Harper and Margot's biggest supporters, and I'm grateful that you gave them a chance and their story a home. You're a stellar editor and anyone who works with you should be honored.

To Shannon Rohrer, Sefanya Hope, and Manu Velasco, my beta and sensitivity readers: The three of you were amazing to work with. Thank you for helping educate and guide me in the right direction and for helping me portray my characters in a clearer light.

To my Page Street family: Jenna Fagan, Hayley Gundlach, Laura Benton, Lizzy Mason, Lauren Cepero, Lauren Knowles, and many others.

To my mom and grandparents: Thank you for all the years of love and support and for always encouraging me to follow my dreams, no matter how silly or seemingly unobtainable.

To Costello: Thank you for instilling a love of music that's lasted for years after my final halftime performance.

To Moo and Shiro: You're the best awful dogs in the world. Thanks for sitting at my side throughout the whole process of writing this book, querying it, and publishing it.

Additional thanks to Monique Vieu, my fabulous copyeditor who helped make this book the very best it could be, Chrissy Godsey for supporting me throughout the years, the McAndrew family for being the absolute best and most supportive in-laws a girl could ever ask for, my uncle Chuck Quinlan, for always being down to exchange queer book recommendations, and to the Red Devils Marching Band for giving me a place to belong and a family to come home to on football Friday nights.

ABOUT THE AUTHOR

SKYE QUINLAN (SHE/HER) WAS BORN IN CALIFORNIA DURING AN earthquake and raised in the Midwest where cornstalks outnumber people. She studied physical and cultural anthropology at Oregon State University with a focus on ancient civilizations and minored in creative writing.

When she's not writing, you can find her at the nearest metaphysics or craft store, dressed up in cosplay at the nearest convention, or ruining the furniture in her basement with epoxy resin and paint. She still lives in the Midwest with her wife, their dogs, and the occasional little human who comes to visit them often (their niece).